18.00

Praise for The Whammer Jammers

A brilliant, hard-edged thriller with sharp, assaulting dialogue...The action is rough, raw and violent but at the same time vulnerable, precarious and human.
Amazon Review

A rip-roaring romantic thriller...Meticulous attention to details, lively prose, and obvious affection for the sport of roller derby shine through in this well-paced, elbow-throwing ride.
Publishers Weekly

With more twists and turns than the roller derby world it penetrates, The Whammer Jammers is a mixmaster of city cops, brave women and betrayal—for love and dirty money. A page-turner that pays big dividends at the bitter end.
Chris Knopf, Author of the Sam Acquillo Mysteries

...and for Who Wrote The Book of Death?

A great book...really fast out of the box and the pace never lets up. You won't be able to put it down.
Kate Flora, Edgar Award Nominee for *Finding Amy*

I was surprised by the author's fresh, new voice...especially his clever, rapidly paced dialogue. His characters were a continual surprise, and the plot held my interest throughout.
Chris Roerden,
Agatha Award for *Don't Murder Your Mystery*

The Whammer Jammers

Also by Steve Liskow

Who Wrote The Book of Death?

The Whammer Jammers

by

Steve Liskow

This is a work of fiction. All characters and events portrayed in the book are products of the author's imagination and any resemblance to real persons or incidents is strictly coincidental. Real locations have been used fictitiously and some locations have been altered for purpose of the plot.

Cover imagery and design by Peter B. Riley

ISBN:9781466364394 97

For Jennifer, my real Roller Derby Queen

Chapter One

Kevlar makes Hendrix itch.

OK, he knows it's nerves, but come on, when you slip your arms into the frigging vest, it means there's a good chance that someone's going to shoot at you. Not to mention that Kevlar breathes half as well as carbon steel and is slightly less flexible. He's been wearing the sonofabitch under his shirt in the back of the unmarked car, the Hartford humidity thick enough to chew. He feels like the Michelin Man; in another hour, people will smell him across the river.

Jimmy Byrne, Hendrix's partner, checks his watch again. His freckled forehead shines with sweat, too, below matted red curls, but the Mossberg 12-gauge he's holding dispels the Ronnie Howard image. The smell of gun oil fills the back seat, along with the sweat and tension.

"What is the goddam problem?" Byrne says. "When you guys said 'raid,' we thought you meant kicking someone's door, not cruising the West End." He cracks his knuckles, which drives Hendrix even crazier.

"Act like you're looking for pussy." That's Sturges, riding shotgun, no joke. He wears a Red Sox cap and baggy jersey that conceals his own Kevlar, and even without it he's one big motherfucker. "Like you don't know Monday is amateur night and you won't even get a decent blowjob."

"Decent blowjob?" Byrne knows every stripper in Hartford County, most of them regularly. "Isn't that an oxymoron?"

"Fuckin' college kids." Owens, behind the wheel, watches the woman striding down the street beyond the parked cars, yellow hot pants disappearing up the crack in her ass.

They've cruised Albany Avenue to the West Hartford line, then down to Homestead Avenue, zigzagging through the side streets for two hours. Three-story houses that were elegant after World War II line the streets, but most of them haven't been painted in years. Guys in wife-beaters and homeboy shorts sit on car fenders. Black and Latina girls in tight tees, their lips and tongue glowing with piercings, lean close to them, hip hop music so loud Hendrix can hear it through their ear buds.

"Lots of kids hanging out," he says. The black Vice and Narcotics cops were surprised to see he's a blue-eyed blond and not a dude like Jimi, but his father, Ray Hendricks, liked the guitar player so much he changed the spelling of his name.

"They're probably studying together for finals," Owens says. "Hartford Public started exams Friday."

"This is fucking crazy." If Byrne looks at his watch one more time, Hendrix may shoot him just on general principles. "How long does it take a judge to sign a warrant?"

"If he's from Waterbury, he probably has to print." Sturges watches the cloud of bugs pulsating around a streetlight.

Owens turns down a side street, careful not to take the same streets in the same order, and coming back in the opposite direction. "And if he's from New Britain, he's gotta find a crayon." The house they want lies on a side street between Albany and Homestead.

“That’s the one.” Sturges nods at a faded gray three-story with a sagging porch. Trees fill the back yard so they’ll have cover when they rush the place, but all bets are off once they get inside. The first car has four guys to kick the front door, and a third car will pull up sixty seconds later.

Hendrix looks at those trees. “How solid is your information?”

“We knew there was crystal in the neighborhood. Just not where.”

A kid on a skateboard zooms from between two parked cars and Owens slams on his brakes. The kid flips them off and keeps going.

Sturges’s phone beeps.

“Gotcha.” He holds the cell away to check the clock. “Eight minutes.”

Owens turns left on Homestead. Three blocks down, he turns left again and goes around the block so he can return on the right side of the street.

Sturges glances over the back of the seat at Byrne and Hendrix. “The lab’s on the third floor. We go in, the stairs are on the right of the door, all left turns. The lights are probably out or broken, so watch out for shit on the steps.”

“How many people?” Hendrix tucks his ID under his shirt. The badges reflect light and make perfect targets.

“Five, they think.”

“Think?”

“Hey, they gave us the time and place, you want the attendance, too, like a fucking ball game?”

Owens stops at the light. “As soon as we get across, it’s show time.”

The light changes. Hendrix follows Byrne out the door by the curb, shotgun heavy in his grip and the Kevlar vest making it hard to move his arms. He trots between houses and through the trees, sweat dribbling down his rib cage and mosquitoes whining around his face. He hears yelling behind him and knows they've been spotted.

The back door of the house, unpainted wood with a broken pane of glass above the knob, hangs ajar. Sturges flashes his Maglite at the stairs and swings around the first landing, Hendrix almost stepping on his heels. The narrow stairs stink of piss and shit, with an overlay of sweet weed. People probably fuck here, too, but he hasn't stepped on any used rubbers yet.

They turn the second landing and Hendrix sees a bare light bulb hanging above them. A shadow appears in front of it and something glitters in its hand.

Sturges yells "Gun!"

Hendrix sees a black ponytail and dark tee shirt, then that gun flashes and he throws himself against the wall. The slug buzzes past his right ear and he brings up the Mossberg, firing as the bead on the muzzle covers the guy's chest.

It sounds like two trucks colliding and the recoil almost spins him off the step. The guy slams back against the wall, an after-image in the brilliant muzzle flash. Hendrix turns the corner and charges up the last flight of steps to the open door, shotgun leading the way.

"Freeze. Right there. Now." He feels his voice in his throat, but he can't hear shit. In front of him, three skinny Latinos hold their hands high, two cops covering them and two others patting them down. Paper bundles and plastic vials cover the coffee table, and a shoe box overflows with cash. Byrne pulls out his handcuffs and Hendrix keeps everyone covered. By the time the third car of cops appears a minute later, the ringing in his ears has faded to a steady jingle.

He retreats to the door and smells the shotgun residue filling the stairwell. Underneath that, he recognizes the metallic smell of blood and the sharper odor of excrement. The guy must have shit himself when he took the blast full in his chest.

Two EMTs huddle over him, going through his pockets for ID. When they hear Hendrix, they look up.

"How is he?" Hendrix asks.

The older EMT stands, his gloves bloody. "If she were still alive, her tits would be growing out of her shoulder blades."

Hendrix feels a block of ice form in his stomach.

"Did you say 'she?'"

He looks again and the bare bulb throws harsh yellow light on the smooth tan face. Her eyes are open wide and she's wearing cherry lip gloss.

Oh, fuck.

"Yeah," the EMT says. "And if she were any younger, she'd probably bleed green."

Chapter Two

Annie Rogers slides her Hyundai into a parking space near the rink entrance and looks in all four directions before unlocking her door. She recognizes the other cars around her, an old Chevy, an older Taurus, a shiny Civic, all dozing in the sun that glows on the streaks in her new windshield.

She walks around to the passenger side and slides the strap of her gym bag over her shoulder, the weight of her skates, pads, and helmet so familiar that she feels her rhythms changing even before she stands up again. She's tied her chestnut hair in a ponytail to keep her hair off her neck, but on a night like this, she'll sweat like a horse anyway.

When she straightens up, Kevin's there.

"Annie, we gotta talk." He's almost a foot taller than her own five-two and twice her weight, red tank top, shaved head, soul patch, eyebrows thick as crayons. When she sees his eyes, she thinks she's going to wet herself, right there on the blacktop.

"It's over, Kevin. Go away. Please." She tries to keep her voice steady.

"There's too much between us, Annie. You can't just toss it away like an old stick of gum. We've got a future."

It's only six-thirty, but his breath smells like Guinness.

"I told you to leave me alone." If he touches her, she'll scream her lungs out.

"Annie, that's just crazy talk. Look, you know we love each other. C'mon."

She wishes she had mace in her purse. Or a taser, a cannon, anything to quiet the terror that's squeezing her chest. She forces herself to breathe. It's bad when you have to think about it.

"Annie, I love you. Shit, I told you often enough."

"You hurt me often enough, too. Kevin. I don't want that anymore."

"Hurt? What kind of bullshit is that?"

"You hit me. Remember? You gave me a black eye." He rolls his eyes, but she forces herself to keep going. "And bruised ribs. Twice."

"OK, so I got upset a couple of times. But that just shows I love you."

"I don't love you, Kevin. It's over."

"Shit, that's just girl talk. You're crazy around that time of the month, right? A couple of days, you'll be fine. Listen, why don't I wait around. After practice, we can go somewhere and talk."

"Jesus Christ, Kevin. You broke my windshield here the other night, remember? I had to get a tow truck and call my insurance company and fill out paper work and get a loaner to get to work yesterday. You had a crowbar. If you'd hit me instead of my windshield, I'd be dead."

He clamps his hand around her arm and her right hand goes numb.

"Goddammit, listen to me. You don't fucking get it, do you?"

He pushes her back against the hood of her car and her eyes burn with terrified tears. His face is only inches from hers. If he were any bigger, he could carry her up the Empire State Building with one hand and swat away airplanes with the other.

"Kevin..."

"Hey, dickhead. Let her go."

The voice slashes through the humidity and Kevin takes a step back. Annie can still feel where his fingers gripped her; she'll see purple marks on her biceps tomorrow.

Roxy Heartless strides over. Her blue eyes gleam like sapphires and a cell phone glows in her hand. "Don't tell me you didn't get the restraining order. And don't even fucking dream of saying you didn't understand it."

Kevin has eight inches on Roxy, too, and his fists look as big as Annie's head. "This has nothing to do with you, bitch. This is between me and my girlfriend."

"Ex-girlfriend. It's over. She told you that, but you keep stalking her."

"Stalking? Where the fuck do you get stalking? I just want to talk to her, make her start thinking straight again."

"This isn't a debate." Annie hears Roxy's phone beep. "The cops are on the way."

"You..." Annie thinks Kevin is going to swing.

"Do it. Please." Roxy's voice sounds like a snake ready to strike. It scares Annie even more than Kevin does. She's the toughest divorce lawyer in Hartford County, which is why her rink name is Roxy Heartless. "Half a reason, and your tiny little balls are on my key ring."

"You want her too, bitch? Is that what this is all about? You a fucking dyke?"

But he stalks back to his car, hidden around the corner of the building. His Hummer spews gravel and roars across the lot to Farmington Avenue, swerving right toward Bristol, Farmington, and I-84.

Roxy watches until the car disappears beyond the pillars to the middle school two hundred yards away. “Well, I’m wet now. How about you?”

Annie realizes her knees are shaking and feels arms wrap around her. It feels pretty good, but she knows Roxy likes guys. She’s divorced two of them.

“I’m all right. Thank you.”

Roxy marches them across the blacktop and into the rink of the New Britain Whammer Jammers, eastern Connecticut’s roller derby team.

As soon as they step inside, Annie feels her heart rate and breathing slow down to normal. Grace Anatomy, black braid falling to her waist, does a Pilates warm-up, and a couple of other girls rest their feet on a bench to stretch their hamstrings and quads. Other girls skate slow laps, Lugg Nutz, the coach, rolling backwards ahead of them. The hair on both sides of his black Mohawk spike is mango orange.

“Keep your hips lower, Molly. You give people a high center of gravity like that, they’ll knock you off balance. Stay low and you can push back better.”

Annie drops her bag by the bench and finds her own skates and pads. Roxy gives her a quick squeeze.

“We’re on your side, OK?”

“I know. Thank you.”

By the time Annie slides her knee pads over her fishnets and laces up her skates, everyone is there and she feels like she’s back in the dorms at UConn.

The space feels big as an airport hangar. A dozen women roll around the room, the thunder of steel wheels echoing off the walls. A new maple floor covers the old concrete, and three rows of aluminum bleachers sit on the far side of the room to match the ones where Roxy talks with the team Captain, Tina G. Wasteland.

At the center of the space, red, white, and orange lines define the rink.

I belong here, Annie tells herself. *This is where I'm me.*

She lets the room fill her with strength and feels Annie Rogers, meek nutritionist, slowly morph into Annabelle Lector, the demon jammer. It's hard to be a demon jammer at five-two, but she tries like hell. Shoot, Tina's only an inch taller, and she really is a bitch on wheels. Annabelle's arm still throbs where Kevin grabbed her. She feels her fear turn to anger and knows that tonight she's going to take no prisoners and eat the wounded.

Tina G. Wasteland wheels over, brown eyes narrow with concern.

"Roxy says he was here again."

"I'm OK." Annabelle Lector fears nothing except earthquakes, tornadoes, and big fuzzy spiders. That last part is a secret.

"If he shows up again, don't talk to him. Just run in here and call for help. We'll all back you, but he's got to understand that what he's doing is wrong."

"It's a hardwired guy thing." Roxy sprays her water bottle into her mouth, and Annie thinks it looks pretty obscene. "He learned his etiquette from the paintings on the wall of his cave."

In the real world, Tina G. Wasteland is a social worker at a women's shelter. Annabelle doesn't know her real name, either, because everyone uses their rink names here, but she does know that at any given time, Tina counsels anywhere from eight to fifteen battered women who have come for refuge.

Tina looks across the rink at the coach. Lugg Nutz is shorter than Kevin, but a little wider. "Let us walk out with you tonight, Annabelle. If there's any more trouble, we may need to hire security."

"How do you think we can pay for that?" Roxy asks. "We still owe the printer for the last posters, and we've got another bout coming up in two weeks."

Tina squirts water from her own bottle and Annabelle smells citrus. Most of the girls like carbonated water for more of a burst. Practice means skating between six and ten miles in the next few hours, so Annabelle's glutes are tighter than they've been since high school.

"Maybe Mr. Keogh would be willing to kick in," Tina says.

Danny Keogh is sponsoring their next meet, a fund-raiser for a new women's shelter. Keogh Contracting & Construction has decided it's good public relations to share some of the family wealth with the community.

For the next two hours, Lugg drives the women like Kentucky thoroughbreds on a muddy track.

"Jesus, Jesus, Jesus, talk to each other! When your jammer is coming around, you gotta know where she is and move your guys to the outside all together. You do this half-assed little dance like you're doing now, Annie and Tina can't get through. That's how you get points, remember? Let's try it again. Tina, start half a lap back and holler when you're about ten feet behind Grace."

Annabelle and the others follow Molly Ringworm's striped helmet. The pivots wear stripes so everyone can see them, and they set the pace. Goldee Spawn and the other blockers slow just enough to stay behind her. Annabelle's a jammer, not a blocker, but Lugg makes them practice other positions so they understand what has to happen.

"Now!" Tina's voice rebounds off the rafters overhead.

Annabelle lowers her hips and leans into Tiny Malice on her right, driving her toward the outside of the rink. She pushes from her lower legs and butt and feels the surge of energy when her forearm slides under Tiny's ribs. Leverage. She keeps her forearm against her side—elbowing is a penalty if you get caught—and slowly straightens up, driving the woman clear off the track.

"Christ," Lugg bellows. "You block like girls! Annabelle, switch places with Tina and we'll try it again. Blockers, trade sides, too."

They do it over and over for the next half hour. Then Goldee Spawn divides the group into two teams by light or dark tees.

"What, you don't want to try shirts or skins?" Roxy says.

"I don't want to corrupt Lugg."

The coach pretends to lick his eyebrows. "Too late, baby." The fluorescent lights make his hair glow like it's radioactive.

An hour later, he tells them to take five and talks with Tina and Goldee. Then they practice weaving back in forth in formation. Then he makes them do it backwards. Annabelle's calves feel like they're on fire. Then they take turns "falling small," curing into a fetal ball so skaters behind them don't run over an extended hand or foot. That's how people get hurt.

They finally call quits at nine, and Annabelle Lector tucks her sweaty gear back into her bag. All the women have helmet head, their hair dark with sweat. They look at each other with glowing faces and happy smiles and clump into a group hug before they drift out to the parking lot in twos and threes, discussing kids, work, and recipes.

Annabelle humps her bag onto her shoulder and strides toward the door, a five-foot-two badass bitch. Roxy Heartless, Tina G. Wasteland, and Lugg Nutz join her and she feels safer than gold in Fort Knox. She tells herself that Kevin's in Bristol, a half-hour drive. And he's gone for good.

Even with the sun down, the humidity still makes the parking lot feel like an armpit. The arc lights throw a blue-gray haze over girls unlocking car doors, waving good night, ready to go home to husbands and kids and real jobs for tomorrow. TGIF, then another practice Saturday morning.

Every step away from the building turns Annabelle Lector a little more into Annie Rogers, and she watches Tina G. Wasteland shrink, too. And Goldee Spawn and Novacaine Dancer. All their names are sexy or violent to sell the persona and the sport. It also makes it harder for groupies to track them down and become a problem.

"You going to be all right, Annabelle?" Lugg's eyes scan the cars. The traffic light up at the exit glows a cheerful green, but there's no traffic. There's a mini shopping center with a Laundromat next door, and that's still open, but the other side of the street and up Corbin Avenue is all residential.

"Yeah, thanks." Annie beeps her door open and slides her bag into the passenger seat. She closes the door before she hears Roxy explode.

"Shit! Mother-fucking shit. That sonofabitch!"

The blond lawyer seethes with rage before her Mercedes. The lights reflect off the diamond fragments covering her front seat.

"The asshole knows I filed the restraining order for you, so he came back while we were all inside." Her cell phone blooms in her hand again.

"You think it was Kevin?" Annie feels stupid even asking the question.

"Well, DUH..." Roxy talks into the phone. "Hello? I'd like to report a vandalized car at the corner of Corbin and Farmington. The roller derby rink. Right, the old Walmart. Someone smashed my windshield, and I think I know who it was."

She turns back to Annie again. "What's your asshole ex-boyfriend's address?"

Annie tells her and Tina steps forward.

"This is it. Tomorrow, I'm calling Mr. Keogh to see if we can get a guard down here."

#

Cavaliers Lounge is less than a mile from the Hartford PD, just go under I-91 and down the road and there you are. Hendrix finds Jimmy Byrne studying a blonde's crotch with the dispatch of an elderly gynecologist. Clearly off duty, he wears a white tee shirt and jeans below a slightly jaded expression. The girl wears a pasted-on smile, a green navel piercing, and white stilettos, a butterfly tattoo hovering over her tailbone.

Byrne sees Hendrix through the blonde's spread legs and waves him over. She shifts her position slightly so Hendrix can enjoy the view, too.

"Trash, this is Tiffany." The blonde takes Byrne's five spot in her teeth between her knees. "Tiff, this is Tracy, but we all call him Trash."

"Hi." Up close, Tiffany's breasts bear a slight scar on their underside that means implants.

Byrne lets the song finish so they don't have to shout. Unfortunately, the next song up is the Scorpions' "Rock You Like A Hurricane," which is even louder.

Tiffany sights down her tattoo at Byrne. "How about another one, honey, now that your friend is here?" The black light off to her right turns her stilettos the bluish white of a full moon, which seems appropriate.

"Sure." Byrne draws another bill from his shirt pocket. "It's on me, Trash."

"I've got money, Jimmy."

"Hey, you're on suspension."

Tiffany grinds her hips with the subtlety of a cement mixer and bends her knees to bring her crotch level with Hendrix's eyes. Her major labes showcase another green stone that matches her belly-button ring.

When a server appears in shirt and shoes—and a G string just so they can tell she's taking more mundane requests—Hendrix asks for a large coke. Even on a hot Saturday afternoon, all three pole dancers entertain a large crowd. Come nightfall, the place may have valet parking.

Byrne finishes his ginger ale. Tiffany moves to all fours and lowers her hips. Hendrix decides she's trying to engulf the empty glass and turns to see the other patrons admiring equally exotic performances around the room. When the song ends, Tiffany smiles at Byrne.

"Would you like another, honey? Maybe back in the VIP room?"

"Thanks, Tiff, but I'm kind of saving myself."

"Someone special?"

"You all are, darlin'. You know that."

Hendrix thinks Byrne could probably sell Saint Peter an Edsel that has gone off a cliff. Twice. He watches Tiffany pick up her discarded accessories and sashay back to the dressing room, then cracks his knuckles.

"How are you holding up, Trash?"

Hendrix has been suspended for three weeks, since the morning after he shot Corazon Losada dead on that stairwell. Deputy Chief Harmon Shields bends like tall grass in the political wind and has decided that the situation is too volatile to assign Hendrix to desk duty.

"My garden's going crazy." The over-dressed server appears with his Coke. "I'm had more time for weeding, so my tomatoes are great. The weather's baking my corn to shit, though."

Byrne watches a woman with purple spikes on the pole off to their left. "It's all Shields. We think that reporter is doing him in his office. He's fucking you so he can keep fucking her."

"What reporter?"

"She's with the *Courant*," Byrne says. "And she's a Latina. She's turned the shooting into a race thing, and she's after your ass."

He faces Hendrix again. "And Shields is going along because he's after her ass."

Hendrix crunches an ice cube between his teeth. "You and Sturges both said the girl shot first."

"Yeah. Shields is sitting on your grievance and Vic is raising hell. We need you."

Lieutenant Walter "Vic" Savickas paired Byrne and Hendrix as soon as Byrne made detective. He was the one who first called Tracy Hendrix "Trash," but everyone in Major Crimes was calling them "Trash and Byrne" within days.

Byrne catches their server's eye and holds up his empty glass.

Hendrix wishes he'd spent an extra hour on the range that morning. He fired fifty rounds and scored as well as usual, but it just reminds him that he's useless as a Braille skin mag. "You called me, Jimmy, remember? Wanted to meet me here? I'm assuming it wasn't just to admire the landscape."

Byrne smiles at a redhead with spikes that don't move when she shakes her head. "You want something to fill your time besides weeding your veggies?"

"Actually, I'm beginning to bond with my peppers."

"Uh-huh. Not to mention your carrot."

"I wasn't going to mention it."

Byrne keeps his eyes on the redhead. "Jenny talking to you yet?"

Jenny Della Vecchia, Hendrix's former girlfriend, called him the night after the shooting to say good-bye.

"All I get is her voice mail, and she's not calling back."

"Shit." Byrne finally turns his eyes back to Hendrix. "You want a job?"

"What kind of job?"

"Security, sort of. In New Britain. I guess someone's having trouble. Vandalism, stuff like that. Anyway, they called the New Britain PD. They couldn't put a uniform on the place, so the people called a guy named Barnes, used to be Hartford PD. He called Vic, and Vic thought of you."

Hendrix pictures himself with a beer gut and a flashlight, punching a time clock. Then he remembers the stack of bills growing on his coffee table.

"What do they pay?"

"Barnes is a PI, and his going rate is six hundred a day."

"No shit."

"Yeah shit." Byrne looks at the platform to his right. Bon Jovi's "You Give Love A Bad Name" blasts from the speakers and the redhead is trying to confirm it.

"How long do they need somebody?"

"I don't know. But it gets you out of the hot sun. Blond guys like you, you burn even worse than us redheads."

"New Britain." Hendrix lives in New Britain, so travel is no problem. "Where is it?"

Byrne digs in his jeans and produces a business card.

"Victoria McDonald. She's a social worker."

"So it's a hospital or something?" Hendrix wonders why a health facility doesn't have its own security people.

"No. She's a social worker during the day. This is a separate thing." Even in the reduced light of the Cavalier Lounge, Hendrix sees Byrne's eyes gleam. "It's roller derby."

Hendrix almost spews Coke across the table. "I watched roller derby on TV when I was a little kid. I thought it died out years ago."

"Yeah, me too." Byrne hands him the card. "But see for yourself."

Hendrix holds it so the strobe to his right flashes on it. Sure enough: Tori McDonald, MSW. He turns it over and reads "The New Britain Whammer Jammers" in ballpoint on the back.

"What I remember from TV, those women ought to be able to take care of themselves."

"Yeah," Byrne agrees. "Shit, those broads were bigger than we are."

"Probably beat us up, too," Hendrix says.

"You wish." On the far platform, a Latina with silver hair is pretending to rub her shaved crotch in some bald guy's face.

"Give her a call Monday if you decide it's worth a shot." Byrne shakes his head. "Fucking roller derby."

"It has to be a joke." Hendrix figures he'll go on line when he gets home, check it out.

A woman wearing a bridal veil and lots of lace over a push-up bra and white panties materializes by the table and looks at Byrne. Sitting down, he's almost as tall as she is in heels.

"I heard you were saving yourself, Jimmy."

Hendrix reminds himself that all the girls know Byrne by name.

"I am, Mona. For the girl of my dreams."

"Want to be the groom in the VIP room?" She leans forward, careful not to touch him in public.

Byrne glances at Hendrix. "We done here?"

Hendrix tucks the card into his pocket and walks outside into the blinding July sunlight.

Fucking roller derby.

Chapter Three

Vito's on Main replaced the Hardware City Tavern in downtown New Britain during the spring, but Hendrix has never visited since the changing of the guard, even though he's heard it offers good service and huge portions. The décor remains funky pub minus the cigarette smoke, staring across Main Street at the downtown campus of Central Connecticut State University and the grassy lot that threatens to become the New Britain Police station and block his view of the Sgt. H. J. Szczesny Parking Garage.

Hendrix sits at a table near the window and sips a Sam Adams. After meeting Byrne Saturday, he Googled the New Britain Whammer Jammers and found a Web site with intelligent commentary, great pictures, and links to several other sites, including the Women's Flat Track Derby Association and the Connecticut Roller Girls. Grrl Power for the New Millennium.

They no longer use the banked track he remembers from TV, stressing the athleticism instead of the side show, and they seem to be distancing themselves from the women who resembled stevedores. Hendrix finds page after page of rules and regulations, and more stuff on training and conditioning. What really flattens him is that there are nearly eighty sanctioned teams throughout the US and an equal number working toward that goal. Including the minor leagues, roller derby has nearly 250 teams in the lower 48 states.

The New Britain Whammer Jammers site has action shots of women in helmets and pads, bios of all fifteen players, and posed portraits that feature power tools and scary grimaces. The names merit loud rimshots, and the team portrait features the whole line-up wearing fishnet stockings and tank tops. He finds it strangely arousing. The first page also announces that the team is meeting the Raleigh Riot from Raleigh, North Carolina in two weeks as a fundraiser for the Patience Randall Women's Shelter.

Hendrix finally figures out that a "bout" is Derbyspeak for what he would call a game or a match. But the idea of a fund-raiser blows him completely away. Unless Victoria McDonald turns out to be a true bitch on wheels—he catches himself realizing how appropriate that idea is—he's already considering taking the job.

A red Civic slides to the curb across the street and a woman in dark slacks and a beige blouse waits for traffic to clear before she approaches the restaurant through the waves of heat rising off the blacktop. She's either a large petite or a small medium. Her brown hair is cut short with bangs, and aviator shades mask her eyes.

She speaks to the host and they both look toward Hendrix's table. She hooks her shades into the open front of her blouse. Her cheekbones are clean and she moves gracefully in heels, but her purse looks huge, little kid with mommy's stuff. When Hendrix stands, her brown eyes read him in the time she needs to take one step.

"Mr. Hendrix?" He's glad he chose a button-down shirt instead of his usual tee. Blue pinstripes enhance his eyes.

"Yes. Ms. McDonald?"

"Everyone calls me Tori."

She takes his hand in a grip that makes him glad she doesn't want to arm wrestle. Even in the ninety-plus heat and high humidity, her palm feels dry. "Thank you for calling me back."

She slides into the chair across from him before he can hold it. "Have you ordered yet?"

"I thought I'd wait for you." He's read the menu six times.

She pushes hers aside as though she has it memorized. "If you haven't been here before, everything is good, but their salads and sandwiches make you understand what 'awesome' is supposed to mean."

A server appears in black, order pad in hand, and the woman turns to him.

"I'll do the Tomato Gorgonzola salad, please. And a vat of iced tea."

Hendrix orders the Caprese salad and another Sam. Tori McDonald rests her chin on her small hands and they study each other across the placemats. He guesses she's close to his own thirty.

"I have to admit, Ms. McDonald, I thought Roller Derby died with big hair back in the eighties."

She gives him a smile that makes him think of a toothy chipmunk. "Yeah, around here, even earlier. But it never went away completely. It evolved to meet the times, sort of like animals. The Southwest, the Midwest, it hung on by its fingernails."

"I surfed the Net," he says. "It's coming back big time, isn't it?"

"Women find something that scratches their itch—if you'll excuse the expression—and they're on it quick. This team only formed last winter because a lot of us were tired of driving to Waterbury to practice and New Haven for bouts. We're practically still learning each other's names, but we all agree this is the neatest thing that's happened to us since we gave it up after the senior prom."

Hendrix manages not to snort beer through his nose.

"Why is that, exactly?"

The server brings Tori's iced tea; she squeezes the lemon into it, tears the paper off the straw, and sips.

"It's a girl thing, I guess. But it gets us in shape. You have to skate 25 laps in five minutes or less before you're allowed to scrimmage, about six tenths of a mile. In a full bout, you'll probably skate four or five miles. And it's a full contact sport, so we feel like the baddest bitches on the block. Actually, we wanted to call the team the Hardware City Drill Bitches, but someone decided the media wouldn't run our ads unless we were a little more kid-friendly. Not that they give us any coverage anyway."

OK, Hendrix thinks. That explains the power tools picture on the site. Tori McDonald keeps going like he's hit her fast-forward button.

"We support each other and feel better about ourselves. A lot of the girls say they feel more confident at work, or even in their lives in general. It's female empowerment without all the New Age woo-woo."

She stops long enough to take another sip of tea. "If you looked at some of the sites, you saw that it's not just hot in America."

"I did. How many teams are there in Europe?"

"I don't know, but it's huge in England. One of the New Haven teams had their first international match with the London Brawling a few months ago, and the Limeys kicked their ass around the block."

She slows down and looks at him. "Am I shocking you? I can act like a grown-up, it's what they pay me for."

"At roller derby?"

"No, that's non-profit. We all pay our own way. Travel, equipment, insurance. I meant my secret identity as a social worker."

Hendrix remembers that the Web site lists the occupations of the Whammer Jammers, and they include a doctor, a banker, a lawyer, a nutritionist, a physical therapist, and a social worker. Not an alligator wrestler or a shot-putter in the bunch, and they range from twenty to forty years old.

"If this is so cool—and I'll admit that it sounds that way from your Web site—how come more people don't know about it?"

"I think most people still have the old image in their heads. The over-the-rails and WWF stuff. It's pretty hard to shake. And we're still inventing ourselves from the ground up. Recruiting players, finding practice times, figuring out how to raise money. We're starting to get a feel for it, but it takes time."

The server brings their salads, and the tomatoes look big enough to build a small castle. Tori takes a bite, then continues.

"TV's what killed the sport in the eighties. The girls had to tour and play five or six nights a week and they burned out. Not to mention getting hurt going over that railing. It's still physical, but it's a lot safer now."

Hendrix shakes his head. "And you're here in New Britain. I've lived here for six years, and I've never heard a word about it."

"Our home rink is the other side of town, on Farmington Avenue near the middle school. We do one home match a month and a couple on the road."

"Which would be...?"

"Boston has a really kick-ass team. So does Providence. We're just starting, so they both clean our clock. Philly has a good team, and Baltimore has a great one. New Hampshire has Skate Free or Die, and another team that started up about the same time we did. Maine has a team or two."

She stops for breath and Hendrix tells himself it's time to talk business.

"I have to admit, Ms. McDonald, I'm not sure exactly what you need. My friend said 'security,' but that covers a pretty wide field."

She watches the server replace her empty tea glass with another full one, then squeezes the lemon and pops the rind into her mouth.

"Well, it wouldn't be full time. We practice two nights a week and some weekends, so we'd only need someone for when we're there, maybe twelve or fourteen hours a week."

"But why do you need anyone at all? You haven't had anyone before, have you?"

She flips over a tomato wedge with her fork. "The last couple of weeks, we've had some vandalism. Broken windshields in cars two nights in a row. And one of our girls is getting hassled by a guy she broke up with, badly enough that she took out a restraining order."

Hendrix shakes his head. "A restraining order is pretty much useless."

"Tell me about it. I counsel battered women. And the jerk showed up again the night after he'd been served. If nobody else had been out there to help, he might have hurt the girl."

She chews another mouthful of salad and Hendrix sees her glance at her watch.

"Counseling, you said?"

"Yeah. I'm at the Patience Randall Shelter. Right now, we've got seven women living there, four with husbands, three with boyfriends that like to hit them."

"Is that the place you're doing the fund-raiser for? The one I saw on your Web site?"

"Uh-huh. But we need more space and at least two more bathrooms. We've got a grant and a new place is under construction over on West Main, but it won't be ready for months."

"Where on West Main?"

"Oh, that's right, you said you live in town. One street over from the Museum of American Art. We'll be right behind the Continental Bank. Nice area again, and most of those old houses are offices now. Quiet, low key. That's what the women need."

She glances at her watch again.

"Are you interested in the job? We'd like to be able to practice without worrying that we're going to come out and find someone else's car has been hit. Even though we think it's the asshole boyfriend who's doing it."

Hendrix attended CCSU for his law enforcement degree and knows that side of town reasonably well.

"You're in that old box store by Corbin Avenue?"

"Right." She slurps the dregs of her tea.

"That's a residential area, down behind you and all around you. It could be just kids doing this, not the boyfriend."

"A few of us saw him break the first one and he's got a track record as a jerk. But I don't care who it is, we'd like it to stop."

"Twelve to fifteen hours a week." Hendrix plays with figures in his head.

"Uh-huh." The woman clasps her hands in front of her and examines him again. The purple stone on her left hand might be an amethyst, and she wears matching ear studs. "If you don't mind my asking, are you a former police officer, or what?"

"I'm still a Hartford detective. I'm on an indefinite leave."

"Injury?"

"I shot someone on a drug raid. A minority."

"Oh." The woman seems to retreat from him without actually doing so. "Did he die?"

"She. And yes."

"Oh," she says again.

"I doubt that I'd carry a weapon if I watched your practice. Just being visible in the lot might make all the difference."

"How tall are you, Mr. Hendrix? Or is it Detective Hendrix?"

"Actually, it's Tracy. On the force they called me Trash."

"I see."

"No, you probably don't. My partner's name is Jimmy Byrne, so we were Trash and Byrne. Cop humor."

The woman's eyebrows arch. "Right up there with the Drill Bitches. How tall did you say you are?"

"Five-eleven. And I weigh one eighty-five. I can bench press three-twenty and run a mile in under five minutes. Which I do regularly."

He hears bitterness creeping into his voice and finishes his beer. "Since I've been on leave, I've been spending lots of time at the gym."

"How long have you been on leave now?"

"The shooting was four weeks ago today."

"Can you legally do something like this?"

"Yes. Lots of cops moonlight."

"How much would you charge?"

Hendrix hesitates. It comes as a surprise to him when he realizes that he really wants to do it. "When is your next practice?"

"Tomorrow night. We usually go six-thirty to nine-thirty Tuesdays and Thursdays, and then Saturday or Sunday afternoon unless there's a match."

"Why don't I come tomorrow night and look around. I can meet the other skaters and they can get a look at me, too. If we agree that we can get along with each other, we can talk about a fee then."

The woman crumples her napkin into her bowl. "That sounds reasonable. Why don't you meet me there at six-fifteen."

He picks up the check and escorts her to her car. Even in heels, Tori McDonald barely reaches to his nose. The soft blacktop grips his sneakers and he wonders how she manages to avoid leaving her shoes sticking in the middle of Main Street. He watches her turn onto Bank Street, then frees his own car from the parking garage.

Just for giggles, he decides to take the long way home and check out the rink.

#

When Hendrix pulls up in front of the rink the following evening, the sun still bounces off the building's façade. It is, indeed the Caldor style, crushed stones embedded in the front so leaning against the wall will draw blood. They've added a second door at the corner of the building to Hendrix's left, probably to satisfy the Fire Marshal, and through the original double doors, he can see a sheetrock wall separating the lobby from what he assumes is the playing space.

Five minutes later, Tori McDonald steps out of her car wearing a yellow tee shirt, red gym shorts, and a Red Sox cap.

"Been waiting long?" She drags a gym bag from the passenger side. If it were any larger, he'd suspect she was smuggling in her dining room table.

"Just a few minutes. I looked around yesterday afternoon. I'm assuming the pizza joint is open when you finish, but how about the Laundromat?"

"I think it's open twenty-four-seven. The package store closes at eight, but a few of us go over to the pizza place sometimes after practice. I'm trying to get people to go down to Vito's instead because they're buying a full page ad in the next program."

She unlocks both the lock and a dead bolt. Considering that the doors are glass, Hendrix wonders why bother with a dead bolt.

"Has anyone tried to break in, or has all the trouble been with your cars?"

"So far, just the cars. There are doors in back so you can get out if there's a fire, but they don't have an outside handle."

"Panic bar on the inside?"

"Yes."

She trips the circuit breakers and lights illuminate the lobby, about twenty feet deep and the width of the building. He sees bathrooms at both sides, and another alcove at the far end that she tells him are locker rooms they only use during matches. Three vending machines flank the entrance to the rink area.

He follows her through an open arch the width of the double doors and into the space, where their footsteps echo off three rows of aluminum bleachers on both sides of the room, enough to accommodate about a hundred people. He sees two doors that break up the back wall, panic bars reflecting the light from two dozen cones hanging off the rafters. He sees a large air conditioning unit, too, but it's not turned on, and there's nothing else except the door they came through and another one that he guesses comes out beyond the locker rooms, near the other exit he's seen.

Tori dumps her bag on the near bleachers and pulls out pads, a helmet, and her skates.

"Lugg ought to show up any minute, and everyone else will be here within another ten or fifteen."

"'Lugg?'"

"Lugg Nutz, the coach. He plays hockey in the winter so he knows skating and full contact stuff. You'll like him."

Hendrix walks out onto the maple floor, new enough that he can still smell the wood and varnish. He stands on an oval outlined with orange paint, white and yellow lines crossing it on the far side.

"The orange lines are the outer and inner boundaries," Tori tells him. "The yellow lines are for jammers and pivots."

"Jammers?" He thinks he remembers the term from TV all those years ago, but feels like he hasn't done his homework.

"Yeah." In her elbow and knee pads, Tori resembles a poorly-constructed robot. "I'm a jammer. They're the only players who can score points. It's a pretty simple game, actually. Your pivot leads the pack and sets the pace. Then you've got three blockers, who try to clear the way for your jammer and keep the other team's jammer from passing them. The jammer starts behind everyone else and has to lap them all. The second time around, she gets a point for everyone on the other team she can pass. You can use a hip to block, or a forearm if it's against your body, but there's none of the punching and tripping you used to see on TV."

Tori slides her foot into a skate and starts lacing it up. "Theoretically, anyway. We all get a little carried away. You know, hold on a little or take a shot in the excitement. It's a girl thing."

Voices echo from the lobby and four more women enter. Two of them are fairly tall, but none of them strike Hendrix as really big, not like he expected. Tori does the introductions.

"Girls, this is Trash Hendrix. He's thinking about becoming our security guard, so look shy and timid. Mr. Hendrix, this is Roxy Heartless, Grace Anatomy, Molly Ringworm, and Annabelle Lector."

Hendrix does a knuckle bump with each of them. "Where do you come up with the names?" Tori called him "Trash," not "Tracy." It fits here better, anyway.

"Tina's idea." The woman with a black braid to her waist sits on the bench next to Tori and slides kneepads over yellow fishnets. "She suggested we use names that go with what we do in our other lives. I'm a physical therapist."

"Grace Anatomy?" Hendrix says, and she nods. "Cute."

"Oh, you're sweet." The woman nods at her companion. "Annabelle's a nutritionist and Molly's a hair stylist."

"How about your real names?"

"Oh, I don't even know most people's real names. Out in the real world, some people don't think we should be doing this. For awhile, we had a nun, she was Sister Twisted, but she got transferred down south in the winter. Too bad, she was a good blocker, but the Monsignor didn't approve."

"What do people say when you tell them you do roller derby?"

Grace adjusts her helmet strap to accommodate her braid. "I don't tell most people. If I do, I almost always get either 'Oh, that's too cool,' or 'you're kidding.' The second one almost always comes out like they think I'm some kind of whack job."

"How did you get into this in the first place?"

On her skates, Grace Anatomy is three inches taller than Hendrix. "Well, someone dragged me to a match in New Haven a couple of years ago and it sounded like a goof. But after about two minutes, I felt like I'd found the missing piece in my life. It's that way for all of us. This is where we can be us. More and more, I only tell people if I get that same vibe off them."

Several more women appear, along with a man, and Tori guides them toward Hendrix, who turns back to Grace.

"Did you call your Captain Tina? The woman I came in with?"

"Yeah. Tina G. Wasteland."

Right, he thinks, *the social worker*.

He meets Denver Mint Julep, Goldee Spawn, Tiny Malice, and Lugg Nutz, the coach. The skates add six inches to the women's height, but Tiny Malice is still shorter than Hendrix. Her eyes dare him to mention it.

"Tiny Malice," he says. "What's your day job?"

She takes out her mouth guard. "I teach theater."

Lugg Nutz's shoulders are wider than Hendrix's, and he's a little taller. His hands are huge and his handshake shows commendable restraint. "I used to play hockey, but not so much anymore. This is my main thing now. And I skate for the men."

"There's a men's team too?"

"Yeah, down in New Haven."

The women stretch and skate around the track to warm up. A few weave back and forth and turn around to skate backwards, too. They seem to grow even taller as Hendrix watches, the sound of steel wheels on the wooden floor like machines in a factory.

"None of these women is really huge," Hendrix says to Lugg Nutz. "Isn't size important?"

Nutz scratches his nose. "If you're good on skates, it can help. But speed and agility are better on a flat track. It's about control and communication. Our girls are still learning how to work with each other. Watch for awhile, you'll see."

"I should go outside in a few minutes."

"Oh, right." Nutz looks across the rink at the curvy brunette in black tights. "Annabelle's asshole boyfriend."

"As in Annabelle Lector?"

"Yeah. He busted her windshield last week, took out Roxy's the other night."

"Roxy?"

"Yeah, Roxy Heartless. She's a lawyer, got Annabelle the restraining order against the bozo. Lot of good it did."

"Do you mind if I talk with them for a few minutes?"

"Go ahead."

In skates, Roxy Heartless is as tall as Hendrix, with eyes that belong on a barracuda. Annabelle Lector's fawnlike eyes make Hendrix rethink his vision of roller girls again. She's only slightly taller than Tori McDonald.

"I filed the restraining order last week," Roxy says. "Wednesday. We all saw him break her windshield Tuesday night."

"Did you report that to the police?"

"Yes. They took his name, but I don't know if they even talked to him."

"I didn't file charges." Annabelle's voice hides under the rumble of wheels on the rink. Roxy Heartless turns to face her.

"Annie, come on. The least you can do is work with me. We're all worried about you."

"I don't want him to get in trouble. He really cares about me."

"Cares my ass. He busted your windshield. And you broke up with him because he scared you."

"But..."

Hendrix decides Annabelle Lector has barely graduated from college. Her helmet gives her face some of the definition that her chin still lacks.

"Where do you work, Ms...Lector? I understand you're a nutritionist, right?"

"Uh-huh. I supervise the meals at a geriatric hospital in Southington. About thirty patients."

"How long have you worked there?"

"Not quite two years. I got the job as soon as I graduated from UConn."

"What's your boyfriend's—ex-boyfriend's name?"

"Kevin Draper. He works for the city of Bristol. Department of Sanitation."

"Does he drink?"

Annabelle shrugs. "I don't know. Not really. No more than most guys, I guess."

"How much do most guys drink?"

"Um..."

"This is bullshit," Roxy Heartless says. "The guy makes her life miserable, I file an order, he shows up here again Thursday night anyway. If a bunch of us hadn't been in the lot when he pulled up, he would have hurt her, no question about it."

"Did you call the police that time?"

"Damn right. When I came out after practice and found he'd busted my windshield, too."

"But you didn't see him do it."

The lawyer's eyes turn colder. "I made an inference. And the guy was in violation of a restraining order anyway."

Hendrix watches the women skating laps and playfully bumping each other. "I hate to be the bearer of bad news, counselor, but you probably know as well as I do that the cops have too much other stuff on their plate to enforce a restraining order unless something serious happens."

"Yeah, I know, and Tina said the same thing. But Annie needs to make the guy understand that 'no' means 'no.'"

Hendrix turns back to Annabelle. "What does Kevin Draper look like?"

"He's big," she said. "A few inches taller than you are, and he works out."

"Hair, eyes? And what kind of car does he drive?"

"Brown eyes. He's shaved his head and he has a soul patch."

"It looks like he's got pubes under his mouth," Roxy says. Annabelle blushes.

"Appealing," Hendrix says. "His car?"

"A black Hummer."

"What are you going to do?" Roxy ask. "Track him down and beat him up?"

"No," Hendrix says. "But when I go outside, I want some idea of what to watch for."

Roxy Heartless and Annabelle rejoin the other skaters and he can feel a bond filling the space, so strong it almost has texture. He begins to understand why the team matters to them. Especially to someone who's still learning who she is, like Annabelle Lector.

Tori—Tina G. Wasteland—skates over to him. "I looked you up on-line after we met yesterday. Did you really shoot that girl?"

"She shot at me and my partner first," he says. "And there was enough crystal in that apartment to re-build the chandelier at the Wadsworth Athenaeum."

Her eyes look him up and down. "You're not carrying a gun now, are you?"

"No." He forces himself to back off. "I don't plan to, either. If the problem is your skater's boyfriend, maybe seeing me around will discourage him."

"So you're going to do the job? You've decided?"

He glances at his watch. "Let me watch tonight and see if anything happens."

"If you decide to do it, give me a price and I'll try to persuade our sponsor to kick in."

"Sponsor?"

She pulls off her helmet and her bangs stick to her forehead. "Yeah, we caught a break. Do you know who Danny Keogh is?"

"The builder? His family's been big around here for years."

"Yeah. He got interested in roller derby and heard we were looking for a space. He knows the guy who owns this building, and persuaded him to rent it to us for a song. And he's actually helping with our next match. Well, you probably saw that on our site, didn't you? The fundraiser."

“Danny Keogh likes roller derby?” Hendrix knows the Keogh family by reputation. “Does he know about the trouble you’ve been having?”

“It’s not really his problem. On the other hand, we’d like to be able to practice for the charity match without worrying about our cars, so I figure Nutz and I will talk to him tomorrow and see if he’ll pay for you.”

Hendrix starts doing the math in his head. The Keogh family gives enough to museums and libraries that the guy probably wouldn’t even notice a little more.

“Let me go outside and look dangerous, OK?”

#

When Hendrix steps out the glass doors again, the sun sweeps down Corbin Avenue to catch him squarely in his eyes and he moves behind the cement column to let them adjust. Seven o’clock, and it still has to be ninety outside. By the time he walks to the end of the building, his shirt has plastered itself to his back.

A chain link fence runs about thirty feet from the side of the building to a steep drop into a wooded hillside, and houses built in the fifties crowd the curving streets beyond the trees. Hendrix returns to the front, where a few cars congregate by the pizza joint. The Laundromat across from it has a few cars, too, and so does the package store.

Across the street, fifty-year old houses stretch as far as he can see in both directions. A light at the corner of Corbin and Farmington gives cars egress from the parking lot, but Hendrix sees no traffic. A quarter mile to his right, Pulaski Middle School overlooks an athletic field where he hears kids playing baseball.

Tori McDonald and Lugg Nutz picked the spot because it lies only a mile off I-84 and has 300 parking spaces, which means their growing fan base can find the site easily. They've told him that access is a major consideration.

New Britain's banner years as the Hardware City, home to Stanley Tool and Machine and a dozen other manufacturing companies, faded before Hendrix was born, but he knows that in those long-ago glory days, the city had a per capita income to challenge anywhere else in the United States. The Stanley family funded two city parks, one designed by Frederick Olmstead, and was a major contributor to the public library. The school system was the pride of New England and a model for systems nationwide. Housing skyrocketed to accommodate the influx of workers with children to fill those schools.

That was then. Since 1970, most of the factories have closed. Stanley—now owned by Black and Decker—has corporate headquarters in the Carolinas and builds its reduced inventory in China. The buyout broke the hearts of five generations of families that worked the assembly lines.

The demographics have changed as much as the economy. A century ago, New Britain mirrored the other industrial towns of the Northeast, built by Italians, Irish, and Polish. Now, the city has the second fastest Hispanic growth rate in Connecticut.

The three quarters of New Britain that surround downtown still boast breath-taking houses built by the manufacturing barons, cozy neighborhoods with smooth sidewalks where kids ride their bikes and draw hopscotch games in chalk. Even the downtown, blighted by drugs and poverty, is fighting to stage a comeback. Hendrix thinks of Vito's, where he and Tori McDonald met, the CCSU technology building, and three performing arts venues, all within two blocks of each other.

He tells himself that New Britain is a perfect location for roller derby, a former hybrid of working and middle class populations with a love of sports. At the other end of town, the New Britain

Rock Cats, a farm team for the Minnesota Twins, holds regular fund-raisers for the community.

Tori says that Danny Keogh supports the Whammer Jammers because his girlfriend is on the team. She pointed out Denver Mint Julep, manager of the Continental Bank over on West Main. Hendrix hasn't talked to her, but has noticed that in full derby gear the woman has at least four inches on him.

He's looked at the Web site more carefully, too, and now he knows that in two weeks, the Whammer Jammers will meet the Raleigh Riot to raise money for the new Patience Randall Women's Shelter being built by Keogh Construction. Tickets are twenty-five dollars instead of the usual ten, and Danny Keogh has offered to donate three dollars for every one the bout earns at the gate—after the first $10,000.

Tori claims it's a slam dunk, but Hendrix finds it hard to believe that four hundred people will show up.

He leans against the cement column just long enough to discover that the sun beating on it has turned it hot as a barbecue. He straightens up, wishing he were back in Hartford doing real cop work. He likes the women, but he can't really believe there's a problem. It's probably just kids. Malikowski Circle, an ancient housing project the New Britain cops call "Maladjusted Circle" because of the drug and domestic problems, is less than half a mile away.

Thinking of drugs reminds him of Corazon Losada. He can still see that tall shadow raising the gun and firing a shot past his ear. Then he feels the butt of his shotgun slamming into his shoulder again. From six feet, the blast was like a baseball hitting the girl in the chest at a thousand miles per hour. She was dead before she slid down the wall behind her.

Until a month ago, Hendrix never fired his weapon anywhere except the pistol range.

The skaters will practice for two more hours, and he wonders what that involves. Certainly conditioning. Lugg Nutz says that a bout is two thirty minute halves of continuous action. It explains why none of the women look flabby and several have legs fit for the Radio City Music Hall Rockettes.

What about tactics and strategy? If the game doesn't rely on brute force anymore, there has to be some kind of plan. So far, all Hendrix knows is that there are three positions and the women skate laps around a track. Only one person tries to pass the others, so it's not like a race. If he takes the job, he needs to learn more about the game.

The names make strippers look boring. Well, judging from Byrne's acquaintances, that's no challenge. Hendrix needs a woman to be entertaining even when she has her clothes on, which is why he hoped he and Jenny Della Vecchia could grow old together.

Jenny is a painter and a good cook, not to mention funny, beautiful, and a passionate lover. But she couldn't accept that he needed to shoot someone, even in self-defense. Especially not a fourteen-year-old girl.

Hendrix walks to the other end of the parking lot and weaves back through the cars, trying to memorize the models and license plates. Tori drives the Civic, and he thinks the Mercedes belongs to Roxy the lawyer. He sees a BMW, too. There's a Hyundai, two Chevrolets, a Taurus, and a couple of SUVs.

He's going to do this. It may be mind-numbing to spend three hours watching an occasional car drive down a street in a white middle class neighborhood, but it can be a little money coming in and it gives him the chance to tell himself he's being useful. Besides, he already admires the attitude and humor that seem to be part of the women's hardwiring.

A black Hummer swings into the parking lot and coasts toward him. It slides into the space nearest the door and a man with a shaved head gets out. He looks taller than Hendrix, and his red muscle shirt shows off impressive biceps. When he draws closer, Hendrix sees a soul patch.

Kevin Draper.

Hendrix intercepts him twenty feet from the door.

"Can I help you?"

The guy sizes him up briefly.

"Nah, I'm just here to meet someone."

"They're busy in there now, and practices are closed."

The guy frowns. "Who the fuck asked you?"

"I'm here to make sure the women aren't bothered. If you're Kevin, you're going to bother them."

"Beat it, guy. I'm just here to see my girlfriend. It's got nada to do with you, OK?"

"Are you Kevin Draper?" Hendrix wishes their positions are reversed so he doesn't have the sun in his eyes. "You look like him, and that looks like his car. Which means you don't belong here."

"Fuck you, Jack."

The guy tries to step around Hendrix, who lays a hand on his shoulder.

"Yeah, you're Kevin. The women told me you have a language problem."

"Hey, you're starting to piss me off."

"Kevin, there's a restraining order out on you. You're within a hundred feet of your ex- right now, so you're in contempt of court. That's a fine. If the judge is in a pissy mood, he might even throw your ass in a cell. You're breaking the law."

"This is such shit. I just want to see my girlfriend. Are you fucking deaf?"

"I think your problem is more basic, Kevin. You don't understand English. The lady is not your girlfriend anymore."

Kevin Draper's face grows red and he clenches fists the size of grapefruits.

"We love each other. You can't stop me from seeing her. So move out of the way before I wipe your face all over the fucking wall."

"Number one, you don't love each other, and two, yes, I can stop you from seeing her. I'm the security guard here. In my regular job, I'm a police officer."

"Whoa, a cop. Bully with a badge. I got friends on the Common Council. You give me shit and I'll talk to them. You'll be pounding a beat down on Broad with the Polacks and the Spics."

"How can I bully you, Kevin? You've got at least three inches on me, and probably thirty pounds, even without your mouth. But I'm telling you to get back into your car and drive away before you ruin a beautiful summer evening."

"She won't answer my phone calls, they go straight to her voicemail. She's not calling me back. I want to get this shit straightened out."

"When did you call her?"

"Today. She hasn't returned any of the fucking calls. She can't do me like this."

Hendrix hopes the guy will talk himself out, but his face keeps getting redder and his voice louder.

"How many times did you call her?"

"Who knows? Four, five? I tried like every hour, but the stupid bitch doesn't call me back. I gotta tell her to answer her friggin' messages."

"Kevin, I hate to be the one to break it to you, but it sounds like she's given you the answer."

"You asshole."

Draper telegraphs a clumsy right hook. Hendrix catches his wrist with his left hand and pivots, forcing his shoulder into the bigger man's armpit. When Draper teeters, Hendrix slams him face first into the stone column and pins the guy's fist against his back.

"Just stay there, Kevin."

"You motherfucker." The voice is still loud, but now it's muffled.

"Count to ten. Slowly."

Draper relaxes for a few seconds, then tries to whirl. Hendrix snaps that captive fist up toward the man's shoulder blades.

"If you try that again, I'll break your arm."

"Bastard." Hendrix yanks the fist up even higher and Draper rises up on his toes.

"I can see why the woman wants you out of her life, Kevin."

When Draper's breathing diminishes from snorting to normal, Hendrix pulls him a step away from the column.

"If you drive away now, I won't tell the police about this little dance. But I will tell them you came by and I had to persuade you to leave. If you stay any longer, you'll be talking to a judge tomorrow morning. And if you try busting any more windshields, I'm going to bust you, too. Understand?"

"I didn't bust that bitch lawyer's windshield." Draper's nose is bleeding. "I told the cops that, and I had a witness."

"Good. Stay where he can vouch for you from now on."

Hendrix marches the guy to his car, then watches the Hummer roar up to the traffic light and turn right toward Bristol.

When he looks through the glass doors, the lobby is empty.

The women emerge forty-five minutes later, their voices a satisfied hum that broadcasts good feeling all around. In the twilight, Hendrix recognizes Roxy Heartless, the blonde lawyer, and Grace Anatomy with her waist-length braid. The little brunette with Roxy is Annabelle Lector.

Tori McDonald strides out the door, her tee shirt blotchy with sweat.

"Well, Mr. Hendrix, how did it go?"

He glances at Annabelle Lector. "You need me. Mr. Charm came back tonight."

"Shit." The brunette sags and her blonde lawyer puts an arm around her.

"I'll call the cops again," Roxy says. "Or did you already?"

"Not yet. Ms...Lector, have you checked your voicemail today?"

"Yes." Even in the shadows, the woman's eyes shine with unshed tears. "He called me fourteen times. He's driving me crazy."

"We'll do something about it, honey." Hendrix doesn't know the woman's name, but three others echo her. "You're safe here."

Hendrix turns to Tori McDonald. "Do you think I should talk to Mr. Keogh?"

"Let me do it. And Denver's here, too. Maybe she can run interference."

They watch Annabelle Lector's Hyundai cross the intersection and disappear up Corbin Avenue.

"Where does she live?" Hendrix asks.

"Meriden. Why?"

"The opposite direction from Bristol."

Tomorrow, maybe he'll drop into the Hartford PD to see if Kevin Draper has a history.

Chapter Four

From the outside, the Hartford Police Department looks more like a poorly-designed high school than a law enforcement facility. Hendrix strides through the tiny lobby with the pillar, the house phone, and an ATM—nice touch—and upstairs to the squad room, nodding to familiar faces and trying to maintain a low profile, just on the off-chance that Deputy Chief Harmon Shields, who put him on leave, steps out of his air conditioned office.

He's been off the job for four weeks, and his desk shows that someone else is moving in. Pencils, file folders, a couple of CDs, and unfamiliar post-it notes cover his blotter and dot his PC monitor. Someone is probably juggling all the cases he was working on when Shields yanked him.

"Yo, Trash."

Kosinski and Mills nod at him from behind their computers. Mills wears jeans and a polo shirt faded to the color of pavement, and Kosinski's once-white shirt has lemony armpits.

"Whose stuff is this, do you know?"

Mills blows a bubble the size of a croquet ball and slowly sucks it back into his mouth. The effect is far more obscene than anything Hendrix saw with Byrne at the strip joint. "Guy on C shift. Jimmy thinks the guy's a hairless dick, but we got no one else."

"Gee, you mean nobody can replace me?"

"We'd have to spend money to get someone good. That's why we had you."

Kosinski stage whispers, "We weren't supposed to tell him that."

Hendrix boots up the computer. A dozen new icons bloom on the desktop, mostly case files. Hendrix double-clicks the top one and watches a word document fill the screen. Sure enough, no privacy, no codes, no nothing. If the PC is on, anyone in the room from a janitor on up can open the file. Nice.

A voice from behind him interrupts his moral outrage.

"Tracy Hendrix."

Deputy Chief Harmon Shields stands in the entranceway, his face shiny with perpetual sweat. Beside him stands a woman in a turquoise tee shirt with a deep "V" and jeans that look surgically applied.

"Hendrix, you have been relieved of duty."

"I'm on leave, Chief, not suspended. I thought I'd check a couple of things while—"

"No. You don't belong here. Anyone at the front desk should have stopped you from coming up."

Prevailing wisdom is that Shields walks through the squad room once a day so he can remember how to find the exit. Nobody remembers him ever handling a case or even being a cop until the day he magically appeared behind his desk. His appearance doesn't help: he's well over six feet tall but weighs less than Hendrix, with greasy-looking hair and a complexion that makes him resemble a waxy candle.

Hendrix closes the file on his screen before he stands up. The woman with Shields has dark curly hair that matches her almond-shaped eyes above clean cheekbones. Her eyes flick back and forth between the two men.

"In the first place, Deputy Chief Shields, you could have put me on desk duty, but you decided to put me on leave. In the second place, I should still be receiving full pay for that leave. Internal Affairs ruled that I acted in self-defense. I assume my grievance is still on someone's desk, maybe even yours."

"Department guidelines prohibit using a firearm against anyone under the age of sixteen, Hendrix."

"Against anyone I have reason to believe is under sixteen." Hendrix sees Savickas, his command Lieutenant, round the corner and stop dead. His hair is as white as paper and now his eyes roll to the ceiling.

"The shooter was between us and a bare light bulb so we couldn't see her face," Hendrix continues. "And we were several steps below the landing so we couldn't judge height. The girl turned out to be five-foot-nine anyway. We couldn't even tell she was female, never mind her age."

"But you shot her at point-blank range with a twelve-gauge shotgun." The woman's words carry a slight lisp and a sharp edge.

"I don't think I got your name, Ms."

The woman draws herself up to her full height. She's less imposing than Tori McDonald, who is probably three inches shorter.

"I am Carmen Ortega of the Hartford Courant."

She digs into her purse and Hendrix realizes she's going to hand him a business card.

"I am here to see that the police are responsive to the needs of the Hispanic community. And shooting a teen-aged Latina doesn't fit that template. You should be facing a murder charge."

Hendrix remembers that Jimmy Byrne thinks Shields is boning this woman.

"Excuse me, Ms. Ortega." Vic Savickas gives Hendrix a look that makes him close his mouth. "The young woman fired at our men first, even though they had identified themselves as police officers. We dug the bullet out of the wall. Even if Detective Hendrix could tell that the shooter was a young female, his action was appropriate under the circumstance."

"He shot to kill. He should have shot her in the arm or leg."

"Jesus Christ, lady." Hendrix sees Vic shaking his head, but keeps going. "When someone shoots at you, you take it personally. All you care about is not dying. Besides, I had a shotgun. At that range, shooting her in the arm or leg would have blown it off, and she might have kept shooting anyway. She had fourteen rounds in that gun."

"Sure, crazy spics versus the racist Hartford police. Heard it, heard it, heard it." The woman would look like a cartoon if she weren't so serious.

Shields curls his fishlike lips. "Detective Hendrix, your leave at half-pay will be rescinded tomorrow. From this moment on, consider yourself suspended without pay pending a further investigation of the shooting."

"One Goddamned minute here." Vic Savickas slides between the reporter and Shields. "That's crap, Shields, and even you have to know it. It's a violation of my officer's rights, and the union will know about it in ten minutes."

"Sure, go to the union." Carmen Ortega sounds like a little kid ragging on someone's mother. "Look out for your own, one bad apple turns the whole barrel rotten."

"It's true," Hendrix says. "Owen, Sturges, me, and all the other niggers on that raid."

Savickas turns the color of library paste and the room becomes silent, like after Hendrix fired the shotgun in that stairway. Vic steps in before the shit gets any deeper. "Ms. Ortega, if you want to work with this department, you'll make your job a lot easier if you treat us as professionals instead of thugs. Just like you want us to treat you as a journalist instead of the Deputy Chief's bimbo."

"Detective...Savickas, you're—"

"Sa-VICK-as, Deputy Chief. I've been commanding the B squad for six years and you don't even know my name yet, do you? I'm defending one of my officers because you won't. And if you want to put me on report, too, I've got several witnesses who will back me when I file another grievance."

"Enough." Shields's face glows red, which makes him look even more like a candle. "Savickas, you're getting a letter in your file for insubordination. And Hendrix, you are now suspended without pay. I'll make sure your access code to the computer system is invalidated, too."

Shields strides toward the stairs, almost dragging the reporter behind him. Hendrix expects her to stick out her tongue at him before she vanishes, but she doesn't.

"Shit." Mills dumps his bubble gum in the waste basket.

"You didn't have to get into it, Vic." Hendrix notices that he's sweating. "I could have handled it."

"Yeah." Savickas sits at his desk and finds a roll of antacid mints. "I noticed."

"It was my battle; you shouldn't get a letter."

"Fuck the letter. He won't write it. He was just waving his dick for that broad."

"Hey," Kosinski says. "He doesn't know who you are anyway, Vic. If he asks, we'll tell him your name is Michael Ross."

Serial killer Michael Ross received the last lethal injection administered by the State of Connecticut.

"I like it." Savickas turns to Hendrix again. "Got a Plan B, Trash?"

Hendrix stares at his screen saver.

" I've just become a security guard for the New Britain Whammer Jammers."

#

Daniel Michael Keogh III is one negotiated "yes" away from everything he's ever dreamed of having in his entire life.

That negotiated "yes" sits across from him wearing an off-white silk blouse and chocolate blazer that matches her hair. Her name is Georgia Leigh Pitcher, but she comes from Louisiana, although she's lived in New England long enough to hide her accent when she wants to. Right now, sipping a glass of white wine, she doesn't seem to want to.

"You look tired, Sugar Plum." Her syrupy vowels slide into Danny's ears and he stops thinking about anything at all to admire her face. Her cheeks are a little too plump so her nose looks a little too small, but her teeth are a dazzling white so that when she smiles, everything falls into place. He first told her he loved her last winter, when the night they met progressed smoothly into breakfast at his place the next morning. He still hasn't figured out how to explain to her that she makes him feel adequate, which his family never quite managed to do.

"No," he says. "It's just this humidity, turns me to mush."

"Not all of you, I hope." Georgia's spaniel eyes flick down and he knows she's looking through the mesh table, outside, so they can enjoy the refreshing evening breeze. The Elbow Room, which bills itself as "An American Joint," is on a main dog-walking route in West Hartford Center and even supplies big stainless steel bowls of water for those patrons who want to stop for dinner outside with their pets.

"I was looking forward to letting the evening go on a little bit." Georgia's wine-fueled drawl makes it sounds like "Lill biht."

"Don't worry." The server refills their water glasses and assures them that their meals will be up momentarily.

"Oh dear," Georgia says. "I do hope we can have them for longer than that." She smiles at the guy in his white shirt and black slacks, seeing that he doesn't have a clue. Danny knows that she will correct people who use "multiple" instead of "many," too. She has a full demonstration built around "Lie" and "Lay," but that's a private tutorial.

The server blinks and asks would they like more wine while they wait.

"None for me, darlin', but thank you anyway." Georgia's voice makes the kid, probably still an undergrad, look like he wants to drop to his knees and have her tap his shoulders with a sword. Or tuck him in, but Danny's got dibs on that.

"Me neither, thank you." The kid floats blissfully away and Danny turns to Georgia again.

"Victoria McDonald called me this morning. She wants to hire a security guard for your practices, and she says she's found someone. Something about more trouble last night?"

Georgia watches the couple walking an English sheepdog across the street. "That same low-life came back, and I gather that he wanted to bother Annabelle again. But a man made him leave. He was a tad ambiguous about exactly what happened, but I got the impression it involved more than his saying 'please.'"

"But no real violence."

"I don't believe so. No."

Danny knows that Georgia can read situations and people as easily as he can read a blueprint. It complements her ability to juggle complex mathematical functions in her head. She manages three New Britain branch offices of Continental Bank and has increased their loans and collateral, even over the last two years with the economy bleeding all over the streets.

"I hate to bring in security." Danny sips his wine.

"You can afford it, Sugar Plum. Why, you have more millions than Miss America has teeth."

Georgia smiles like they're already naked in bed. "You just want a whole boatload of people to see your girlfriend on skates, right?"

Before Danny can think of a clever reply, the server arrives with their entrees.

"Diver sea scallops," he intones. He might be conducting mass. "And Chilean sea bass. May I take your salad dishes?"

Georgia sends him off with another one of her stunning smiles before Danny continues.

"I want to see the place packed for the fund-raiser. I don't want people to think their cars are at risk when they park or that some jerk is going to cause trouble."

"I think the gentleman last night made it clear to the jerk in question that it was a bad plan." Georgia watches a pair of schnauzers prance by with their owners. "Why are you so concerned about this, Sugar? You could just write a check if you want to."

"It's not just the money as money. It's how people will look at it. Perception is everything."

"Not quite," she murmurs. Her eyes make him glad that they aren't playing poker. "But it's pretty darn close." It comes out "purdy durn close."

Danny's grandfather established the moving and storage business after World War I and slowly engulfed several other competitors. His son, an apple who didn't fall far from the tree, took up where his father left off and expanded into plumbing and heating after the second Great War, then into building. He made even fewer friends than his father.

Daniel Michael Keogh III has inherited his mother's sense of humor in place of his father's hunger and was stunned when the old man finally died and left him in charge. His two older sisters—either of whom could play the rich bitch on any soap opera ever written—expected to inherit control and haven't forgiven Pop for passing them over in favor of his only son, six years younger than either of them. Patricia now lives in Palm Beach with her third husband and Katherine lives in Lauderdale and cheats on her fourth. Neither gives a shit about building or moving or any of it, but there's a principal to uphold.

Danny looks at the tasteful gold necklace Georgia helped him pick out for her birthday present two months before.

"I guess I've just answered my own question, haven't I?" Georgia dips a scallop in the melted butter.

"I can see the new building out my office window," she says after chewing. "It looks like things are moving along like a bee through a rose garden."

"We're catching up now." Danny's sea bass almost dissolves on his tongue. "All that rain last month put us behind, but this heat means the ground's dry enough so we can sink the supports and get the basement settled. We should be back on track in another week or so."

Part of the problem has been getting a zoning variance to put a shelter among the Roaring Twenties homes that are now mostly office space for lawyers, dentists, and realtors. But the Museum of American Art is one block over and two churches are in walking distance, so it's a quiet neighborhood. Besides, having one of his main construction projects next to the bank means Danny can stop in to see how work is progressing, then walk next door to visit Georgia, whom he decided months ago is more than a girlfriend.

"How did practice go last night?" he asked. "Outside of the dickhead?"

"Well, a couple of the newer girls are starting to fit in, and Nutz is making us talk to each other more. We still need to be in better shape, though. Late in a match now, all I want to do is lie down."

"Lugg is a pretty big guy. Can't he handle the clown himself?"

"Not if he's inside, teaching us delicate little blossoms how to play like the big boys.

And this man does seem to be awfully determined. Annie's told him that she wants out, and I know for a fact that she doesn't stutter."

"Annie?"

"Annabelle Lector."

"The only two skaters I know by your real names are you and Tina. And I only know her real name because she got me to help out with the rent and the building."

"No, sugar." Georgia dips another piece of scallop in butter. "I got you to help out with the rent and the building. After you saw me in my red fishnets, you were so smitten I could have asked you to buy us the Hartford XL Center for practice and you would have done it."

"No," he says. "I can't afford that."

"But you would have tried to raise the money." Georgia's brown eyes look wicked. "Admit it; you would have come back to Continental for a loan."

"Wouldn't that be a conflict of interest?"

She finishes her wine. "I do so love a man who thinks with his...heart."

Danny turns his attention to the sea bass until he gains control again. He knew Georgia Leigh Pitcher only as his banker for nearly a year before he discovered that, by night, she's Denver Mint Julep, a blocker with a roller derby team he didn't even know existed. They took their relationship beyond her polished mahogany desk only weeks later.

He lays his Amex on the black folder with their check, then tips in cash so the kid can afford another textbook. He and Georgia link arms and weave through the tables and out among the trees and huge planters lining the curbside. A few doors down, Reigning Cats And Dogs displays a sign announcing that they will close before the end of the month. Their display window showcases a stainless steel bowl like the ones at the Elbow Room.

"This place is the closest thing animals have to Neiman Marcus," Georgia comments. In heels, she's three inches taller than Danny. They stroll around the block to his Porsche and he holds the door. Her BMW is back in his garage, and her overnight bag is already in his bedroom.

"So you won't pay for a security guard?" she asks.

"I'd rather not." He looks through the CDs in his case to buy time.

"Be a real nice idea if we could concentrate on practice. You want publicity, think of your girlfriend and her wheel bitch buds seriously kicking Raleigh tush."

"Let me think about it, OK?" He puts back the CDs. "I told Tori to call me if there's a problem again tomorrow night."

Her hand wanders beyond the gear shift and strokes his forearm. "Anything I might be able to do to make you think more favorably in our direction?"

"I don't think I can think any more favorably in your direction."

"You never know." Her fingertips slide up his arm.

"You have any ice in that nice big house of yours?" Her drawl makes the word sound like "oz."

"I can send the servants out to grow some."

"Oh, that's very good, Sugar Plum." She tightens her seat belt. "When we get back to your place, you find some of that ice, and I'll show you another way a pitcher is worth a thousand words."

#

From the Hartford PD, Hendrix takes I-91 South. By the time he peels off onto the Berlin turnpike and cuts through Newington and into New Britain, he no longer wants to stuff Harmon Shields into the shredder next to his desk. He's still pondering Carmen Ortega, though, who strikes him as more of a firecracker than a journalist, but the few people left in print need a gimmick to compete with the Internet. The Courant, which bills itself as the oldest continuously published newspaper in the country, has reduced its size and coverage twice in the last two years, so maybe the woman's days are numbered anyway.

In summer, the nine million school buses that turn New Britain's residential thoroughfares into a parking lot are hibernating, so Hendrix cruises down the tree-lined streets with no difficulty.

Except for fresh paint and sealer on the driveway, his house probably looks pretty much the way it did during the Vietnam War, a three-story frame with a small screened porch in back. The houses for blocks in each direction are variations on the same theme. They convey a serenity that the town is trying to regain after forty years of municipal laissez-faire that turned downtown into an asphalt cesspool.

He squeezes his Accord down the driveway between his own and his neighbor's house, narrow enough to use for a sobriety test, and trots to the back door. The sun beats down on his vegetable garden, which peers over weeds tougher than a street gang. His clothes stick to him and it isn't even noon. He unlocks the back door and turns on the AC, then trots upstairs.

With the rising heat and the window on the sunny side of the house, the air in his bedroom is even heavier than downstairs. He watches the AC gently move the curtains and tells himself it will make a difference. Then he changes to a tee shirt and cargo shorts and goes outside to check his garden.

No rain for over two weeks of ninety-degree heat has turned his back yard to a wire brush and his garden sags under the weight of direct sun. His tomatoes glow fiery red, but the leaves on his zucchini, summer squash, and peppers all look more gray and brown than shiny green, and the weeds that he spent hours hacking a week ago already resemble a jungle again. He spends the next two hours trying to conquer Mother Nature. He might as well try to fly.

"Spencer Tracy, you work too hard. Come over here and have some iced tea."

Across the driveway, Paola Roccapini wears a hat with a floppy brim the size of a manhole cover. Her crimson shirt hangs open over a white Foxwoods tee, and her cut-off jeans reveal legs that women a third of her age would kill for.

"I'm almost done, Ms. Roccapini."

"The sun is too hot. You come over here and cool off." When she holds up the glass, he can see the condensation beading up like an old Kool-Aid ad and his work ethic goes belly up.

"Remember," she tells him, "turn on your hose when you finish dinner, soft, just a trickle then come out and shut it off after dark. About three hours, very soft. No nozzle, just trickle. Let the water soak in."

Hendrix cuts the woman's lawn and shovels her snow in the winter. In return, she buries him in a steady stream of homemade bread and pasta. He's told her that he likes to cook, but the idea of a man cooking seems to violate her understanding of the sacraments. If he can ever figure out the last ingredient in her spaghetti sauce, he will have the most important secrets of the universe.

She watches him sip. “That’s good, you just sip. Don’t gulp. You want I should go get you some lemon?”

“No, thank you, Ms. Roccapini. This is great.”

“Spencer Tracy, we live next door to each other, what, five years now?”

“I think so, yes.” He was walking a beat in the South End when he decided his job was secure. New Britain’s prices were already sliding, and the house is near two different entrances to the highway, so he can reach Hartford in twenty minutes.

“So how come you still don’t call me ‘Paola’ like I tell you?”

“I don’t know, Ms.—Paola. It just sounds funny.”

“So what’s funny? We friends, yes?”

He’s on the point of mentioning the age difference, but that will start her stand-up routine about her age. He walked into that one the first summer and still believes it’s probably true.

Wearing a bathing suit that did nothing to hide her still considerable charms, Paola Roccapini graced the nose of her husband’s jet fighter during the Korean conflict. After his discharge, they supported the Baby Boom enthusiastically—six kids—and Hendrix suspects that Dominic died blissfully in bed. When Hendrix complimented the woman’s beauty, she gave him a smile like Scherazade.

“I just eighteen, you know.”

“Eighteen?” He doesn’t look that gullible, does he?

“That’s the last birthday I celebrate. Two years ago. Now I’m eighteen ana half.”

The year was 2006 and Hendrix felt a click in his head. “Ms. Rocca—Paola—is your birthday in February, by any chance?”

“Thatsa right. The twenny-ninth. So I only have eighteen birthdays. I just eighteen.”

Her smile almost made it plausible.

“I no see your young lady ina while.” Paola Roccapini’s gifts don’t include subtlety. “You two have a fight?”

The summer sun leans on Hendrix’s shoulders and threatens to bake his brains through his Red Sox cap.

“A handsome young man like you, lonely no good.” Ms. Roccapini takes back his empty glass. “You should come over for supper. You like, I call up my grand-daughter. She’s a pretty girl, nice. About your age.”

“Thanks, Paola, but that’s OK.” The last thing he needs is an Italian grandmother setting up his dates.

“I just saying, you know?”

“Yes. Thank you. I appreciate it. But if your grand-daughter is anything like you, she has all the boyfriends she can handle already.”

Paola Roccapini gives him that amazing pin-up girl smile. “Spencer Tracy, you a real gentleman.”

He returns to his garden. The few ears of corn he planted are only a foot tall and he yanks them up along with the remaining weeds. He weighs the economics of working security for the roller girls. If he charges the same eighty-five dollars an hour that Byrne says is that PI’s going rate and covers three four-hour practices a week, it will cover his expenses. He’ll make his offer to Tori McDonald tomorrow night. If she can’t persuade Danny Keogh to kick in, he can come down a little. He’s already picked up on the group’s vibe and he likes the way the women take care of each other. They seem to have a sense of humor, too, so that even though they play everything over the top, they don’t take themselves seriously. There’s probably a lesson in there.

He still wants to see if Kevin Draper, Annabelle's boyfriend, has a record. A twenty-something sanitation worker who drives a Hummer and can be a first class asshole may have had practice. But if neighborhood kids are part of the problem, too, Hendrix may have the job for longer, which wouldn't suck.

Then he remembers that Draper broke his girlfriend's window in front of witnesses.

At the very least, Hendrix figures he can watch the cars until the fund-raising match in two weeks. And he'll get to learn more about the sport.

He goes inside to get a beer and call Tori McDonald.

Chapter Five

Danny Keogh's mornings glow a little brighter after Georgia spends the night. He loves shaving in the morning after they've made love, watching her wear one of his old shirts as she glides by him to take her own turn in the shower while he goes downstairs to make coffee.

He's never asked a woman to move in with him before, and she still won't do it, but they sleep together three or four nights a week and her clothes have gradually taken over two drawers in his bureau and most of the closet in one of the spare bedrooms. Her shampoo and various cosmetics claim space on his bathroom counter, too.

"Delayed gratification keeps you alert, Sugar Plum," she tells him whenever he asks her to move in again, which is about every two weeks. "I don't ever want you to stop wanting me."

He's been with enough women in his thirty-five years to be fairly sure that won't happen, and he says so. But she gives him a slow wink, sips coffee and a small glass of grapefruit juice, munches two slices of lightly buttered whole wheat toast, skims the Hartford Courant, kisses him demurely on the cheek, and plunks her Pierre Cardin overnighter into the trunk. She aims her

BMW at the bank, looking so prim that her underlings probably suspect she's still a virgin.

Thursday dawns hot again, but less humid than the last week, and Danny glories in the difference when he greets his receptionist for the morning he'll actually be in the office. The dry weather means all the building projects are going at warp speed, and he'd rather lay shingles or drive screws than sit behind a desk, but that's the price he pays for being Number One Son. His sisters may forgive him on his deathbed, and he figures they'll outlive him just so they can spit on his grave. Then they can claw out each other's throats over the business again unless he has a kid of his own to leave it to.

Which makes him think of Georgia Leigh Pitcher again. If she marries him, he won't even ask her to give up working unless she wants to. Shit, he won't even ask her to give up roller derby.

The phone on his desk buzzes.

"Mister Keogh, there's a Mr. Hendrix here. He wants to see you for a few minutes, and he says it's about the Whammer Jammers."

Mr. Hendrix looks like a rehabbed surfer dude in a white tee and jeans under a safari shirt, but something in his blue eyes gives Danny the feeling that he can whip ass faster than he himself can drive a nail. In sneakers, he's got a couple of inches on Danny and his voice sounds like he's used to being listened to. Once.

"Mr. Keogh, Victoria McDonald told me you're sponsoring the Whammer Jammers' charity match and offering matching funds for the shelter, is that right?"

OK, this is the guy Tori's told him about. Danny watches Hendrix slide into a chair and take in the office with one glance that never seems to leave his own face.

"That's right."

"Can you tell me more about that?"

"Can you tell me why you're interested?"

Hendrix, Tracy Hendrix. Danny never forgets names.

"You're the detective that reporter mentioned in the Courant this morning."

Hendrix doesn't move. "I haven't seen today's paper."

Right, Danny thinks. And my mother's a pelican.

"Something about you being suspended by the Hartford PD after shooting a kid."

"That's me." The guy doesn't offer any excuses and Danny's impressed. "How did you get involved in roller derby, Mr. Keogh?"

"How about you, Mr. Hendrix?"

"Someone called me. I understand the team's had a couple of incidents in the last week or two. They asked the police to do something about it, and one thing led to another."

Hendrix's body language reminds Danny of Georgia Pitcher conducting business across her desk. He doesn't seem to move at all, but he gives off the vibe like he hears and sees and smells everything within a half mile. If he's guarding the girls, Danny gets the feeling that they're safer than they'd be in a convent with a moat full of sharks.

"So, where is it leading now?"

Hendrix still hasn't moved. "I was there two nights ago to check things out. A man showed up who already has a restraining order on him, and I had to persuade him to go away. I'm worried that it might happen again."

So this is about money. Danny stays motionless, too. "If you've made him go away, I'm sure he'll stay away."

Hendrix hitches up his sleeves and lets his hands dangle over the arms of his chair. "This guy's used to doing what he wants. I have coping skills, but I don't get the impression that the team can afford my expertise unless you help out a little."

Danny shakes his head.

"I'd rather not. I think you've probably already done what was necessary. We've never had any trouble before, and I'd hate to give people the impression that we have any now."

"Ms. McDonald tells me the bout—is that what you call them?—is a fund-raiser for a new women's shelter. Seems ironic, doesn't it? That you're willing to give them money, but not pay for protection now. Especially since I get the impression I'm chump change compared to what you're offering them."

"You've got a point there." Danny wants to be on the road, visiting places where the smell of sawdust and the screech of power saws fill the air. "The Fire Marshall gets acid reflux every time he walks into the old place. Building the new shelter is actually going to be cheaper than trying to rebuild the dump they're in now."

"And you're building the new one." Hendrix's voice makes Danny feel like a robber baron.

"Yeah, but a lot of it is with grants. We found another building that was ready to be condemned and razed it. Now we're building the new facility in a nice location."

"Good PR, right?"

"Well, yeah." Danny wonders why he feels defensive. Shit, he's said almost the same words to Georgia. "My family was making money in New Britain even during the depression. It's time we gave something back."

"So why the fund-raiser?"

Danny wants to look at his watch, but won't give Hendrix the satisfaction.

"Like you said. Good PR. Besides, I've gotten into the derby in a big way. I think it's good for the women to get some attention, too."

Hendrix leans back in the chair. "I didn't even know roller derby still existed until a few days ago. How did you find out about it?"

"One of my work crew guys mentioned it to me. Someone he knew told him about it, he went to a bout, thought it was cool, and now he's the team's announcer. I thought he was putting me on until I went to a bout, too."

"I haven't seen a bout." Hendrix sits up straight again, his vibe like a kid who's been promised a trip to the circus if he's a good boy. "I watched some of the practice the other night, though. The women really get into it."

"Wait until you see an actual bout." Danny tries to find the words. "You get seven, eight hundred people, it feels like the high school gym in a basketball game with the cross-town rivals. And the girls have people selling cupcakes, tee shirts, jewelry, all kinds of shit. It's like the Guilford Craft Fair meets the World Wrestling Federation. Only the snacks are better."

Danny couldn't imagine it himself until he walked through the doors down in New Haven. Then he went to the after-bout party and realized the blocker he'd cheered for all night was the woman who wore pinstripes behind the desk at the Continental Bank six blocks down the street from where he sits now. And she drove her car behind him all the way from New Haven to West Hartford.

"The women get a lot of self-confidence and support from each other," he says. "That's very cool."

Hendrix stares out the window as though he's talking to himself. "Then it would probably be even better if they didn't have to worry about some asshole smashing their windshields while they're practicing, don't you think?"

Danny realizes he didn't even see it coming.

"Concentrate on practice, making this match a real good one for the women who need that new shelter." The guy's still looking out the window.

"And you're calling it the Charity Jam." Hendrix turns back to Danny. "I don't quite get the name."

"A jam is what they call each play, when the jammers try to lap the other team and get points."

"OK. They gave me a crash course the other night, but I haven't got it all down yet."

"Once you watch it, things start to make sense in about two minutes."

"I'll bet." Hendrix shifts gears. "Do you know Annabelle Lector? She's the woman with the boyfriend problem. Brunette, on the small side?"

"I don't remember her by name. Besides, on skates, most of the women are my height. Some of them would be even taller than you are."

"True." Hendrix stands. "Look, Mr. Keogh, I'd like to help these women, but I can't do it for free."

Danny hesitates. "How much are you looking at?"

"I was thinking four-hour shifts until the fund-raiser in two weeks. That's three practices this week, two and the match next week. Three-fifty a shift."

What the hell, Danny tells himself. Tori McDonald seems to want it, and Georgia does, too. She thinks it's a good investment, and he knows that keeping Georgia happy is an even better one.

"Could you see your way to two-fifty a pop?"

"How about three?"

Danny looks the guy over. "Do you have a license for this kind of stuff?"

"I've still got a badge. Will that do?"

Danny remembers the article. He's suspended without pay, and the article in the paper didn't mention for how long.

"We'll do the three-fifty," he says. "You want me to sign anything?"

Hendrix stands and puts out his hand.

"Why don't you call Ms. McDonald and tell her she doesn't have to come up with the money on her own. I'll whip up an invoice and e-mail it to you to look over."

#

Hendrix cruises into the parking lot about one minute before Tori McDonald's Civic, and Lugg Nutz's beat-to-shit Dodge truck pulls up next to her before she kills her engine. Hendrix holds her door.

"Whoa," she says. "This is going to cost extra, isn't it?"

"That's only when I wear a tie," he tells her. He's in a black tee shirt and jeans, with black sneakers to complete the look.

"Oh, OK. But you look like a real bouncer now. I'd be scared of you."

"It's the Red Sox cap that does it, isn't it?"

"Yeah, probably. West of here, most of the people are Yankees fans." She slides her gym bag's strap over her shoulder. "No tattoo?"

"I never show that on the first day."

"Oh, cool." Her aviator sunglasses make her seem taller. "Something to look forward to."

"You wish," he says. "Danny Keogh says he'll pick up the tab for two weeks. At least through your fund-raiser."

"What are you charging?"

"Three-fifty for four hours, six to ten. You're all done by then, aren't you?"

"Yeah, more like nine-fifteen, nine-thirty."

He holds the door for her and she steps into the building. "What if we're still having problems then?"

"One day at a time, OK?" In the stuffy semi-darkness, Hendrix watches Lugg Nutz flick the circuit breakers. Tori goes into the arena and parks her stuff on the near bleachers before he turns to the coach.

Lugg Nutz, a plumber in Hartford, has a pale face under his neon hair and his left nostril sports a small silver ring. His introduction to roller derby is so similar to Danny Keogh's that Hendrix wonders if someone handed out scripts.

"How do you think you'll do next week/" Hendrix asks him.

Nutz makes sure Tori's out of earshot. "They'll kick our ass. They've been together for three years. Some of our kids only qualified for skating a few months ago, and only six of them were in a match before February."

In the rink area, Tori has turned on the ceiling fans and the air moves sluggishly around the room. Hendrix doubts that it will help much.

"We don't have exactly what we need for positions, either," Nutz continues. "I could use one more jammer. I'm working with Tiny Malice, but she's still got lots to learn."

"Who are your jammers?"

"Tori and Annabelle. Tori's OK, but Annabelle's not quite quick enough."

"Or big enough?" Hendrix remembers the Bay Area Bombers on TV.

"All our jammers are small, but I like it that way. They can maneuver better. Big kids are better for blocking. Our best blocker's probably Denver Mint Julep."

"Which one is she?"

“Brunette. She’s got a little southern drawl. With her skates on, she’s taller than either of us.” Nutz pulls a clipboard from his bag and studies his notes. “She and Tina got Danny Keogh to throw down with us.”

“How did they do that?”

Nutz digs in his bag for his skates. The previous session, Hendrix felt jealous watching the guy drift forward and backward at will. Put wheels or blades on his own feet and he’s on his ass in five seconds.

“Danny came to a match in New Haven last winter. Some of the girls invited him to the after party—everyone’s starving after a bout, so we hit a bar, preferably one with decent food—and I think Denver went home with him.”

“Is that why you’re in it, too? The camaraderie?”

The coach watches Tori stretching her hamstrings and quads against the metal bleachers. Two more women walk in, their voices echoing in the space. They wear tee shirts and gym shorts, too, and one has a braid that falls nearly to her waist. Hendrix can’t put names to either of them yet.

“I think we all are. The girls found something that Girl Scouts and the Pep Club can’t give them. Then someone dragged the guys here—like me—and we found out just how ballsy and smart the girls are.”

“They don’t mind being called ‘girls?’” Hendrix asks. Not ‘women,’ or ‘ladies?’”

“Not here. They’re like the eighties punk girl bands, you know, riot girls with three ‘R’s. It’s a major turn-on.”

“Like mud wrestling?” Hendrix remembers Jimmy Byrne’s ongoing romance with thirty strippers.

Nutz cocks an eyebrow at him. “News flash for you, guy. These women are all white collar. Lawyers, social workers, bankers. You can’t tell with the helmets and pads, but a lot of them are pretty, too, and you know they're in condition. Before the league even lets you scrimmage, you've got to be able to skate twenty-five laps in five minutes or less. Unless you get a serious injury—which doesn't happen too often, you can do this for years. I've heard of a woman on the West Coast who's in her fifties."

"You're kidding." Hendrix watches Tori and the other women exchange hugs.

"I think they call her 'The Hot Flash.'"

More women trickle in as Tori McDonald and the woman with the braid skate slow laps to warm up. The rumble of wheels echoes around the big room.

Nutz laces his other skate in a double bow knot.

"You know the most dangerous animal on earth? A human female. They can take three times the pain a guy can stand, they have higher resistance to disease, and their life expectancy is about nine years longer. But we treat them like friggin' crystal. They're going crazy for a way to let the shit out, and roller derby is it. They'll beat the crap out of each other, then come back to the bench with their eyes like a golden retriever and say, 'oooh, did I do that?' when what they mean is 'did you see me put that bitch down?' I love these girls."

More women enter and start putting on their armor. The one with the braid leads others in stretching exercises and Hendrix tries to remember her name from the other night.

"Do you get a lot of problems like the guy who's bothering Annabelle now?"

"Nope." Nutz digs into his bag and finds a whistle. "There was a guy out in the Midwest a couple of years ago, but the girls called the cops and that ended it pronto."

Voices bounce off the walls and raise the energy level in the room. A couple of women blow kisses at Nutz; Hendrix decides they may be greeting him, too.

"Besides," Nutz adds. "That asshole's not about roller derby at all."

"Do you know him?" Hendrix thinks the slim woman with the long dark hair is Grace Anatomy, but he's not sure. She wears a black leotard and red tee with a bulls-eye on it.

"Nope. I hope he stays the hell away now. Or you can get rid of him. That's pretty much your main job here now, isn't it?"

"It looks like." Hendrix hopes it's that easy. The women seem to be happy and the sight of a dozen toned young female bodies rolling around is refreshing. For the first time in weeks, he's not thinking about Jenny Della Vecchia

"How much strategy is there to this?" he asks. "I understand the basics, but that's all."

"It's not exactly rocket science. Help your jammer through the pack and try to stop the other one."

"I got the feeling it's not as rough as it used to be."

"Not with the flat track. You can't heave someone over the rail. Which is fine. I've been doing derby for about two years now, and the only serious injury I've seen is a broken collar bone last year. Outside of that, a few twisted ankles and stuff, but everyone has to learn to fall small, it's part of the training."

"What are you working on tonight?" Hendrix counts fifteen women in the place, and two men, which means he should get outside.

"Endurance. And some drills to help the blockers clear a way for our jammer better. Swear to God, there are a few teams, clear the lane so fast it's like their jammer is coming down a pipe. Two minute jam, they can get about fifteen points."

"Is that a lot? I don't even know."

"Yeah. The bout's sixty minutes, like a football game. Figure a team getting two touchdowns in two minutes and multiply it by fifteen jams in a half."

Hendrix picks out Annabelle Lector, the tiny brunette, even smaller than Tori—sorry, Tina G. Wasteland. It's easy because the blonde with the assassin's eyes—Roxy Heartless, the lawyer—is holding her by the shoulders and talking right into her face.

Nutz waves at a woman in the flesh-colored tank top, a dirty blond, maybe in all the senses of the word.

"Two hundred points in a half?"

Hendrix watches Tori McDonald put her foot on the top row of bleachers and slowly bend forward. After fifteen seconds, she changes feet and does it again.

"Doesn't happen." Nutz rolls his head around on his shoulders to loosen his neck. "If the teams are evenly matched, your scores are about the same as a high school basketball game, maybe sixty or seventy points for the winner."

The sunlight bathes the double doors and Hendrix sees dozen of smudged handprints on the glass. He wants to stay and watch, but he knows he has to get outside.

#

Emilio Losada still doesn't understand what he's doing in the car with these two assholes, and he's not sure where they are except swirling somewhere around downtown New Britain. He's from Hartford, so while he knows there's a New Britain—it's only like eight miles southwest—he's never had any reason to go there, and now doesn't really change things all that much.

The asshole driving doesn't seem to know much more than he does, either. Emilio knows he's already seen this same intersection twice because he recognizes the sign in the shop window. He doesn't speak Polish, but the sign sure has that look like it's telling everyone they're going out of business. Several other store fronts along the street have plywood covering what's left of the glass, too.

"Fuck," Tito says. He's doing figure-eights around blocks, but New Britain doesn't seem to have signs on the cross streets, so they think they're on Broad, where everybody seems to speak Polish, but they aren't sure. Emilio's thought about telling Tito to stow the bandanna since it's gang colors and who the fuck knows what gangs these Polacks have, but Tito likes the way he looks, like a pirate, especially with the nine piercings in his left ear. He thinks it helps him get laid, too, but that's probably just his hand talking.

"You said you know New Britain." That's Manny, riding shotgun. He's got a Mac 9 tucked under the seat and when they find where that cop lives, he's going to give it to Emilio and have him waste the motherfucker who killed his sister.

"I do," Tito says. "I got customers in Malikowski Circle, buy lottsa product, know what I'm saying? Every two weeks, I come down, sell them a few grams, regular as fucking clockwork."

"So where's Mali, whatever, Circle?" Emilio asks. "How far away?"

"Over there." Tito jerks his head.

"How far?"

"Over there, I told you. Shit."

Tito takes another right, and Emilio knows he's seen these buildings before. He remembers the roses climbing that trellis by the window.

He's willing to forget the whole thing, which was never his idea in the first place, but that reporter put it in the paper again this morning and Tito saw it. Thought he'd get his bones if he could burn a cop. Tito's got no hassle with Tracy Hendrix, but he figures if he helps Emilio waste the guy, he'll get points anyway.

Tito's got the personality of crotch rot and half the intelligence, so arguing with him, you might as well teach a ghetto rat to sing freaking opera, and Emilio does not have the time. When he thinks about it, he doesn't have the time for this shit either, but Tito's driving and Manny's packing, and he's just in the back seat and it's eight miles back to Hartford so he's fucked no matter how you look at it.

Damn reporter.

Emilio sees an old woman sitting on the steps of what looks like a miniature church, three toothpick-skinny kids with butter-blond hair chasing each other around the cracked sidewalk. They yell at each other in Polish.

"Fuck," Tito says again. He turns left and finds himself going the wrong way in a side street, cars coming at him honking their horns like fucking geese. He flips them off and swerves into a driveway. Soon as the other assholes go by, he guns it back out to the intersection. Fucking Broad Street again.

Manny's trying to read his BlackBerry, but the car's rocking so hard he can't hold it still.

"I think we're on the wrong side of town," he says.

"Swell," Tito says. "So where you want I should go?"

"It looks like Farmington Avenue takes us there."

"We came in on Farmington," Emilio remembers. "It was the exit off I-84."

"Yeah," Tito says. "That's how I come to Malikowski."

"You shoulda stayed on that other street, Corbin," Manny says. It would've took us all the way across town, come out near where we going."

Emilio doesn't care that much about his sister, whom he hasn't even seen for three months. She stayed with Mami the crack ho. He's been getting decent grades, though, and he's managed to stay out of the gangs and shit, and he's going to graduate next year, so he decided to chill with Papi, but Tito's got this hair up his ass about a cop killing Corazon and how Emilio's got to maintain the family honor. Secretly, he thinks Corazon was blowing both Tito and Manny and probably half of Albany Avenue, too. He knows his mother still is, and he hates remembering what it was like when he was in middle school, stepping off the bus and finding mom on her knees in the living room, the landlord with his pants around his ankles, mom going out to get a taste while he had to dig through the kitchen for bread that wasn't blue with mold and fix himself a PB and J sandwich.

Tito tries another side street and turns down a hill steep enough to somersault the car if he's going a little faster. Fucking Polack cemetery on the right, names full of z's and skis.

"Don't you worry, Emilio." Manny reaches down and strokes that Mac 9 like he thinks it's his cock. "We gonna find that motherfucker."

Emilio doesn't think Corazon's worth killing anyone for, already two grades back at age twelve, which is hard to do in Hartford. But she probably didn't get to school a hundred days any of the last four years. Emilio wonders if she even knew the names of her teachers. She wanted to be a gang-banger and started banging them early. She came home when she was only ten, Emilio was thirteen, and she smelled like Mami, like sex.

That was when Emilio called his old man and said he wanted to move in. Papi comes by the next day in his '86 Nova, Emilio tosses a garbage bag with his clothes and books into the back.

Now Corazon is doing gang shit, gets killed trying to stop cops when they raid a crystal meth store. Fourteen years old. Emilio wonders if his mother even knows she's gone. It's only been a month, she might not have tumbled to it yet.

"Holy shit." Manny reads the street sign by the gas station. Big old church on their left. Nice looking one, grass and trees and houses ahead of them. "This is Farmington Avenue. Tito, you a fucking genius."

Yeah, Emilio thinks. *And I'm Lady Fucking Gaga.*

Tito turns right. Six blocks later, they hit a fork and he hesitates. He takes the right fork and two minutes later they're back by that fucking going out of business sign and Broad Street again.

"Turn left here," Manny says. "We gone right before, maybe this'll do it."

They drift down another hill and they're on Main Street. That's got to be a good sign, it means they're in an important part of town.

Emilio remembers the funeral home, flowers filling the room, aunts and uncles and cousins and the priest rattling their beads and saying Novenas and Hail Marys and staring at the closed casket and the pictures of Corazon as a cute little kid, first communion dress, Mami with clear eyes before the crack ate her soul. Papi with a smile and the love. He brought Emilio to the funeral home, stood next to him at the cemetery, watched his wife rock like a chair and hug people she couldn't even remember by name.

Tito stops at a red light and Manny reads signs. Main and West Main. Tito turns right on West Main. They know Shuttle Meadow Avenue is in the Southwest Corner of New Britain.

Corazon the cute little girl. Somewhere along the line she shot up, almost as tall as Emilio, five-nine when she was twelve, and heavier than he is. Probably living on the junk food Mami kept around. Sugar and cigarettes, the two basic food groups. And dick, the other white meat. Or not.

"We gonna bust a cap in this cop's ass," Tito promises. "Emilio, you gonna teach him what it means to kill a Latina. One of ours."

Emilio's not so sure. He remembers his father not even touching his mother at the funeral, not even over the grave, which is where he said the only words he's said to her since he moved out five years ago.

"You did this. I hope you understand how evil you are. Then I hope you die."

Corazon made her own choices, though, Emilio tells himself. Mami was too fucked up to lead her to this. Corazon was a fool.

But he's in a car in a strange town with two assholes and a gun so he can kill the man who killed her. Maybe he's a bigger fool than she was.

Two hours later, they still haven't found Arch Street, which is supposed to be the fucking landmark that will get them to where they want to go. They've passed a plaza with a Rite Aid about six times and the New Britain Diner even more often. They go back down West Main, see a bank and a building under construction on the right, signs to the New Britain Museum of American Art on the right and Walnut Hill Park, and the Hospital for Central Connecticut. Everything else has a fucking sign on it, why not Tracy Hendrix's house?

An hour later, it's too dark to read the street signs that aren't there anyway. Tito blunders onto Main Street again and turns left. There's another plaza ahead, but a sign says I-84 is to their right, so he takes that turn and they fight their way back to the highway. Emilio figures if they drove a straight line from Hartford, by now they'd be somewhere around Poughkeepsie, New York.

#

Annie Rogers AKA Annabelle Lector watches the blond security man from the other night talk to Lugg Nutz for a few minutes before he disappears outside. He's not huge, but his shoulders and chest move under his tee shirt like there's some serious muscle there when he needs it. Annie returns her attention to Grace Anatomy, counting while some of the other girls twist from the waist to loosen their lower back.

Kevin hasn't called her voicemail for two whole days, so maybe he's finally figured things out. Annie checks the lace on her skates and adjusts her helmet. It mushes up her hair a little, and even though it's just psychological, she always feels like it takes away her peripheral vision. On the other hand, since she's one of the smaller girls on the track, she prefers it to Molly Ringworm giving her a booty block into the next zip code.

The hollow roar of wheels on the maple floor fills her head and she slides into the swarm cruising counter-clockwise around the track at half-speed. Lugg hollers at them and she squats, feeling the pull on her hips and thighs. She's been doing this three days a week since last fall now, and getting on a treadmill or an elliptical trainer at the gym twice a week, too. She's in the best shape of her life. Even the bruises from Kevin are almost gone.

Tina G. Wasteland twitches her butt and Annabelle watches her drift to the outside of the track and Roxy Heartless weave to the inside. She follows Tina and senses someone sliding to her left tail light. They weave like that for the next ten minutes, then Lugg pairs them off to work on tandem blocking.

"You block like girls." His voice bounces off the high ceiling and around the room. Well, they ARE girls, Annabelle reminds herself. "Get to the inside, lower your center of gravity—DMJ, that's your booty, in case you don't know—and push off on your inside foot. Keep your arm against your side and drive your booty into her hip. Push her clear over the line. That's how you clear the way for your jammer."

After fifteen minutes, he blows his whistle again, the shrillness cutting through the rumble of the wheels, so hypnotic Annabelle's almost in a trance.

"OK, Annabelle, you jam now. Nova, take the pivot."

Tina peels off the rubber skin like a shower cap. It has the star on it to show that she's the jammer, and Novocain—No Fuckin'—Dancer slides the striped pivot covering into place over her own helmet to lead the pack.

"Remember," Lugg tells them. "Raleigh's fast. That means you've got to get lower than they are so you can drive them off-balance. You try to take them straight up, they'll put your scrawny butts into the bleachers. It'll get old quick. Listen for my whistle. Two blasts means I want you to speed up like they've broken on top. One long whistle means slow down, got it?"

Annabelle takes short running steps to start and feels her whole body finding the rhythm of the space. Her feet feel the boards on the turns and she senses the bodies swirling around her in a ballet of hips and elbow pads. The rumble of skates fills her head and vibrates in her ass, the squeals and grunts of the other girls becoming the sound of a team. It's all good.

"Faster, Annabelle." That's Tina, always the cheerleader. She can speak distinctly around the rubber mouth guard, something Annabelle hasn't quite mastered. She wonders if Tina had braces and a retainer when she was younger, like maybe that helps you learn to talk with something in your mouth. She catches herself thinking dirty thoughts and yanks her mind back to the track.

"You've got her," Tina yells. "Keep coming."

Annabelle leans forward, the air cool on her face. Her tee shirt sticks to her ribs and her legs burn. Faster.

Lugg's whistle shrills. "OK, looking good. Take a break."

Everyone coasts to a stop and they find their water bottles on the bleachers, next to their bags. Annabelle aims a stream of water between her lips and swishes it around. It's lukewarm, but it's wet.

Goldee Spawn sinks to the bench next to her and takes off her helmet so her hair stands up in dirty blonde spikes.

"Whoa." Her forehead shines like a mirror and she wipes a towel across it. She digs into her bag and finds her watch. "Seven-thirty. If I weren't in such terrific shape, I'd be dead by now."

"You're a legend, girlfriend." Annabelle swishes another mouthful of water around before swallowing it. "You're the youngest old broad any of us has ever seen."

Goldee's pushing thirty-five, but Annabelle can't remember from which side now. Annabelle knows she has two children—or is it three?—and is probably the only OB/GYN at Hartford Hospital who wears a clit ring.

Annabelle looks around the room again. Fifteen skaters, three trainers and coaches, a ref in training, and Amber Alert, who does most of their publicity, are talking together, leaning into each other, laughing, joking, giving girlfriend hugs.

These are my friends, Annabelle tells herself. The last time she felt as comfortable was sharing an apartment with three classmates her senior year. She wonders if those other girls have anything like this in their lives now.

"How do you like those new bearings?" she asks.

"I'm still getting used to them," Goldee says. "But I feel like I've got more control on the turns."

Most of the girls have the Swiss bearings on their skates because they can be cleaned a few times before they wear out. They cost about a hundred dollars, but the cheap bearings from China wear out so fast they eat up the lower price in two months. Goldee the Doctor has enough income so she's decided to try the really good ceramic bearings they've all heard about. They cost about two-fifty, but last longer than the average marriage.

Like most of the girls, Goldee maintains her own skates. She put in the new bearings a week earlier, so now she's ridden them three times.

"You can feel that much difference?" Annabelle asks.

"Yeah." Goldee tries to flatten her sweaty hair. "Maybe it's wishful thinking because I know what I spent, but I think so. There's a little more resistance I can push against. It's kind of...anchoring, I guess is the best way to put it."

They talk about wheel bearings and mouth guards. Most of the girls wear shorts for practice, but they prefer fishnets or even tights for matches to hide some of the bruises. Hey, people are watching.

Kevin Draper saw her in a bout for the first time three months ago. She'd told him she skated, but he didn't get to a bout for two months.

"Jesus, Babe," he told her at the bar for the party. "On skates, your ass looks so tight, I felt like I could fuck you all night."

Her beer turns sour in her mouth. "That's not what derby's about, Kevin. It's about...teamwork. And fun. And working together."

He looks at her like she's just offered him a lap dance.

"In those fishnets, all of you are just so hot."

When they go back to her place, he really does try to fuck her all night.

Lugg Nutz's whistle shrieks and they regroup.

By the time he calls quits an hour and a half later, Annabelle feels the good tired that a hard practice always brings. She knows she can get lower, and now they all seem more connected. She wishes they had a couple more big blockers, but you take what you've got. DMJ—Denver Mint Julep—has agreed to work with a couple of the newer kids over the weekend and help them break the habit of throwing an elbow. It's pretty effective, but you don't help your team with your butt in the penalty box.

Annabelle dumps her sweaty gear into her bag. She takes a last squirt of the lukewarm water, then puts her bottle in, too. Her hair sticks to her forehead and the back of her neck, and her shirt is dripping. Never mind her sports bra. And especially don't mention her panties. The whole room smells a combination of girl sweat and estrogen. Annie would never tell Kevin because he'd take it wrong, but a night with the team makes her glow like good sex.

They do a group hug, lots of lips brushing cheeks—or other lips in a few cases—before everyone finds her car keys and humps her gym bag onto her shoulder.

Tina, Lugg, and Roxy Heartless approach, Molly Ringworm on their heels. Molly's shoulders and hips are wide, but she's solid as a bank vault.

"Want an escort, Annabelle?"

The sun is down, but it's still sticky hot in the parking lot. The houses across Farmington Avenue have lights on and the skaters' alter egos fade as they approach their cars. Annie Rogers sees a shadow moving between the cars, but when she sees blond hair, she realizes it's the guard, not Kevin's shaved head.

"Anyone feel like a slice and a beer?" Molly asks. "It's still early."

Annie's opening her mouth to vote yes, when she sees movement to her left. A shadow charges from the corner of the building and slams into Lugg Nutz, knocking him to the blacktop.

"Stay away from her, motherfucker." The guy kicks at Lugg, who's rolling onto his knees, and Annie recognizes Kevin's voice, the same feral growl he uses when he's on top of her.

"Kevin. No!"

The security guy sprints toward them from between the cars and Kevin dashes back the way he came. Both men disappear around the corner and Annie joins the other girls clustered around their coach. He shakes them off and gets to his feet. He looks more mad than hurt, but blood drips from his chin. Tina digs in her purse and finds a tissue.

"Who the hell...?"

Annie hears a rattle around the corner as both men vault over the chain link fence and scuttle down the hill. It's dark and there are lots of trees and rocks. She hopes nobody breaks his neck or his leg. She amends that to only mean the guard. She hopes Kevin Draper falls on his face and scrapes it all off before he reaches the bottom of the slope.

Roxy has her cell phone out again and is talking to the cops. God, they must be getting sick of her. The security guard returns a minute later, puffing a little and looking hungry.

"I think it was your ex again, wasn't it?"

Annie can only nod. All her joy and vitality turn to shit.

"He had a car stashed down there, a black Hummer. Does that sound right?"

"Yes," she sighs. Will it never fucking end?

"There are a dozen little side streets down there." The guard wipes sweat off his forehead. "But he's got to go home sometime. What's his address?"

Annie tells him. "It's in Bristol, do you know how to get there?"

"I've got a GPS in my car."

A police car pulls into the lot and they all tell their story. The security guy produces his badge and talks to the local cops, then they all take off together.

Annie doesn't feel like a slice and a beer anymore.

Chapter Six

Jerry Machowski's biceps threaten to burst through the sleeves of a Rolling Stones tee shirt, and his shoulders probably don't fit through the doorways of older houses. He wears work boots and a yellow hard-hat, too, with the tanned face of a guy who spends most of his time outside. To Hendrix's surprise, his voice is a rich tenor that would make him a fortune if radio stations still used announcers.

"I fucked up my back on a job," he says. "About a year ago. The doctor sent me to a physical therapist, and during a massage one day, she told me she skated. I remembered roller derby on TV when I was just a little kid, so I thought she was just yanking my chain."

"But you went to see for yourself?"

Machowski waits for a truck full of dirt to grumble out of earshot before he continues.

"Yeah, down in New Haven. They didn't have the space up here yet. All those women kicking serious butt, having a ball. It blew me out of the water. I told them I wanted to join up."

Another truck pulls up and two guys with shovels appear from a hole near the corner.

"We lost about three weeks with the plumbing." Machowski wipes the back of his neck with a bandanna. "The pipes were shot to hell, we had to bring in some people, get more permits, move the old ones out. Pretty much start over from square zero. It was a major cluster fuck, but now we're catching up."

Hendrix leads him back to the girls, not a hard task.

"You wanted to get involved."

"Yeah. I used to sing in a band. We broke up years ago, but I still had a microphone and some decent speakers. They told me the guy they had announcing was getting transferred to the west coast in a few months, so I offered to take over. I sat in with him on a few bouts, got to know the girls, learn the rules, get a feel for everything. Then when he left, I was ready to step in."

Hendrix visualizes Machowski exhorting the crowd to give it up for Amber, who comes out in a helmet and pads. That's probably not quite right.

"So exactly what do you do at these matches? Play-by-play?"

Behind Machowski, guys in hard hats are dropping plumb lines and surveying what will become the new Patience Randall Domestic Center by Labor Day. The summer sun smells of sawdust, dirt, and motor oil. Not to mention sweat. Twelve of the last fourteen days have topped ninety degrees.

"Oh, it's a fun night. I get the crowd psyched up to cheer, get them to buy stuff at the concession stand, support the local sponsors. We do contests at the half-time, a raffle, stuff like that, too, so I keep on them to buy tickets."

"How many people are we talking here?" Hendrix still can't believe the sport has an audience.

"Down in New Haven, usually about six hundred. They had the London Brawling in the spring, their first intercontinental bout, and you couldn't have got anyone else in with a shoehorn and a tube of KY. They probably had about eight hundred for that one."

"It's in Europe, too?" The joke keeps getting bigger and Hendrix feels like he still isn't in on it.

"Yeah. I don't know how many teams, but enough so they have tournaments. Those babes won the Rule Britannia last year. And they whipped our girls' butts."

The sun isn't directly overhead yet and everyone's sweating. Hendrix reminds himself that he's got beer back in the fridge.

"How many here in New Britain?"

"We had three-fifty in February, but about four-fifty in March and almost five hundred in May. Danny's said he'll give the shelter triple the gate next week if they have five hundred. I think he's gonna write a major check."

Hendrix shakes his head. Incredible.

"Do you see anyone hassling the women?"

"Uh-uh. There are a lot of friends and family at these things, and they all look out for their girls. But that's part of why they all have the crazy stage names, so nobody can find them in the phone book or on-line. I guess it happens, but not around here."

"How about the guy Annabelle Lector has the restraining order on? Kevin Draper?"

"He's an asshole. I only know the girl a little, but she's a sweetheart. And she's growing up in front of everyone."

Hendrix thinks Annie Rogers already has a college degree, but maybe he's wrong.

"What do you mean? I just assumed you'd have to be an adult to skate. Legal issues, liability if you're hurt, stuff like that."

"Oh, yeah, I just mean she's getting stronger now. She was this shy little kid when she came in, wouldn't say dick if she had a mouthful, and now she's more self-confident. I see that a lot. The women start cheering each other on, and it carries over to work, too. Well, you must have seen the Captain, that little brunette?"

"Tina G. Wasteland?"

"Yeah, God, more balls than a driving range."

Machowski looks like a redneck, but he's definitely an enlightened man for the New Millennium. Hendrix wonders if he's hooked up with any of the skaters.

"So how many bouts do you have?"

"Usually a home bout every month and one or two away. We're trying to pick up more regular opponents and develop a season. But we have to pay our own way on the trips, so we usually car-pool."

"Are you married, Jerry?"

"Almost, once. Then we both sobered up."

"Dating anyone?"

"Not steady. Grace Anatomy and I kid around at the matches or the bar. She's the one who got me interested in the first place."

Hendrix remembers Grace leading the Pilates. "Long braid down her back?"

"Yeah. She's another one like Annabelle. Really quiet until her buds are around. They bring out the spirit."

Two other workers step away from the far corner, where Hendrix sees a back hoe.

Machowski's tenor turns even warmer. "I love these girls, all of them. I mean, they have a shitty day at work, OK? Then they put the wheels on and they're all beautiful, and everything's all right again. Who can complain about something like that?"

"Kevin Draper, for one."

Machowski pushes back his hard hat and shakes his head.

"Like I said, total asshole. Guys like him are why we're building this place."

The night before, Hendrix and the Bristol cops were waiting for Draper when he finally got back to his apartment. He reeked of cigarettes and beer, but they made him do the balloon and he passed. He looked at Hendrix with enough heat so Hendrix is sure they'll meet again.

"Your boss said he got involved in derby because one of his crew mentioned it. Was that you?"

"Could've been. I told him when I started announcing. He came down and saw a match. He and DMJ hooked up right away." Machowski sticks two fingers in his mouth and lets out a whistle that cuts through the machinery. When the guys with the plumb line turn, he points to the other corner and they wave back.

"Denver Mint Julep," he says. "She's the manager of the bank right over there."

"The names are great," Hendrix says. "What do you call yourself as an announcer?"

Jerry Machowski grins, big white teeth in a tanned face.

"Lee Da Vocal."

#

Hendrix thinks of New Britain, Connecticut as an urban doughnut. The entire perimeter of the town is residential, and some of the houses, dating back to when over a dozen factories fueled the economy, would triple their asking price if they sat a few miles away in either Farmington or West Hartford. The downtown, the center of the doughnut, is a quilt of shuttered businesses, civic offices, and a few renovated buildings and churches now calling themselves "Art Centers" in a desperate ploy to get federal funding. The local economy has been bleeding out for as long as Hendrix can remember.

The town also boasts a street system that would make Lewis and Clark throw in the towel. Main Street runs North and South through the center of town, but becomes South Main as soon as it crosses West Main, which runs East and West and becomes Bank Street when it crosses Main. East Main runs east from Main Street, but starts two blocks north of West Main, and calls itself Myrtle Street west of Main. South Main passes South Street, which runs East and West near the southern border of the city, and East Main ends at a stop light and "T" turn that becomes East Street. That's just for starters.

Hendrix can name at least a dozen other streets that change their name for no particular reason. Arch Street, which has become a Latino enclave, disguises itself as Kimball Drive when it crosses Shuttle Meadow Avenue, only a few blocks from his own house. The citizens voted to change the name of the Upper Arch Street area so potential house buyers didn't realize they were near a high crime district. It works, but now nobody can find the place.

The current Patience Randall Domestic Center nestles among three-story frame houses off East Street. Most of them have cracked driveways and small garages that enclose parched back yards, venerable trees providing shade. Hendrix knows that most of the houses in this area have been taken over as office space. The same is true of the houses around the area where Jerry Machowski and his crew are building the new center. It makes sense. Even if you don't advertise your location so the predators can find their prey again, businesses mean less legitimate traffic at night. And the bank has surveillance equipment that might do double duty.

When Hendrix enters the large old vestibule, the faded glamour of the house hits him instantly: dark varnished woodwork, wide curving stairs to the second floor. The banister is that same dark wood, and the worn green carpet gives the impression of moss over it. A large room opposite those stairs holds a TV and heavily-upholstered furniture. Three women look up from their viewing to watch him warily. He guesses that none is older than he is, but the fear in their eyes adds another decade. He approaches the reception desk and asks for Tori McDonald, his nose detecting the brittle smell of dry rot around him.

A woman who looks too frail to evict a kitten takes his name and speaks into her Blue Tooth. Her PC has a screen-saver of azure surf rolling across golden beaches.

Tori glides down that curving staircase, clad in jeans and a white tee shirt with a pocket. She wears a necklace of what might be jade to convey a more professional vibe, but her short hair makes her look more like Tinker Bell's evil twin. When she sees him, her eyebrows arch over her brown eyes.

"I just wanted to check a few things with you," he says. "Kevin Draper wasn't home last night when we got to his place, but he showed up about half an hour later. Do you know if he smokes?"

Her eyebrows arch even higher. "Why?"

"He jumped over that fence and ran down a steep hill to get away from me last night. I'm in pretty good shape, but he left me for dead. I guess it hurt my pride."

"He didn't help Roger's pride last night, either. That's for sure."

"Is that Lugg's real name, Roger?"

"Yeah." Tori motions to their left and he follows her down a short hall. "Did the police arrest him last night?"

"Yes, but he posted bond on the spot. And you know as well as I do that the judge will probably slap him with a piddly little fine for violating the restraining order."

Tori's office has a hanging plant in the bay window overlooking the street and two file cabinets facing a loveseat that might have escaped from curbside pickup. A hooked rug almost the same green as the carpet on the stairs gives the place a restful feeling, and Hendrix remembers that Tori counsels battered women in here. A framed degree hangs on the wall between the two filing cabinets and a laptop is open on her desk.

"Guys like him are the reason I've got this job," she says. "We've got seven women here now, and three of them have been here before. They really think hubby's going to stop hitting them if they tell him it hurts."

"How many people can you accommodate?" Hendrix asks.

"Ten, but a couple of the rooms are really small. The mildew's terrible there, too. Anyone with asthma or any kind of respiratory problem can only stay here for a couple of days before the building starts eating them up."

Despite her petite frame, she generates a nurturing warmth that fills the room. "This place should have been condemned years ago. I think the counselor before me must have been making friends with the building inspector every time he came by."

Hendrix knows enough of the town's politics to know she could be right.

"The new place will hold eighteen and have space for counseling and medical, too," Tori continues. "And a bigger kitchen. I can hardly wait until it's done."

"I was over there this morning, but it's just a big hole in the ground right now. What's it going to look like when it's finished?"

"Three stories. Sort of a pseudo Tudor like the apartment building across the street. We're going to have a sun porch in the back so people can get fresh air without being visible from the street."

She glances toward her window. "Believe me, sunlight helps. Otherwise, you feel like you've traded one dungeon for another one."

Hendrix remembers patrolling Albany Avenue when he first joined the Hartford PD.

"Danny already has enough paper filed with the building inspectors so we can get the certificate of occupancy before the sawdust has even settled."

Hendrix watches her eyes. "You know abuse cases, they're what you do. How likely is Kevin Draper to come back again?"

Tori looks at her hanging plant.

"Annie has all the behavior patterns of an abused partner. She's shy, she doesn't have a lot of self-esteem, and I'll bet there's abuse in her family. She has the mindset that tells her she really deserves this, and Kevin Draper has probably seen it all from the other side. People in abusive relationships repeat the pattern they know, just like substance abusers and criminals."

"So you think he'll be back."

"Hell yes. The only reason he's even got that restraining order is because Lynn the lawyer—Roxy Heartless?—was in the parking lot the night he busted Annie's windshield. Lynn called the cops because Annie wouldn't."

"The cops have better things to do than enforce restraining orders," Hendrix says. "They're right up there with seat belt checks."

"You already know all of this." Tori picks up a Bic pen from her desk and starts twirling it through her fingers. "Why did you drop by, really?"

His face feels hot. "I just wanted to be sure. I'm going to talk to Annie at work now in Southington, but I wanted to see if I was over-reacting."

"You aren't." Her eyes look like she's interviewing him and writing the answers on a clipboard.

"When I was a little kid, I thought a social worker helped guys find a date."

"No, we call that a 'pimp,'" she says. "I led a sheltered life, and even I knew that."

When they reach the bottom of that curving staircase again, she thanks him for coming and turns to the women watching television.

"Aneta? Why don't we talk for a few minutes?"

Chapter Seven

The Patience Randall Shelter is an old house, but Greenfield, in Southington, is so new Hendrix wonders if the ink on the blueprints is dry. The place exudes that manufactured warmth he associates with rest homes; sure enough, no one he sees in the lounge looks younger than seventy-five and two have walkers. In spite of the enlightened architecture, the smell is that archetypal perfume of age, decay, and medicine, not quite hidden by air freshener and cheerful plants.

Someone directs him to the kitchen, a modern masterpiece with a skylight and enough windows so it's like cooking on the beach.

When Annie Rogers rises to shake hands, Hendrix congratulates himself for not stopping in his tracks to gawk. Cleaned up, she has the innocent beauty of a fairy tale princess, with chestnut waves that fall to her shoulders and brown almond-shaped eyes. Her nose and chin have the delicacy of a little girl, and her red and white striped shirt brings out the roses in her complexion. She's even tinier than Tori McDonald, but curves under the stripes announce that she's a full-grown woman even though she conveys the delicacy of a glass slipper.

She sits carefully and when she extends her hand, she moves like an old woman. She turns her head and a sunbeam highlights redness on her cheek. It looks like four fingers.

Hendrix feels anger bubbling in his chest. He's guessed right.

In the kitchen behind them, two men and a woman in white clean up the remnants of the meals for thirty residents, average age seventy-one—five of them through a straw or with an orderly—that Annie has designed with the help of several primary care physicians. Cooking smells fill the area, so good Hendrix almost forgets why he's there.

Annie's eyes avoid his and her fingers riffle through a wooden box of file cards that he finally realizes contain recipes. Her hands never stop moving.

"Ms. Rogers, I'm concerned about Kevin Draper."

"There's no problem now." Her voice has a tremolo that he bets she wasn't born with. "Lynn made me file a restraining order, so he'll stay away now."

Sure, Hendrix thinks. *And the Easter Bunny lays his own eggs.*

"Ms. Rogers, he came back last night, remember? He sucker-punched your coach. You were right there when it happened."

"He doesn't like other men looking at me, it makes him worry that I might..."

The recipe cards scatter all over Annie's desk and her lip trembles.

"They might think I like them."

"Are you attracted to Lugg Nutz? Roger?"

Draper claims he received a text message that Annie's now sleeping with her coach after the practices. The cops didn't find it on his phone last night, but he said he deleted it.

No!" Annie shakes her head violently. "There's nothing between us. I mean, he's nice, but he's old. He's probably almost, what, thirty-five?"

"Yeah." Hendrix is thirty. "He could be your older brother."

She doesn't get it. Hendrix realizes the cards have several different handwritings, some of them in pencil or colored ink, and a few were cut out of magazines or newspapers. It occurs to him that they aren't in a computer file because Annie's accumulated them from family and friends.

"Kevin and I...well, I understand he cares about me, I don't do what he..."

"You mean 'didn't,' don't you?"

"Um, yes." Annie's blouse and slacks fit perfectly and Hendrix wonders if she shops in the Junior Miss department or has to have them tailored. If she looked any younger, he would check to see if she still had braces.

He tries to make her look at him.

"Ms. Rogers, this isn't easy, and I know it isn't really part of the job, but I've got some free time and I want to do the best I can. Does Kevin Draper smoke?"

"Excuse me?" She reaches for the recipe cards again.

"Cigarettes. Tobacco. Does he smoke? You were together for several months, so I think you'd know his brand."

"No. I never saw him with a cigarette, and his apartment doesn't have any ashtrays."

Hendrix was afraid of that. He knows Annie didn't go home with the coach last night, because Lugg spent two hours in the emergency room getting stitches in his chin and a prescription for Tylenol III.

"Ms. Rogers, the New Britain police called the Bristol officers when you gave me Kevin Draper's address, and I met them at his apartment. He didn't show up until after midnight, and he smelled of both beer and cigarettes."

Annie's terror is so palpable that he waits to see the wall of thorns spring up around her castle.

"He had half a pack of Marlboros on the front seat and the smoke in the car was so thick it coated his windshield. We didn't find any beer, but there are dozens of bars in the area. I think he was trying to cover something with the cigarette smell."

Annie's head rotates on her neck, back and forth, back and forth, back and forth.

"No," she whispers. "No, no, no."

Through the door, Hendrix watches the orderlies wipe their hands on dish towels and toss them into a bin. They leave the room, speaking what he thinks might be Polish.

"Ms. Rogers, would you do me a favor?" He waits for her to look up, but she doesn't take her eyes off that pile of recipes. She seems to be folding into herself.

"Would you give Tori McDonald a call when I leave? Just touch base with her?"

"Why? Tori—Tina—and I don't even know each other outside of derby. Shoot, I don't think any of us know any of the others. We're from all over central Connecticut, we're different ages..."

"But you support each other and watch each others' back." Hendrix waits until that sinks in. "Lugg Nutz says so. I've talked with your sponsor and your announcer, and they say the same thing. They really admire that, and I think right now you need someone to talk to."

He pulls out his card and circles his cell number before he lays it on her desk.

"Mr..." Annie flicks a finger across her cheeks and glances at his card. "Hendrix. I need to get back to work now."

"Of course." When he stands, he's nearly a head taller than she is. "And whether you talk to Tori or not, please program my number into your phone."

"Why in God's name would I want to do that?"

Hendrix feels like a bully. He wonders if he should stay out in the parking lot and follow her home later. Or even offer to follow her now.

"Because a lot of your friends are worried about what you're not telling me."

He watches that sink in, then he walks back down the hall to the reception desk. Three patients watch TV, the volume slightly lower than a heavy-metal concert.

#

Annie Rogers watches Tracy Hendrix's shoulders under his polo shirt and his trim hips in tight jeans as they disappear through the door.

Slut! You're looking at other men, just like Kevin thinks you are. Tramp!

She forces her numb feet to carry her back to her chair. Two animals are fighting to the death under her rib cage. If she had any food in her stomach, she'd throw up.

Last night, she told those New Britain police about Kevin and how he kept calling her and showing up. Roxy and Tina kept urging her to tell them more, but she dug her nails into her palms and insisted that Kevin wouldn't be back. She couldn't remember feeling so mortified since her father insisted on meeting the boy who brought her home late the week before and asked him if he was tooling her.

Lugg Nutz holds a bloody tissue to his gashed chin. His eyes look more worried about her than about himself even though everyone is trying to get him to go to the hospital.

Then the police leave, the security guard following them, and Annie knows they're going to find Kevin in Bristol and he's going to be so pissed. She hopes he doesn't do something stupid like try to punch out one of the cops.

Everyone is oohing and ahhing at Lugg's cut chin and Roxy finally uses what Annie thinks of as her courtroom voice to tell him to get his butt over to the emergency room for stitches before he has a scar that makes him even uglier than he is already. Everybody laughs, including him, and he says OK, then they all pile into their cars and head for home.

What with all the brouhaha with the police, it's after eleven when Annie guides her Hyundai into her space and humps her bag onto her shoulder again. She's thinking about nothing more than a hot shower and bed when Kevin Draper comes around the corner of the Dumpster and grabs her arm so tightly she feels her fingers go numb. His other hand covers her mouth.

"You fucking that coach, you little slut? Answer me."

Ice forms in her stomach and she shakes her head frantically.

"Then why'd someone say you were? They told me you're fucking him, old guy like that, like he can give you more than I can. You cunt."

She feels tears on her cheeks.

"Get inside."

He clamps his hand on the back of her neck and she knows if she makes a sound he'll hurt her. Then he makes her unlock the outer door and drags her through the lobby and up the stairs. When she unlocks that door, too, he shoves her inside and kicks it shut. She hears the dead bolt, loud as a slap.

"That guy, he can't possibly love you like I do, Annie. Why don't you believe me? We can have the love of the ages, you and me, but you won't give me a chance."

"Kevin, I'm really tired. And you're scaring me. Please leave. Please." Her voice feels like a squeak and she realizes again how big he is.

"I gotta make you understand, Annie. That fucking restraining order, why'd you do that shit? I love you. Why don't you believe me?"

He turns her around, still in the middle of her living room with the soft blue love seat and the big puffy pillows behind the wicker coffee table, the worn leather recliner her dad let her have so he could get a new one, all the comforts of home, her very own apartment, paid for with her very own money from her very own job, and now Kevin's in it and she doesn't want him to be and she doesn't know how to get rid of him. His tongue forces itself between her lips.

"C'mon, Annie, kiss me like you mean it." He forces her mouth open, and his teeth bruise her lips. Then his hands are grabbing her breasts, her butt, sliding under her sweaty shorts and soggy bra.

"I want you so much." His voice is a feral growl. He yanks her tee shirt over her head and kisses her neck and throat. His tongue laps up the sweat that's chilling her so much she's shivering. Or maybe it's the terror that keeps humming in her ears like a storm.

"Kevin, please..."

But he shoves her into the bedroom, pictures on the walls and her clothes for tomorrow already laid out on the chair. He pushes her back on the bed and she feels his fingernails scrape her hips when he pulls down her panties and gym shorts in one soggy clump. He looks at her body and licks his lips.

"God, you are so beautiful, Annie. I love you so much. Touch me. Come on, honey, you know how I like you to do it."

He tosses his tee shirt near the door and leans on her chest with one hand while the other one unbuckles his belt. When he slides down his jeans and his boxers, he's already hard, even bigger than she remembers.

"Come on, baby, does that fag coach have anything like this? Betcha he doesn't, you can't forget what a real man is like, can you? Someone who really loves you."

He kicks off his shoes and steps out of his jeans, then bends over to ram his tongue into her mouth again. She thinks of biting him, but it might make him mad.

"C'mon, bitch, kiss me back. You know what I like."

His hand guides hers to his hard cock and makes her stroke him. He groans while he's kissing her.

"God, baby, you turn me on like nobody else. You and I belong together, don't we? Feel what you do to me?"

She turns her head away from his. "Please, Kevin. I don't want this."

"Sure you do, Annie. I love you. You have to know that. Feel how much I love you? Look at what you've done to me. You can't just get me turned on like this and send me home, what kind of cock-teasing shit is that?"

"Kevin, Please." She's afraid she's going to cry. He grabs her bra with both hands and tears it in two. He kisses her between her breasts, then he squeezes her left one and bites her nipple so hard she cries out.

"Kevin..."

He slaps her. Her head rings when it snaps back against the mattress. She tastes blood in her mouth.

"Annie, Annie, Annie."

"Please stop, Kevin. Please, please, please. I'm afraid and—"

"You fucking bitch."

He slaps her again, her head snapping back and forth with each blow. She reaches up to shield her face and he grabs her arm and forces it down. His fingers feel like steel. He bends over her and his mouth covers hers until she's afraid she's going to swallow her own blood.

"Come on, baby, you gotta get wet for me. Gotta get wet so I can love you all night long. Come on, Annie. This is me, the one you love, the one that loves you, too."

He rubs her crotch until she's afraid he's going to draw blood down there, too, then he bends down and spits. He slides his fingers into his mouth, then jams them into her. She wants to scream, but his mouth covers hers again.

Then he's inside her, his weight pressing her down into the covers and her head between her big fluffy pillows.

"Oh, yes, Annie, oh, it's so good. Tell me it's so good. Tell me how good I fuck you."

She tries to move with him so he doesn't hurt her even more, but he's so heavy and his tongue almost chokes her. He pulls out for a second, but before she can say anything, he grabs her hips and flips her over, her face in the pillow. She feels him probing her rear.

"Kevin." But her voice is caught in the pillow that closes around her face so she can't breathe. He rams into her again and she can hear his voice faintly, but it's disappearing under the roaring in her ears. The blood is hot and metallic in her mouth. If she doesn't get air...

"Kemminn," she tries. Big blue dots float before her eyes and the hum gets louder. He's saying something in the background, but nothing else matters except getting air. She forces her palms flat and her elbows up, manages to get her face out of the pillow.

"Kevin," she gasps. "I can't breathe. Please stop."

"Oh, it's so good." His hand slams the back of her head and drives her face into the pillow again and he's pumping into her harder and harder. That hum starts up again and she feels her right hip burn when he slaps her again. He's fucking her from behind and spanking her and she's not sure which one hurts more but she still can't breathe and he's going to kill her.

"Kemm." She tries another push-up, but his other hand slams between her shoulder blades and drives what's left of the wind out of her. He drives into her again, harder and faster and deeper than he ever has before. But he's never been so turned on before and now she wonders how much longer until he comes and gets off her. The blue dots before her eyes get blurry and she knows she's going to pass out and she's so scared...

Then he pulls out and she feels something touch her tight little anus.

"Open up for me, baby, show me how much you love me."

She can't help it. The pain and fear are too much. She loses control, all her sphincters releasing and she's wetting herself and messing the bed and almost throwing up, blood and bile mixing in her throat.

"Jesus, Annie, Jesus fucking Christ, look at you."

He punches her, first on her butt, then in her back. But he's not trying to shove his cock into her ass anymore.

She lifts her face out of the pillow. Cool air rushes into her mouth and fills her chest and she breathes deeply until the big dots go away. Then she feels the blow on the back of her head and bright lights explode in her eyes.

"Stupid bitch. Stupid, stupid, stupid."

He hits her again and another flash bursts. Then he turns his attention to her back again, knuckles landing between her shoulder blades again and again.

He finally gets tired and moves away from her. It's not until then that she feels the wet between her thighs and on her stomach, soaking her sheets. She smells her excrement and feels it on her butt and she's so ashamed.

"Jesus Christ, Annie. Look at you. Just like a little kid."

He pulls up his jeans and finds his shirt in the corner. Then he walks out of the room. Annie sobs softly into the pillow, lying in her own filth, feeling disgusting and dirty and helpless. She wants to die.

Kevin reappears with a bottle of beer, the last one in the refrigerator. She doesn't like beer, but she bought it for him. Since it's the last one, maybe he'll never come back.

"See how much I love you, Annie? See how good we are together? God damn, why'd you have to go and spoil it? That's just so...Whatever."

He slides the bottle into his mouth and sucks half of it down in one gulp. "Why you have those assholes at the practice? Why you got to fuck up this beautiful love we got for each other? You belong to me, Annie, you're my woman, so why you want to fight it, huh?"

His nose wrinkles. "Christ, clean yourself up, will you? Disgusting."

He sits on her clothes in the chair to put his sneakers back on. Then he picks up the bottle and she hears it clink in her sink. Then the door swooshes closed and he's gone.

The room smells like a sewer and she can't move and she can't stop crying, not even to wipe herself. She cries until big green clumps of snot drip from her nose and she feels her stomach stop churning. Then she carefully rolls off the bed and wraps the covers around herself so she won't ruin the carpet, too. She strips the bed and takes the soaked and fouled sheets to the kitchen, where she stuffs them into two large trash bags and ties them shut.

She goes into the bathroom and takes a long shower, covering her whole body with soap and rinsing herself clean, then covering herself with foamy suds again, four times and shampooing three times, until cold water blasts from the nozzle and she's shivering again. She dries herself off and finds a clean tee shirt and clean shorts—fuck underwear—and looks at her bed again.

The mattress pad only has a little stain on it, so she peels it off the mattress and drops it on the rug. She opens all the windows and turns on the AC as high as it will go. It's hot out there, even after midnight, but she has to get rid of the smell, she'll go crazy if she has to live with it another second.

She puts on sandals and makes sure she has her key, then carries the garbage bags down to the Dumpster. Kevin was hiding behind that Dumpster when she came in, and it takes her fifteen minutes to work up the courage to approach it, but then she tosses the bags with her ruined bedding in and runs back to the door, locking it behind her, then running up the stairs again to her apartment. She locks the dead bolt before she remembers she has to wash the mattress pad, too.

Fuck it. She drenches the spot with Spray N Wash and washes it in the bathroom sink. She drapes it over her shower rod to dry. She pulls out clean sheets and looks at her defiled bed. Then she drapes a sheet over her love seat in the living room and curls up on that, instead. She gets up and pushes her chair in front of her door and makes sure the dead bolt is on. She goes back to her kitchen and finds an eight-inch carving knife. Then she returns to the love seat and wraps the sheet around herself.

She can't stop shivering until the sun comes through the windows in the morning. Her back and hips ache and she takes another shower to loosen the stiffness. When she looks in the steamed-up mirror, the bruises look like bunches of grapes all over her back and buttocks. She makes coffee so strong the water can scarcely force its way through the grounds and into the carafe. She drinks three cups and washes down Ibuprofen to kill the pain, and forces herself not to throw away the clothes Kevin sat on while he put on his shoes last night. She dumps them into her hamper and picks out something else to wear to work. Long sleeves will cover the fingerprints on her wrist.

She takes in the box with her family recipes to use as a talisman to get through the day and it works not one little fucking bit, even before Mr. Hendrix shows up.

When he leaves, she sits at her desk until her phone rings and she forces herself to answer. Then she forces herself to hide behind all the little clerical shit she never thought about before but can use now so she doesn't have to look at anything important, like the fact that she forced Kevin Draper to hurt her again. Her back still feels like the Whammer Jammers did laps over her all night.

She leaves notes for the meals for Saturday and Sunday, knowing they've got everything they need to prepare them before she shuts down her PC and steels herself to walk out the door to the parking lot.

She prays that Kevin Draper won't be hiding behind that Dumpster, too.

Chapter Eight

Hendrix finds a parking space along the curb facing the Hartford PD twenty minutes before the shift change. With any kind of luck, Shields has found some useless meeting to attend so he won't blunder into the squad room again.

Clouds are rolling in and there might actually be rain to break up the humidity that makes the air smell like a highway construction site. Hendrix is sure Annie Rogers won't talk to Tori McDonald or the lawyer, so now he needs to go to Plan B.

He eases by the cops signing in or out without drawing any attention and boots up his PC. It rattles and hums through its usual starting sequence and he punches in his password. A message with a red exclamation point fills the screen.

Invalid Password. Access Denied.

Shit. He feels like kicking something, but everything in the room is older than he is and petrified so he'd break his foot. He scrounges through the drawer, but whoever is using his desk now has even found his stash of gum drops. Just as well, the heat probably melted them into a disgusting blob anyway.

"Hey, Trash, I thought you weren't supposed to be here." Byrne punches his shoulder and plants his butt on the corner of the desk.

"I'm meeting the union steward in a few minutes," Hendrix tells him. They both know he wouldn't have a meeting late on a Friday afternoon, but it's his story and Byrne will stick with it. That's what partners are for.

"Sure, good luck." Byrne glows like he's been laid in the past few hours. Knowing that one of the strip clubs in the area offers what they call "Lunch With A View," it's a distinct possibility. "What's shaking with the roller derby? Cushy job or what?"

"Actually, Jimmy, I could use a favor." Hendrix points at the PC Monitor. "Shields pulled my password, and I'm trying to check on something. Can you go in for me?"

"That asshole." Byrne takes Hendrix's seat and punches in his own access code. The screen flips through some elaborate color changes before welcoming Detective James Byrne. "Where do you want to go?"

"I'm checking on a guy," Hendrix says. "He's been giving one of the women trouble enough that she's got a restraining order on him, but he keeps showing up anyway. Busted a windshield last week, which is why they hired me, and he jumped one of the coaches last night."

"Big guy?" Byrne looks like he's ready to hear a bedtime story before Hendrix tucks him in and leaves his door open a crack.

"Big enough. I think he's the source of all their problems, though, so if I can make him go away, the next couple of weeks could be cake and ice cream."

"Not a problem. Just Taser the asshole."

"I'm trying to stay away from weapons for awhile, thanks very much."

"Good point." Byrne opens the top drawer of the desk, then frowns. "No gum drops?"

"I think whoever's using the desk found them."

"Well, how bad does that suck?"

"Maybe Shields put him up to it."

"Has to have something to do beside hump that reporter. You seen her? I think she's got the IQ of salsa, but she's seriously hot."

"We've met." Hendrix looks at the monitor. He's tempted to ask Byrne about his new partner, but decides he really doesn't want to know.

"I'm wondering if this guy's got a record, anything I can use for leverage to make him go away. I talked to the girl a couple of hours ago, and she's scared cross-eyed. I think he roughed her up again last night."

"Motherfucker." Byrne adores women, in the collective and abstract sense more than the specific, but Hendrix has seen him pull out a chair for women wearing ensembles he can fit in his wallet.

"Yeah. Can you look him up for me? His name is Kevin Draper."

Byrne moves the mouse, taps in his name and badge number, and watches a screen come up. "Got a date of birth or social security number?"

"No, but he drives a black Hummer and he's probably in his mid-twenties." Hendrix gives Draper's Bristol street address. "I think he works for the Bristol Department of Sanitation, too. Maybe we can find him in municipal records."

Byrne checks the Hartford files first, and none of the Drapers are named Kevin. He tries State files and gets no hits there, either.

"Shit," Hendrix says. "I was hoping for anything, even a DUI. The social worker who hired me agrees that he's not going to stop by himself."

Byrne finds Kevin Draper in the Bristol directory and copies down his social security number and date of birth. DMV has a blurry photograph that does the soul patch justice, but the flash reflecting off the guy's shaved head makes him look like a Q-tip.

"You want, I can look a little more in my plentiful spare time," he says.

Hendrix copies down the information. "I'd appreciate it. Maybe I can dig a few other places, too. Thanks, Jimmy."

He stands just as a dark-skinned brunette appears from the hallway. She wears a translucent white top and a skirt that threatens to catch its hem in her earrings.

"Detective Hendrix." Her voice feels like an emery board. "I thought Deputy Chief Shields suspended you."

"He did, Ms. Ortega." Hendrix hasn't noticed the squad room filling up while he's been talking with Byrne, but now every cop in the place is listening. "It's great to see you again, too."

"Should I tell him you're violating his orders? He could have you fired."

"Is he violating you, too?" Byrne's voice slides into the discussion like a slim jim opening a locked car.

The woman's green eyes narrow and chill. Hendrix thinks of the olives in a martini.

"I'm here to meet with my union representative," he says. "I'm updating my grievance against Deputy Chief Shields for wrongful disciplinary action. If that doesn't bring redress, we'll be looking at harsher legal measures."

He knows the woman will scurry back to Shields, but it's the best cover there is, forcing the guy to take defensive action that might actually be justified. Besides, Hendrix wants to see how Carmen Ortega looks from behind in that short skirt. Then he realizes that any of the women he's watched for the last few nights could knock her on her ass in the blink of an eye. They probably have twice her intelligence, and they sure as hell have more sense of humor.

The woman doesn't say anything and he can tell she's memorizing it. Maybe she doesn't know how to write yet. In the digital age, anything is possible.

Byrne speaks up again before Hendrix can say too much and blow his cover.

"Ms, you are so out of place here. Dressed like that, you should be out on the town, sitting on some nice high barstool with your legs crossed so some silly young man will buy you expensive drinks, maybe offer to take you somewhere."

The woman turns her eyes to Byrne. Nightfall isn't for another four hours, but Hendrix is sure he sees fangs behind those full lips.

"What you implying? Where do you think he would want to take me?"

"That's his problem, not mine," Byrne tells her. "So long as he doesn't take you seriously."

#

The television is silent at the Patience Randall Women's Shelter on Saturday morning. Apparently the women aren't into cartoons. Hendrix wonders if the animated violence is hard for them to watch. A woman who appears slightly younger than yesterday's receptionist dials Tori McDonald's office, and she appears down those curving stairs a few minutes later.

It's hard to make a regal entrance in a linen shirt and khaki cargo shorts, but she rises to the challenge. She looks crisp, comfortable, and professional all at once. And, Hendrix catches himself thinking, sexy as all hell. He remembers Jerry Machowski's comment about women on wheels and has to admit the guy is right. Roller skates trump camisoles and garter belts any day of the week.

“I wasn’t sure you’d be here today,” he says. He’s proud of how smoothly the words come out.

“Just a half day,” she says. “We keep a couple of large younger types on for the weekend—that’s when lots of shit hits the fan—and we do less counseling and more sheltering. But everyone has our cell numbers in case something comes up.”

“Our?” he asks.

“Four of us rotate on the counseling.” Her eyes don’t ask why he’s there, but he hears it. They have a snap crackle and pop to them, even early on a Saturday morning. He wonders how she banks the energy to talk with a severely depressed and battered woman who is probably older than she is.

He follows her up the stairs to her office again.

“I’m trying to cover all the bases,” he says. “Your problems started when Annie broke up with her boyfriend, is that right?’

“I think so. She told some of the girls that she was leaving him a couple of weeks ago, and he showed up at the next practice with a really ugly attitude.”

“Who did she tell, do you remember?”

Tori leans back in her chair. “Um, Roxy—Lynn the lawyer. She’s kind of taken Annie under her wing. And...maybe DMJ.”

He can’t place her, and says so.

“Denver Mint Julep. Tall brunette. Danny Keogh’s main squeeze. She can be sweet as a Cadbury bar, but I definitely wouldn’t mess with her.”

“On skates, you mean?”

“Anywhere. She’s a banker. If she had to, I think she could slice out your liver with her fingernails and feed it to the piranha. But gently, of course.”

“Of course.”

Tori straightens the pens in the mug on her desk. It has a picture of Jonathan, the UConn Husky mascot.

"Annie's really shy; that's why we're so good for her. We're bringing her out of her shell. She might have said something to Novocain, too."

"Is she a dentist?"

"Good guess. Dental hygienist. None of us got the whole joke until she explained it. There's a punk version of the Beatles' 'Helter Skelter' that says 'you ain't no fuckin' dancer,' and that's what she's really saying."

Tori can curse like a cop without even seeming to notice.

"I don't think I know her yet, either."

"Hey, with skates and helmets, we all look alike."

"Not quite." He forces himself back to business. "I went to the PD yesterday. I've got someone looking up Draper, but we haven't found any kind of trouble before, not even a parking ticket. I'm just wondering if anyone else might have a reason to bother the team."

"Not that I can think of."

"How many of the women are in relationships, do you know?"

Tori leans back in her chair.

"Not exactly. Five or six are married. One of the husbands is a referee and another one is the DJ at our bouts. A few have boyfriends, but I'm not sure how many are what you'd call serious."

"You aren't one of them."

It bursts out before he even can think of stopping it, and he feels his face getting warm.

"No." She looks out the window.

"Then maybe you'd like lunch when you're done. To discuss business, of course."

"Of course."

She hands him a plastic watering can and sends him down the hall to fill it. When he returns, she waters the plant hanging in the window.

An hour later, they study menus under an umbrella at Cavos on the Berlin Turnpike. The building still betrays its earlier incarnation as a Moto Photo. Tori says she lives in the area, but Hendrix knows of three condo complexes—one of them on the hill directly above them—within walking distance, so she's not giving much away.

If the server looked any younger, Hendrix would send her back inside to take a nap, but she takes their salad orders and bustles back inside for iced tea. Tori steeples her hands on the table in front of her and Hendrix notices that she keeps her nails short and wears no polish.

"Too tempting to claw someone in a jam."

"That's probably a penalty, isn't it?"

"Yeah, two minutes in the penalty box if you draw blood. And you pay for the girl's tetanus shots." She squeezes the lemon into her tea. "I'll bet you want to talk to me about more than my manicure, don't you?"

He takes a deep breath. "Did Annabelle Lector call you in the last twenty-four hours?"

"No. Why?"

Traffic goes by on the turnpike, sixty feet away. Down the road, a package store has a steady stream of customers. Beyond that are a Wendy's and a Dunkin' Donuts, and behind Hendrix are a Burger King, a Subway, and Joey Garlics. The food smells in the air blend so thickly that the atmosphere probably has calories.

"I talked to her yesterday afternoon after I visited you," he says. "She moved like she was very stiff, and I don't think it was from practice. I think Kevin Draper caught her at home after he got away from me."

"That son of a bitch."

Hendrix agrees.

"She's terrified. I suggested that she call you or Roxy—Lynn?—but I didn't think she would. I gave her my card, too, but I don't think she'll call me, either."

"No." Tori's teeth close on her lower lip for a second. "If she's used to an abusive relationship, she doesn't know how to change. Deep down, she believes that she deserves to be punished. That's part of the cycle. Is there anything else you can do?"

"Legally, no. You know her better as her team mate, so she might talk to you. Besides, you know more about abuse."

"Shit, shit, shit. If she won't speak up, I can't do a damn thing."

"Not even call her up as a friend? If the guy hurt her again, maybe we can slap an assault charge on him, do a little more than that pathetic restraining order."

Tori shakes her head. "Even if he did hurt her, she won't admit it. And if it ever went to court, she'd probably refuse to testify."

"That's why I'd like you to call her. Maybe she'll tell you. She sure as hell won't tell me."

The server brings their salads and asks if they need anything else in a voice that shows she's memorized the line all by herself. They tell her they're fine and she skips back inside.

"I'll call her, see what I can do. But don't expect much."

Hendrix pours his dressing over croutons. "It's a start. You still can't think of anyone else who might have a grudge against the team?"

"We've only been together a few months, so nobody's quit or been kicked off the team. We'd actually like to find a couple more players. I don't think anyone bets on our games, and certainly not enough to lose a bundle."

"How about someone having a grudge against Danny Keogh?"

She shrugs. "No idea. I know his company—companies, actually—have been around for years. I think his grandfather started the ball rolling."

Hendrix tries the salad, a light balsamic dressing, just enough to enhance the vegetables. They look and taste as fresh as his own.

"If you find something, our troubles might be over." Tori's sunglasses reflect Hendrix's face back at him. "But then you'd be out of a job."

"I may be able to go back to being a cop soon," he says.

Tori munches so carefully that he wonders if she counts how many times she chews. He almost finishes his tea before she speaks.

"How did you come to be a police officer?"

"It's a family thing," he tells her. "My grandfather was a fireman. He was on the first engine to reach the Ringling Brothers Circus fire. My dad and my uncle were fire fighters, too. I was going to be one, but when I was twelve, my uncle was trapped in a burning house. When we left the funeral, my mother made me promise I wouldn't be a fireman."

Tori's sunglasses watch him impassively. "So you took a safer job and joined the PD."

"Right."

He watches her devour her huge salad. "How did you become a social worker?"

"My mom was a teacher. A guidance counselor, actually. I just took it one step farther."

She puts down her fork. "The downside is that all those psych classes kind of torpedo your belief in Prince Charming."

She looks toward the cars zipping by and Hendrix sees her touch her finger for just a second. He doesn't think she even knows she's done it.

“Are you divorced?”

“Are you just guessing?”

He shrugs and looks at his salad. “It’s none of my business, of course.”

“I was married. We were two horny kids sleeping together in college, and by the time I was finishing up my MSW, we’d run out of positions and divided up the furniture. I decided to keep his name so I didn’t have to file all the paper for my license again.”

“Was that around here?”

“My mom taught in Wethersfield. I was Vicky Passarelli all the way through high school. Once I was out of the house, I sort of re-invented myself. Tori Amos was big, and I liked the sound of Tori with McDonald.”

“You’re a Tori,” he says. “Not a Vicky.”

“Is that good or bad?”

“Well,” he says. “I asked you to lunch, didn’t I?”

She watches traffic whiz by on the Turnpike.

“My grandfather did plumbing and heating in New Britain. I think Danny Keogh’s grandfather bought him out back in the fifties. ”

“So you knew Danny.”

“Well, I knew who he was. I only met him last winter when he started coming to matches. Then he and Denver hooked up and we got him to kick in the money and help us out.”

The server materializes to ask if they want dessert. Tori shakes her head and Hendrix picks up the black leather folder with the check. He figures the tip in his head.

“That was really good,” she says. “I swear, you could use the tomato slices for Frisbees.”

“Yeah,” he agrees. “You can’t beat fresh out of the garden, can you?”

Tori slides her sunglasses to the top of her head. "Spoken like a gardener?"

As a matter of fact, yes. It's how I relax after a rough day."

"Really."

"Yeah. Tomatoes, peppers, summer squash. Zucchini. I had some corn, too, but this year's been so hot it all burned. I expected to hear it popping."

"I'll bet the tomatoes are going great guns, though, aren't they? And I'll bet your zucchini's outstanding."

The traffic sounds get even louder and Hendrix looks at the people going in and out of the package store.

"Oops." Tori's face is scarlet. "I...um...just oops."

"It's OK." His face feels as bright as hers.

"Dangers of the profession." She wipes her face with her napkin. "I guess my mind was already on that road or we wouldn't have ended up there, would we?"

"I guess not." He watches her crumple her napkin and they fight their way back to higher ground.

"So you probably cook, too, don't you?"

"Some. I'm no chef."

"Do you like Italian?" Tori plays with her napkin again. "Maybe some night, you know, I could do pasta. Lasagna, ravioli, whatever. Just maybe somewhere down the road."

"That would be great," he says. "Probably not a good idea before a practice, though."

"Ah, no. Probably not."

Hendrix leaves money and a tip and they walk out together. They're parked side by side, facing the exit and they both slow down just a little until she beeps her car open and he holds her door.

"Thank you for lunch, Mr.—that sounds silly, doesn't it. What's your name, Tracy?"

Her face slides into full social worker mode behind her shades. “I’ll bet there’s a story there. Don’t tell me now. It gives us something to discuss next time.”

“It does, doesn’t it?” She slides behind the wheel and he admires her clean small nose. “Thanks for coming out with me.”

“I had a good time. And I’ll call Annie when I get home.”

“I appreciate that.”

He watches her car hesitate at the entrance, then accelerate into the open lane.

#

Kevin Draper’s apartment in Bristol has the ambiance of a fratboy hangout, the smells of cold pizza and warm beer filling the kitchen and crusty dishes rising to a peak in the sink. The living room is decorated in Cruise Missile Chic, rumpled clothes covering random areas of the carpet and a coffee table hiding under beer cans and more pizza boxes. The DVD player under the TV in the corner holds a dozen cases, the covers featuring busty blondes in various states of undress.

Draper hasn’t shaved today—his bloodshot eyes suggest that it might be risky—and his breath could crack a windshield. He doesn’t so much let Hendrix in as forget to close the door in his face.

“Nice place, Kevin.” Hendrix sees an open door that looks like a bedroom and wonders if the guy can find his bed under all the crap. If Annie Rogers is half as domestic as he suspects, she probably got sick of cleaning up after the guy. Kevin has that spoiled air of a kid who never picked up his toys. The toys are more expensive, now, but they’re still all over the place.

“What the fuck do you want?”

"Well, you looked pretty pre-occupied the other night, so I thought we might get along better if we could just put our feet up and chat a little."

Looking around, Hendrix realizes there really isn't any place to put their feet up because there's no place to sit until they bulldoze the place.

"I got nothing to say to you, motherfucker."

"Kevin, you look like you really need a beer."

Draper finds the kitchen on his first try and opens the refrigerator. He returns aiming a can of Budweiser at his mouth. He doesn't have one for Hendrix, who decides to cope with it.

"Kevin, when we came by the other night, you said someone texted you that Annie was seeing her coach, right?"

"Yeah." A one-word sentence, but all the words are in the right order, so it's a beginning.

"Who sent it?"

Draper kicks at the debris on the couch until he's cleared a place to sit. When he does so, his boxers gape open.

"I dunno. I deleted it."

"Right away? Or did you keep it around for awhile and read it again."

"I don't know. Maybe."

"Maybe which? You kept it or not?"

"Yeah, whatever."

Hendrix decides to move on. "But you thought it was true."

"Hey, the bitch isn't getting any, so she's not gonna sit around at home, right? She wouldn't pick up when I called, that means she's found someone else, right?"

Hendrix feels his mouth fall open. It's hard to believe this guy actually has a driver's license. Then again, he's not dressed yet, so maybe his keeper has the weekends off.

"So you just figured it was someone she knew, someone from work or another skater, right?"

Draper sips at his beer and seems to think about the question. Or maybe he's still trying to focus. After all, it's only two in the afternoon.

"I don't know. I suppose."

"Or maybe just one of your buds, yanking your chain, having a little fun?

"Hey, none of my friends would play me like that."

"These the guys who were with you last week when Lynn Kulak's windshield got broken?"

"Who?"

"The lawyer, the one who filed that restraining order against you."

"Fucking bitch. You know I gotta go to court in two weeks. A guy can't even talk to his girlfriend now without the Gestapo getting into it. What's this country coming to? Oughtta let everyone have a gun, settle their own differences. Fuckin' courts. This country, becoming thought police on every corner. Assholes."

Draper interrupts himself to take another drink. Hendrix waits until he has the guy's attention again.

"Kevin, two nights ago, when the cops and I dropped by, you weren't here, remember? We waited a good half an hour before you showed up."

"I don't know, man. I wasn't here."

"Right, right. That's what I mean. You ditched me back in New Britain, had your car parked down in those little side streets. I was still tangled up in those trees when you drove away. Pretty smart."

"Fuckin' A." Draper tosses the empty can toward the corner of the room. Hendrix sees a waste basket buried under all the other debris.

"You ought to put that can in the kitchen, Kevin. Recycle it. Maybe have enough cans out there for another six pack. You never know."

"Yeah, maybe later."

"No," Hendrix coaxes. "Do it now, and get yourself another one. I can wait."

Draper goes through the kitchen door, letting out a fart that would have earned cheers back in the dorms. He returns wrinkling his nose.

"Christ, who died in here?"

He finds his spot on the couch again.

"Kevin, after you got away from me Thursday night, where did you go?"

"Here. I came back here."

"Not right away you didn't. Think about it."

In his boxers and a sweaty tee, Draper's size is hard to ignore. He has a good four inches and thirty pounds on Hendrix. Well, he humps garbage cans into a truck all day, so he's in shape. Hendrix tells himself he's smarter, and it's hard to doubt that. What in the world did Annie Rogers see in the guy? Oh, right, the boxers.

"You took off, and we called the cops because you assaulted the coach. He didn't press charges, by the way. But we had to talk with those cops and tell the story over and over for a good hour. And then it took me time to make the New Britain cops call the locals, and I needed about forty-five minutes to find my way here. But we still beat you, so I'm just wondering where you went."

Draper settles into a sullen slouch.

"I don't remember."

"Sure, you do, Kevin. Think about it. You went somewhere and had a beer or two, you bought some cigarettes. The inside of your Hummer smelled like a smokehouse when we met you the other night. But nobody I've talked to says you smoke. What's that all about?"

"I..." Draper takes another swallow of beer. "I had places to go. It's none of your fucking business anyway."

"Yeah, Kevin, I know. I'm just worried that you're going to make a really bad choice here. I mean, if the coach changes his mind and charges you with assault, you could be looking at jail time. You might lose your job, you know? Municipal employee with a criminal record?"

"What the fuck you saying?"

"Just trying to keep you out of trouble, Kevin. Hell, you bother the woman anymore, they'll probably ratchet up the fine, maybe even give you jail time for that, too."

Draper crunches the beer can in his fist, not the brightest move, since it's still half full. Beer sprays around the room, like someone will notice.

"OK, asshole. I hear what you're saying. So now you can leave."

Draper stands and Hendrix does the same. Draper sways on his feet, but he can do some damage if he even lands on Hendrix.

"One more thing, Kevin, then I'm out of here."

Hendrix takes a step closer and grabs Draper's tee shirt in his fist. The guy looks down at him and tries to focus. The effect is sort of like a rhino staring past its horn.

"Do not go near Annie Rogers again. Understand? Don't call her, don't text her, don't write or email. Don't drive your car within a mile of the roller derby or where she works or her apartment."

Hendrix steps forward and Draper rocks on his heels. He lets out a putrid puff of breath that Hendrix forces himself to ignore.

"Because if there's any more trouble with the roller derby or the woman, I will be all over you, Kevin. I will be on you like stink on shit, and I will make your entire life a nightmare. Do you understand?"

"You—"

Draper swings the crushed beer can at Hendrix's face, but he telegraphs the move before he can even shift his feet into position.

Hendrix lets go of the guy's shirt and steps back. The jagged can whooshes past his face, missing by nearly a foot. Before he can punch, Draper's hangover drags him after it and he falls on his face in the debris on the couch.

He lets out another enormous fart and Hendrix decides it's time to go.

Chapter Nine

Emilio Losada rides shotgun this time but Tito's driving again, which is only because he's got the car, such as it is. When he guns the ancient Buick up a hill, it grinds like a food processor in mortal agony.

"Shit, Tito, this car going to blow up, swear to God." Manny's in the back seat with his Mac 9 on the floor and his head hanging out the window. He got demoted when Emilio went down to the Rite Aid and bought a street map book of Hartford County because MapQuest bites the big one.

The problem is that the maps have to fit on a page, so the bigger the town the smaller the scale. New Britain's smaller than Hartford, but the street names are still small enough so you could probably jam the text of Emilio's whole American history book from last year onto this one page.

"OK," Tito says. He turns onto Ellis, left off East Street. "Look at all the trees, shit, I never seen so many trees."

"This like the fucking country, bro." Manny's looking up and down the street, lots of kids and big wheels and some people got laundry hanging in the back yards. Most of the houses only got two or three stories, and none of the people around here look Spanish.

Up ahead, Emilio sees an arch over the road between two buildings that look like factories. He holds the map close to his face.

"Tito, slow down a little so I can read this, OK?"

Tito does, but the car starts grinding even worse. "We gotta check my oil when we get back."

"Oil, shit." Manny pulls his head into the car and Emilio can smell his cologne, like piss with sugar. "We should just shoot this fucking heap and leave it here."

"Then how we gonna get home?" Tito stops at a stop sign and looks at the hill ahead of them. The Buick takes it like it's towing the Traveler's Insurance Tower behind it.

"Shit." Emilio leans over and sees the red light on the temperature gauge. "We oughtta stop for oil now, Tito. Your car's burning up."

"I don't want to stop so people can see our faces, bro. We smoke a cop, people might remember us. We'll do it after we out of New Britain."

"If we make it out of New Britain," Emilio says.

"If we find that fucking cop's house," Manny says.

"Shut up," Tito tells him. "C'mon, Emilio, man, talk to me. Where we go from here?"

Emilio turns the map sideways so he can get the same perspective they have in the car, but now he can't read the street names.

"Was that South Main we just crossed? That traffic light?"

"I dunno. I think."

What looks like an elementary school is coming up on the left, yes, big letters, Northend School. It's July, so who gives a shit. Emilio holds the map two inches from his face and Tito hits a pothole.

"Fuck." The Buick lurches from the direct hit. Tito slows down a little more, but there's another grade ahead of him so he speeds up again. He does a New York stop through the intersection and cruises down another block. Trees still look like a green tent over the streets and lots of the houses have kids out playing on a Saturday afternoon.

"Fuck," Manny says. "We're on Monroe now, when we get here? Tito, go back."

Tito swings right and they see houses ahead of them. The street doesn't go straight through. There's another stop sign and he turns right again. A few blocks later, that street ends at a busy intersection and he slows down.

"Right?" he asks. "Or left? C'mon, Emilio, fucking talk to me, man."

"Uh, yeah. Right."

The traffic is thicker here, and they see a Spanish sign on the building to their left. Manny sticks his head out the window again and looks for a street sign. Four blocks later, he sees one that says "Arch," but by then they recognize the corner they went by before.

"Go straight," Emilio says. He hopes the cop isn't home. He still doesn't want to do this, but Tito and Manny and everyone else in the neighborhood is up his ass about how he's got to kill the cop that killed Corazon. Otherwise, he's never going to be able to get through the frigging day. And never mind school. He wonders if Papi will let him transfer somewhere, Wethersfield or Rocky Hill. Or maybe Mars.

Tito sees a steep slope ahead of them and slams his foot down on the accelerator. The Buick sounds like pieces are falling out underneath as they roar up the hill. The temperature gauge light pops to full red.

"Fuck, we gotta do this," Tito says. "My car ain't gonna last much longer. Where the fuck we going?"

"What street we on now?" Emilio has his face buried in the map again.

Manny looks out the window. "Kimball Drive. This is nice, bro, these houses, you know? Nice yards."

"Kimball Drive?" Emilio looks out the window. "You sure?"

"Fuck yes, bro. I can read."

They pass another sign. Sure enough. Kimball fucking Drive.

Emilio shakes his head. "I can't find it on the map. It isn't here."

"Fuck you say." Tito slows down and the Buick groans like it's trying to give birth. He speeds up again and takes the next left because it's downhill. There's a stop sign at the bottom, but he doesn't dare stop, so he cruises into a sharp right turn. Straight ahead would slam him into another house.

"Work with me, Emilio." Tito's voice is grinding worse than the car. "You got the fucking map."

Emilio turns the map upside down again and squints at the flyspeck street names.

"OK, Kensington Avenue. This will work. Take a right on Corbin, it ought to be coming up in a few blocks."

Sure enough, there's a light and heavy traffic. Somehow, they've found the Chamberlain Highway. Meriden straight ahead, Berlin to the left. Tito takes a right and speeds up. The Buick smells hot and the red light glows steadily. A park and lake come up on the right.

"Yes," Emilio feels mixed blessings. He hates being lost. It means he's just as fucking dumb as Tito and Manny. He'd rather die than think that. But if they find the cop's house, he's gonna have to smoke the bastard.

"This light, it should be Shuttle Meadow Avenue, Tito. Take another right."

The cop's house is off Shuttle Meadow. They pass Vance Elementary School, ducks in the park across the street, people throwing bread and shit. When the park disappears behind them, Manny digs through the food wrappers and towels and coffee cups and panties in the back seat and finds the gun again. Emilio wonders how Tito got a girl's pants off in this heap. Maybe he brought the panties back as a souvenir. Or maybe they're his mother's and she hasn't missed them yet.

Emilio counts intersections. Why the fuck doesn't the city of New Britain have signs on the cross streets? How you supposed to find where a homey lives so you can kill him?

"That one, Tito." Manny points to his right and they count houses.

"You sure we got the right number, yo?"

That would be all they need, hit the wrong house. At least the houses seem to have numbers where you can read them. Emilio sees 82 and Tito pulls to the curb two houses down.

When he takes his foot off the accelerator, the engine wheezes and dies.

"Fuck," he says. "I hope we can get started again."

Emilio feels Manny's hand clamp on his arm. The house is a three story, looks nice. Grass in the yard is brown, but what else is new? Last night was the first rain in three weeks.

"Well?" Manny has a towel wrapped around his hand, the gun hidden in it.

"Well what?" Emilio says. "You want me to ring the fucking bell? Ask the guy to come outside? I never done this shit before, remember?"

He doesn't want to do it now, either. He looks down a driveway toward the garage. The door is down. Around the corner, in back, he sees a vegetable garden and takes a closer look. Yeah, tomatoes, cukes, peppers. Stuff looks pretty good, someone weeds it.

"Spencer Tracy's not here right now. Can I help you?"

Manny and Emilio jump a foot. A woman wearing a big floppy hat like they've only seen in old pictures, a pink tee shirt with flamingos on it, and white shorts. Parts of her look really old, but her legs and her smile aren't among them. The old broad looks seriously hot and Emilio struggles to figure what's up with that.

"Uh," he says. "Excuse us." He's careful to speak English, even though the woman sounds like an Eye-tie. "We were wondering... We wanted to...um, maybe we should have called first..."

"Oh, he probably be back soon, you know. He not working now, you know. Or maybe you don't know, huh?"

The woman stares at Emilio, her eyes like she's coming on to him. Too fucking gross. She's probably twice as old as his Mami. Three times, even.

"So, uh, you don't know when he'll be back?"

"I see him leave, but that's, what, a few hours ago, I'm baking. Before the house gets too hot, you know? Hesa probably back in a while."

Emilio knows that for old women like this, "a while" can be anything up to a month.

"Yeah, right." Emilio feels Manny pulling the back of his shirt. "Well, we must have missed him. We'll try again later. Maybe we should call next time."

"Oh, you call his cell, he probably answer it right now."

"Um, yeah, good idea. We should do that." Emilio backs up and the woman brushes back her hat to wipe her forehead. Hair still blonde, but not yellow like the Albany Avenue whores. This blonde might even be real. And those legs. Emilio feels like he's caught in a time warp.

"I got my cell in the car," he says. "I'll call him right now, see when he'll be back."

"You want I should tell him you come by?" The old lady smiles. "Whassa your name?"

"Uh, no, thank you. That's OK. I...we'll... later. Thank you."

Emilio and Manny head back to the car as fast as they can without looking like they're running away.

"Fuck," Manny says. "What you doing talking to that old bitch? Why didn't you leave her your fucking calling card?"

"Hey," Emilio says. "Cut me a little slack, all right? I was trying to be polite to an old lady. She was nice."

"Fuck, you leave your phone in the car? What kinda thing is that to say?"

"I bet she don't got one," Emilio says. "Old lady like that."

"Hot fucking old lady," Manny says. "I think she wants you. Maybe both of us. How weird is that? That just so wrong."

Emilio has to swallow. It's just been that kind of day, and it's not over yet.

"Don't even go there, bro. We get in the car, I pretend to call, then we get out of here. We stay around, someone'll get the license sure as shit. Everyone in three blocks must have heard us already, never mind seen us."

"I don't think you want to do this, bro." Manny clamps on Emilio's arm again and they stop in the middle of the sidewalk. "What kind of pussy are you? Cop smokes your own sister, you don't even care. You don't wanna do this, you just a piece of shit."

They can smell the car from thirty feet away. Tito has the hood up, so much steam billowing around they can only see his legs.

"I don't hear no shooting," he says.

“The cop ain’t home,” Manny tells him. “The old lady next door told Emilio here to call him before we come visiting next time.”

“Yeah.” Tito pops the trunk. “My ass we’ll call.” He finds a quart of oil and a gallon water bottle and pours them into the engine.

“Hope this will be enough to get us home.”

It isn’t.

#

Danny Keogh realizes he’s holding hands with Georgia Leigh Pitcher as they ride up the escalator and he feels like a high school kid, only better. There are a half-dozen jewelers in WestFarms Mall and he’s been trying to get her into one of them—any of them—for two months to pick out a diamond. She keeps putting him off.

“We don’t know each other that well, Sugar Plum.”

They’ve only been sleeping together three or four times a week since February and finding that they can talk about anything and everything. She can look interested when he’s discussing how to build a dovetail joint, and she can make the intricacies of a balloon payment mortgage border on the erotic. They both like movies but prefer books. She even has a library card.

He’s even getting used to finding a bra or panties in his laundry, which always set his teeth to grinding with other girlfriends. But they all seemed interested in a ring and a name change, and Georgia doesn’t see those as a high priority. Danny’s the nail now, instead of the hammer, and it’s making him crazy.

“We love each other,” he says.

“I don’t want to hurt you, Sugar Plum. Ever.” Her voice turns serious. She’s wearing sandals with her cut-offs because heels make her taller than he is. He's never said anything about it, but he's aware of it. Hey, he's vain, what are you going to do?

"How could you hurt me?"

"When you love someone, you're setting yourself up to hurt them. Or let them hurt you. It raises the stakes higher than cotton in August. Trust me, I know."

"George..."

"And even if we do love each other, we both love what we do, too. That's a problem waiting to happen."

"Come again?" She always does this to him, makes him feel like he's three moves behind on the board.

They reach the top of the escalator. "Sugar Plum, you love building houses and hospitals and things, don't you?"

"Well, sure. The family's been doing it for sixty years. I give a client the best there is. Good materials, good work, and we stay on schedule. People know me and trust me."

"Besides, it pays the bills. Very well."

"Yes. But I love it. I still like to get into jobs and get my hands dirty. I can do the front man stuff and carry blueprints around, but..."

"Sugar Plum. Danny." She never calls him by his name unless she's serious, so he shuts up.

"I know. It's in your DNA now, your granpappy and all. But I love banking the same way. I love helping people and working with figures and working with money. It gets me almost as hot as you do."

She holds up a palm before he can say what's on his dirty little mind.

"You've got a family business here, Sugar Plum. You don't have to move. But I've only been in New Britain for two and a half years. And if the powers that be decide they need me somewhere else...."

"You could retire, Georgia. If you don't want to, you don't have to work another day in your life."

"But I love my job. If I give it up, what am I going to do all day? Shop? Go to the gym?"

Danny tries not to sound like an Irish Neanderthal. "I'd like children. Someone to keep the business in the family."

He holds his breath and realizes she's watching a couple with a stroller across the court.

"I'd like babies," she says. "But not yet. I'm not ready. I'm still learning who I am."

"You look like you've got a pretty good handle on that."

"But it all depends on things I can't control, not like you. You own the business. But what if I get a promotion to someplace like...Oh, Minneapolis. That's a pretty serious commute. And I'd want to take it. You can't just pick up and go, Sugar Plum. You're too excited 'bout getting those big strong hands dirty. Still."

"I love you, George." He slows down in front of a jeweler's window and gently turns her toward it. When he puts his arm around her waist, she melts against his side.

"I love you, too. But let's not rush things, all right? Let's just have us a good ol' time for as long as it lasts, can we?"

"How long do you think that will be?" He tries to be an adult and keep the hurt out of his voice. The hell of it is that she's right. They've only known each other five months and he's never met any of her family. She doesn't talk about them much, but he thinks they're around New Orleans.

"Nothing good lasts forever. I'm trying to live every day like it's going to fall apart tomorrow. That way I don't hold anything back."

"Can we go in and look at a ring, George? Anyway?"

When she leans over and brushes her lips across his, her eyes look sad. "For you, Sugar Plum, anything."

They look in two other stores, too. And he watches her try on shoes. He tries on sports jackets. They examine dining room furniture in three stores and cutlery in another. They buy nothing.

Back in the center court, they see a hot dog vender near the Starbucks. Georgia slathers mustard on her hot dog, and Danny thinks it's the sexiest sight he's ever seen. They sit at a table and watch families mill around with the spoils of commerce.

"We've got an extra practice tomorrow afternoon," Georgia says. "Lugg thinks we're going to get our cute little behinds spanked next week."

"I hope not." Danny doesn't want anyone spanking Georgia's cute little behind except himself. "What's he calling the practice for? New strategy or something?"

"Well, Tiny Malice needs more time. He wants to work her in as a jammer, but she's not ready. He wants to take some of the weight off Tina and Annabelle. And he is still vastly underwhelmed with our blocking. I'm guessing we'll spend time on that."

She holds up the remains of her snack and her eyes turn wicked. "Work off some of this wiener. Have to get my exercise, my job being so sedentary and all. Settin' round in that chair goes right to my butt."

"I've never noticed."

"Sure you have. If my headlights were as big as my caboose, I couldn't even stand upright. It's good on the rink, but I have to do some serious mix and match on suit sizes."

A couple herds three small children toward the family restrooms near Lens Crafters. Danny thinks Georgia would probably be the greatest mother in the Western Hemisphere. If the kids take after her, they'd be tall and smart as hell. Maybe they'd be good with math, too.

"Not to mention," she mentions, "I suspect that he wants to have practice in the afternoon so we can leave in daylight."

Danny picks up on it instantly. “Is that asshole still around? I thought I hired security.”

“You did. And he was there, but the good ol’ boyfriend hopped the fence and came up behind us. Sucker-punched Lugg before the Lone Ranger could do anything. He went after him, though, and we called the police.” She pronounces it “Po-leese.”

“Did they do anything?” This creep is getting Danny seriously pissed off. If Hendrix can’t do the job, maybe he should turn Jerry Machowski loose. Jerry communicates very well.

“They talked to us, took all sorts of serious notes on clipboards. And, I do have to say, the security guard was righteously outraged. He followed the guy over the fence like he meant it. And I’m sure Roxy has added a little spice to the court order. If the guy comes back and Mr. Security doesn’t kill him first, Roxy will let him have sloppy seconds.”

Danny shakes his head. Georgia licks mustard delicately off her thumb, then wipes her hands on a napkin.

“I keep thinking how ironic it is,” Danny says. “Here you’re doing the bout for a fund-raiser, I’m building the shelter for battered women, and the team’s getting hassled by this jerk.”

“He’s a pain in the behind, Sugar Plum, but nobody’s really been hurt. He took out a couple of windshields, but that is definitely not going to happen again.”

Georgia’s wearing little gold leaves as ear studs, and the light hits them just right so they glow.

“How is the building going by the way? I look out my office window and see lots of big buff men in tee shirts and hard hats. Lots of machines making lots of smoke and noise, but I can’t tell what’s actually happening. Might as well be ducks out there for all I can tell.”

“Jerry tells me they’ve got the water pipes moved now. That cost us about three weeks, diverting the sewer pipes for that whole street. But he figures we can pour the cement for the basement in another week or so. After that, it'll go fast."

"Good. You going to have a copy of the plans at the bout? Picture of the new shelter? People like to see what their money's going to buy."

"I hadn't thought about that," he says. "I'll see what I can do."

She takes his hand and they pass through Nordstrom's and out to the parking garage. Nice suits on mannequins a little taller than he is. But he's more comfortable in his jeans and sneakers. When he holds her door, she turns into him and puts her arms around him for a serious hug and kiss. The whole world stops when he tastes the hint of mustard on her tongue and feels her pressing into him.

"Oh, Sugar Plum," she whispers. "I don't ever want to hurt you. Not ever."

Chapter Ten

Hendrix checks the chain link fence where Kevin Draper both appeared and escaped three nights before, but nobody lurks back there today. The pizza place up and to his right has a few cars, but it's too early for serious pizza. The serious pizza freaks don't go there anyway. If they stay in New Britain, they do Vito's, where he met Tori. If they're really serious, they do Harry's or Luna's in West Hartford or someplace on Franklin Avenue in Hartford.

Tori and Lugg Nutz show up within minutes, the coach with four stitches and an embarrassed look on his face, especially when Tori makes a fuss about it. He unlocks the door and takes care of the lights while she frowns at Hendrix.

"I called Annie twice yesterday and only hit her voicemail. She never got back to me."

Before he can say anything, a white Hyundai hums into the lot and takes the place next to his own Accord. Annie Rogers emerges with her bag over her shoulder and a face that looks like she's trying hard to be Annabelle Lector, Goddamit, and not quite succeeding. She sees Tori and breaks stride for a second before she comes over.

"Um, Tina, I forgot to check my messages until this morning. Then I figured I'd see you in a few hours anyway, so I didn't bother to call. I'm sorry." Her brown hair is pulled back in a ponytail and her black tee and shorts make her look slim as a garden hose. She's wearing black tights, too, so her white sneakers look bigger than suitcases.

"It's all right, Annabelle. I just wanted to touch base with you after the other night. But you're here."

"Yeah." Annie says it like she's not quite convinced. "I am, aren't I?"

She skitters for the door and Hendrix can't help thinking about how completely she ignored him. And how well those black clothes can hide bruises.

"Damn," Tori says. "If she were any more scared, she'd pee on the pavement."

"Yeah." Hendrix sees a black Mercedes and a blue Ford Edge enter the parking lot. The black one is Roxy Heartless, blood red seats, but he's not sure about the other one. "But unless you or the lawyer can make her say the guy roughed her up again, nobody can do a thing."

"So much for restraining orders." Tori looks even more pissed. "I get this all the time. I finally help someone work up the courage to fill one out, then they discover that the cops are too busy checking seat belts to enforce it. They look at me like I just killed Santa Claus."

More cars gradually fill the spaces. A Chevy, a Taurus, another Chevy. Roxy strides over in a red tank top and white gym shorts. Her hair is in pigtails the color of wheat.

"Nice upholstery," he says.

She gives him a smile that makes him think of a cobra. "I picked it in case I can't leave all the blood inside."

"I didn't think lawyers bled," Tori says.

Roxy Heartless watches a tall woman emerge from the Taurus.

"I didn't say it was *my* blood."

Hendrix amuses himself by trying to put names to the other women as they arrive. Some of them wave at him and he recognizes Grace Anatomy, the physical therapist with the long braid, and Molly Ringworm, the hair stylist. A woman in a designer track suit who looks like she could kick his ass clear into Litchfield County gives him a wave and he can't be sure if she's Goldee Spawn or Novocain Dancer.

She stops at the glass display case by the door.

"Ooh, nice."

When she's inside, Hendrix goes over and looks at the poster that has magically appeared since Thursday. Sixty-point type proclaims CHARITY JAM. Below, superimposed over a stylized skater that reminds Hendrix of the busty female silhouette on truck mud flaps, slightly smaller letters announce New Britain Whammer Jammers vs. Raleigh Riot. The date is Saturday, six days away, above a notation that the proceeds will support construction of the new Patience Randall Women's Shelter.

"Whammer" is spelled with a block "W" and a hammer. Above it is a team picture with the women carefully posed to resemble Amazons from Hell. They all grimace like a heavy metal band and show as much cleavage or leg as neighborhood zoning laws probably permit.

"We're asking twice the goin' rate. You think we're worth it?"

Hendrix turns and finds himself nearly eye-to-eye with a brunette in a Red Sox jersey. Her complexion is flawless and her eyes look mean as Roxy's.

"What's the going rate?"

"Ten in advance or twelve at the door." The woman's voice makes him think of honey, a slight drawl that says she definitely wasn't born here.

"This one's twenty-five either way."

"Danny Keogh told me he's willing to triple the gate if you get four hundred people."

"Oh, don't you worry, Sugar." The woman gives him a megawatt grin. "We'll pack the place. They love us. And so does he."

She strides inside like she means business, and he suspects he's just met Denver Mint Julep. If he's right, Danny Keogh has both terrific taste and the luck of the Irish.

He spends the next three hours watching the occasional car go by on Farmington Avenue and a few customers go in and out of the Laundromat next door. Corbin Avenue extends sharply uphill from the exit fronting the Whammer Jammers rink, and Hendrix knows there's a huge low income project that has been decaying for the last half-century above them, then the Hospital for Special Care, which treats patients with traumatic brain damage. The area looks so peaceful he has to remind himself that Kevin Draper has busted a windshield and terrorized Annie Rogers—and he may not be working alone.

He weaves through the cars and his sneakers stick slightly in the tar. He's glad he's not wearing a gun because then he'd need another layer to conceal it, and he'd die in the humidity.

He wonders if Carmen Ortega has told Shields about their second meeting. Shields has earned a reputation as a political chameleon, willing to appease any group that gets upset in the name of Public Relations, and now he's hooked up with a Latina.

Both Sturges and Jimmy Byrne testified to the Internal Affairs officers that Hendrix fired in self-defense. They dug the girl's shot out of the wall, too, and the angle shows that she missed both Hendrix and Byrne by inches and sheer luck. If she'd kept shooting, she could have filled that stairwell with bullets and killed or wounded all three officers if Hendrix hadn't shot her.

Her.

Hendrix reminds himself that the only light was behind her and that they were looking up stairs so they couldn't judge height—she was five-nine, anyway—and she had a weapon.

The woman with the Southern accent who spoke to him about the poster is tall, too, and she drives a BMW. Hendrix wonders why he and she are alive while Corazon Losada is dead from a shotgun blast at the age of fourteen.

Sometimes shit just happens.

He forces himself to think of happier things. Maybe Byrne will find something on Kevin Draper that will keep the guy away. Yesterday's meeting might have been a mistake, but the asshole isn't around today. It's a step.

Hendrix checks his watch. When he gets home, he'll water his vegetables again. The drought has wiped out his corn, but his tomatoes are threatening to outgrow grapefruit and his summer squash are thriving. So are his peppers. If he and Tori ever really do have dinner together, he'll take her some of his zucchini. He forces his mind off that track with a serious lurch.

A few more cars go by, their exhaust hanging in the heavy air. Hendrix checks the chain link fence again and looks down through the trees. He can scarcely see the houses fifty yards away and marvels that neither he nor Kevin Draper broke his neck on that steep slope in the dark.

The sun is high above the telephone pole across from the exit when the first women come through the doors. They chatter like teenagers and give each other sweaty hugs before they dump their gear in the trunk or the passenger seat and drive away to shower and re-connect with their real lives. Hendrix wonders how many of them have workplace buddies who cheer at bouts. Tori McDonald and Annie Rogers certainly don't, but how about the others? Does Roxy Heartless have former clients—or opponents—who come by to see someone put her on the boards?

Roxy and Annabelle Lector come out together, Roxy talking and her body language showing that she's upset. Annabelle looks like she wants someone to read her a bedtime story and tuck her in, but she finally nods before both women get into their cars and drive off in opposite directions.

Tori is the last one out. Her hair is plastered to her forehead and her eyes have the gleam of the undead. She punches Lugg on the shoulder and strides toward her car, her bag bouncing against her hip.

"God, I love this sport," she says. "Where else in the world can you really be a total bitch on wheels and get away with it?"

"Good practice?" Hendrix reminds himself that he's a detective.

"Effing-fantastic." She beeps her car open—including all the windows to let out the heat—and dumps her stuff on the seat. "We were working in Tiny Malice as another jammer, and she's a natural. She doesn't have the technique yet, but she's going to pick it up. She should be our poster child. She's a drill bitch down to her toenails."

"Drill bitches." Hendrix leans against his own fender, but it's hot and he stands again. "I like it."

"Yeah. But Whammer Jammers is more family-friendly, and we get lots of kids here."

"Really?" He looks at her, her entire body still glowing. "I wondered about that."

"Yeah, we're role models. It's all about the attitude. It's why we all love this."

"I'm beginning to figure that out." He looks at the poster in the display case. "But I still haven't seen a match. What's it really like out there?"

"God..."

Tori takes off her cap and wipes her hair into random clumps. "It's like...you get into this zone. You hear the crowd cheering and the wheels rolling and you feel the vibrations in your feet and all the way through your body and you're just...there. It's all about right that very second, no past, no future. Everything goes into slow motion. You're absolutely in the moment and you know everything and you just process it with your whole body, just doing it because it feels like what you have to do. Someone tries to cut you off and you're like part of the track and you know where to move. And when. You put someone on her ass—in the kindest and most gentle way, of course, because we're girls and we all love each other—and it's fine."

Hendrix remembers the few seconds before he fired that shotgun and went deaf. He tries to see it again and realizes that even in that adrenaline-stoked stop action there was no way he could tell that the hand holding the gun shooting at him belonged to a child. A blazing gun makes everyone a grown-up on the spot.

Tori catches her breath and goes on. "I'm in the best shape of my life, and all the oxygen pumping makes me think more clearly. I think I'm the best at my job I've ever been, too. We all talk about how derby makes everything else better. It's like this incredible estrogen high."

She stops. "You wouldn't know about that, would you?"

"Not really. No." In her sweaty gym clothes and glorious smile, she looks so beautiful he wants to put his arms around her and breathe her in like a freshly baked cake.

"On her way in, one of the skaters told me the audience loves you and you'll pack the place. She doesn't think you'll have any trouble getting four hundred people."

"Shoot, Danny picked that number because he knows we get that many people anyway. He figures if it's for a good cause we can jack up the price and not scare them away, and I think he's right. Danny's no dummy. Well, he likes us, so how can he be?"

"Good point." Hendrix looks at the street, not a car in sight. "I'm not sure who I was talking to. Tall woman, slight Southern accent?"

"Brown eyes like pudding?" He nods. "Yeah, that's Denver Mint Julep, Danny's girl."

She tries to straighten her hair again, but gives up.

"Listen, I've got to get home, take a shower. I know I stink."

"I've been standing out here for a few hours, so I'm probably worse. It's a guy thing."

"Yeah, maybe. But remember we were talking about dinner? How's Wednesday?"

"This Wednesday?" Like he has other plans.

"Right. I'm off early that day, so I figured you could come over and I can do lasagna. Interested?"

"Sure." He looks at her. "You don't want me to cook first? I've even got fresh vegetables."

"No, I'm...it's too weird coming to a man's house for supper first." She twirls her car keys on her finger. "I'm an old Eye-tie girl, and we don't do things like that."

She opens her door and looks at him across the roof. "But bring some of your vegetables for a salad."

He sees her catch herself before she mentions zucchini again.

He's still thinking about that when he pulls into his own driveway. When he comes out of the garage, Paola Roccapini greets him from over the fence.

"Spencer Tracy, you working on a Sunday? Or you out playing the golf? Beautiful day like-a this."

"It is, isn't it, Ms. Roccapini?" Seventy-four, he tells himself. She's wearing a tank top and her arms still look firm, her white shorts fit perfectly above blue sandals that match her top. "Yes, I was out working, sort of. Killing time."

"Paola," she reminds him. "You want to kill time, I know lots of other ways, Spencer Tracy." She winks lasciviously. "More fun, too."

"I'll bet, Ms.—Paola."

"But, I meant to ask you, did those young men get back to you yesterday?"

"Excuse me?" Kevin Draper is the only young man he can think of at the moment.

"Two young men. Well, tree. Yesterday afternoon. They wanted to see you."

"Um, no. What time was this?"

"Oh, I dona remember, exactly. Middle of the afternoon. Two teenagers, maybe sixteen, seventeen. I canna tell anymore."

"Did they say what they wanted?"

"No, but they wanted to see you. Very polite, one of them was. Spanish, I think, but the polite one, he spoke very good English."

"I don't think I know them, Ms.—Paola. Did they give you a name?"

"Uh-uh." Paola Roccapini blinks flirtatiously, but Hendrix can tell she's really watching the scene again, trying to play it out in her mind.

"One of them had a hurt hand. The one who dinna talk much. I remember that, he had it wrapped in a towel. I think they were in a hurry, on the porch, look through your door, I see them coming down the driveway when I'm-a water my plants."

"Uh-huh." Hendrix is completely lost. "And no names. But they were Spanish, you think?"

Not even a blind idiot would mistake Kevin Draper for Spanish, and Paola Roccapini is neither blind nor stupid.

"I'm sure. The one with the bad hand is maybe your size, the other one a little shorter."

"And the middle of the afternoon, you say."

"That's right. They drove up, their old car was ready for the junkyard. Rusty, blue. An old car, a big one."

"Do you remember the make?"

"No, I dona know cars much. It had a big brown spot on the back by the tail light. Brown like, what do you call it?" She moves her hands like she's waving away smoke.

"Primer?" Hendrix tries.

"That's right. Primer. An old, old car. They had to put oil and water into it to start up again before they could leave."

"Did you happen to notice the license number?"

"No, sorry. I told them to call you, and the polite one, he say he'sa call you on his cell from the car. But I guess he didn't, did he?"

"No. Um, where did they park, in front of the house?"

"Two down. The Belliveaus." Paola Roccapini's smooth forehead wrinkles for a second. "So he not call you back?"

"No. I'll check inside and see if he tried my answering machine. Thank you, Ms—Paola."

Two houses down, there's a fresh oil slick on the pavement. He knocks on the Belliveaus' door to ask them about the car, but nobody's home.

He goes into his back yard and turns his hose on gently to water his vegetables, which makes him think about Tori McDonald again.

His answering machine has no messages. He channel surfs through three baseball games, then goes out to turn off the hose again.

By the time the sun sets, he's forgotten all about the young Spanish men who missed him.

Chapter Eleven

A few young kids cluster near the corner of the lot to watch the bulldozer and dump trucks, and Danny remembers what it's like to be seven years old and have these cool machines practically in your backyard. Most of the stately neighboring houses with their shrub-lined lawns and still-proud maple trees are offices now: realtors, a dentist, a chiropractor. Across Vine Street, a pseudo-Tudor apartment building peers down at the bank where Georgia works. A few remaining mom and pop stores lie farther up West Main, remnants of an earlier time. Thirty years ago, Danny could have stood almost anywhere in the United States and seen pretty much the same sight.

Jerry Machowski has spread the plans on the hood of his pick-up, a screwdriver weighing down one corner and pliers holding the other.

"The tap on the main is here." His pencil points to the map, but Danny can see the fresh mound of dirt near the corner of the lot. With this heat and humidity, grass will appear in a few days. Now it resembles the grave of a giant worm.

"The Building Inspector says we're copacetic now," Machowski continues. He has to shout over the compressor and jackhammer. “We lost a few days, but they’re not talking more rain for another week.”

He flips up the blue print to reveal the drawing underneath it. “Besides, it gave us a fifty-foot head start.”

“We don’t have much time left,” Danny says. “We aren’t done by Saturday, we’re fucked.”

“We’re fine.” They’ve had to readjust the cornering of the foundation by about six feet because of the septic system that serves four of the houses, too. A truck is two thirds full of dirt. Danny figures it’ll move out not long after he does.

“Wish we could work double shifts,” he comments. “Get a little wiggle room.”

Machowski sips from his water bottle. “I can do something about that.”

Jerry’s background is a lot like Danny’s, with less working capital. He’s a master carpenter, plumber, and electrician and can read blueprints as easily as newspaper headlines. Denny’s amazed that the guy isn’t married, but that’s unknown territory for both of them. Like this project.

“Georgia said they had a good practice yesterday,” he says. “And that asshole who’s been giving the girl all that shit didn’t show up.”

Two men in hard hats wield pick-axes to help feed the bulldozer.

“You want, I can do something about him, too,” Machowski says.

“I think it’s taken care of.” Danny looks across the parking lot. “Tori McDonald talked me into hiring a guy for security, a Hartford cop. He talked to the guy a few nights ago, looks like he got his point across.”

“I met him last week,” Machowski says. “Blond guy, a little taller than you?”

"That's him."

"If he's a cop, what's he doing with this gig?"

"He's on leave. Shot someone in a drug raid last month. I saw it in the Courant."

Machowski studies the blueprints again. "If he's such a hot rock, it's probably good that he's going to be busy at the match."

"Yeah," Danny says. "But he could be a problem there, too."

"Not if we know about him."

A car glides up to the drive-through ATM, and Danny wonders if they have a Braille pad. Only in Connecticut. Or maybe not.

"I'm going to the practice Thursday, see how things are shaping up. If you come by then, I can help you set up your speakers."

"That sounds good." Machowski wipes his forehead. "It's gonna be a real circus, isn't it?"

"Well that's your job, just like a ring-master." They are in so fucking deep, and they've never done anything like this before. Lady Luck opens the door and she's got no clothes on, who's going to walk the other way?

Danny looks across the parking lot at the bank again, one hundred thirty-eight feet from the corner of what will be the new Patience Randall Domestic Center. Inside that bank, Georgia Leigh Pitcher is sitting at her desk, probably checking financial figures on-line and looking cool and professional in a power suit, not like she looked last night, not cool at all, hot and sweaty after their lovemaking.

But she won't marry him.

Maybe he'll ask her again after Saturday night. The Whammer Jammers have only been together as a team for six months, and they're still learning to work with each other. He and Georgia have only known each other for five.

He wonders about her family again. She's only made a few vague references; he's not even sure if she has brothers or sisters. It's like she was beamed down from a space ship only days before he met her. His own parents would love her. Pretty, smart, polite, successful. His mother would tell him that Georgia is the woman he needs to keep him in line, and maybe she's right.

God knows, Georgia would kill him if she knew what he's doing now.

Machowski picks up his pliers and screwdriver. The blueprints roll up with a snap. Danny watches him join the guys by the 'dozer.

He considers dropping in at the bank, but Georgia's busy on a Monday morning. He'll call her later.

So much they still have to worry about.

#

Hendrix is turning the pages of Sports Illustrated in bed when Tori calls him. He pulls on a tee shirt and slides into jeans almost as quickly as his firemen forebears, stuffing his feet into loafers to save time struggling with laces, and grabs his car keys.

By the time he reaches the smoking remains of the Patience Randall Women's Shelter, the streets and sidewalks are overflowing with neighborhood spectators. Smoke lingers in the air, but the fire is out. The firemen managed to contain it before it spread to any of the neighboring houses and—except for the receptionist and her hunky boyfriend, who inhaled a little more smoke than the Surgeon General recommends—nobody has been hurt. That's the good news.

The bad news is that the fire isn't an accident.

Tori McDonald stands beside a kid who looks young enough to be in college. He's wearing a sooty white shirt and jeans, and racking like he's stripped a gear. The girl next to him sips from a bottle of water one of the firemen has brought her. She wears wire-frame glasses above a pale yellow polo shirt and khaki shorts.

All three have laptops open on the hood of a car, and Tori and the girl are talking on cell phones. The guy sticks a flash-drive into his USB port and his face picks up the flickering colors on his monitor.

A few yards away, several women huddle like lost sheep. Hendrix thinks they range from twenty to maybe late forties, but it's hard to tell in the dark. Some wear clothes, but a couple are wrapped in blankets and may not have anything else under them. Their eyes all look blank and they move awkwardly, as if they don't quite remember how to do it.

The Fire Chief and a New Britain cop join Tori's group and Hendrix hovers close enough to listen in.

"No way," the Chief says. "Nobody's going back in there tonight. We need to go through it in daylight and see if there's any structural damage."

"But where...?" The girl in the polo shirt looks at the huddled women.

"I don't know, Ms." The Chief looks at the smoldering mass. "But you don't have any electricity. And you've got lots of smoke and water damage in the back. That's for starters."

The flashing lights from three fire engines and as many cop cars turn the place into a dark circus. As far as Hendrix can tell, every house for a block in each direction has its lights on, and most of the inhabitants are out here watching. Tori called him and beat him only because she called from her car so she had a head start. Her shirt is buttoned wrong and she's not wearing socks, but she still looks as heart-breaking as she does heart-broken.

Hendrix walks to the back of the building where the smoke still cloaks everything and most of the men wear face masks.

Floodlights shine on the charred mess that was the back door, and burn marks reach the second story window. Two firemen and three men in coveralls are raking piles of soggy ash and broken glass while a cop tries to take pictures without being able to see what he's doing. Hendrix tries to avoid the puddles.

He flashes his Hartford ID at one of the firemen. "What's it look like?"

"Some asshole poured accelerant all around this door and along the back wall," the guy answers. "Nothing fancy, but it worked."

"Anybody see him?"

"Nobody's come forward yet. He probably came through back yards and left the same way. I haven't heard any dogs barking, so maybe nobody even heard him. If he parked on the other side of the block, he could have been long gone before the flames got high enough for the kids inside to notice them and call us."

"But it was definitely set."

"Fuckin' A." The guy looks around again. "At least they got everyone out."

Back at the car, Tori is talking to a man in a rumpled suit. He looks like someone who can't change a light bulb without filling out the order in triplicate and whose best skill is probably delegating.

"I've already called the Marriot." He sounds proud of himself. "They can take two of them."

"I've called CCSU," Tori says. Central Connecticut State University, on Stanley Street, is only fifteen minutes away. "I've talked to the head of campus security, and he says they'll open one of the dorms. They've got bedding. Everyone can stay together that way. And Sarah and Tom will join them."

Sarah and Tom look up from their laptops.

"All right." The suit nods like he thinks it was his own idea. "Will the Fire Chief let them take their effects with them?"

"Not until they check out the building tomorrow." Tori looks at her cell phone. "We can get back in then and pull what they need. And Tom has their records on his flash drive. I've already called the hospital and we've e-mailed the prescriptions. I'll pick them up on the way over."

"Senseless, senseless, senseless." The man shakes his head. "Do they have any idea who did it?"

Hendrix joins them.

"Excuse me," he says. "If whoever did this knew that the place was a shelter and not a residence, maybe he was targeting one of your current occupants. Tell the police to get names and check on all the assholes these women were staying away from."

"And you would be...?" The man looks down his nose at Hendrix, an impressive feat since he's only a few inches taller than Tori.

"I'm a Hartford detective," Hendrix tells him. "But I'm off duty and I don't have any jurisdiction here, anyway. I'm just offering you a suggestion out of the warmth of my heart. And because I hate firebugs."

He watches Tori slowly create order out of chaos. She seems to grow taller and everyone defers to her. Her arms go around two of the older women and she talks to them like a combination nanny, big sister, and drill sergeant. He's seen some of it at roller derby practice, but not as clearly. It's like she was born to make things better. Even with her shirt buttoned wrong, she radiates control and confidence.

Eventually, Tom and Sarah and two police cars leave with the women, en route to a dorm. Mr. CEO strides back to his car—Hendrix notices that it's a Porsche—and drives back to Olympus. The firemen roll up their hoses and the trucks growl back to their fire station. The neighbors go back to their houses and Hendrix sees lights in many of the windows disappear, along with the glow of TV sets.

Smoke fills the night air and puddles surrounding the building flow into the street, but everything else seems normal now. So to speak.

Tori sags back against Hendrix's fender and he puts an arm around her before she slides to the ground.

"Shit," she says. "Why would someone do this?"

"I don't know." His watch says it's nearly one a.m. "You need some rest."

"I have to go to the hospital, pick up the women's meds. Then take the stuff over to CCSU."

"I'm closer," he says. "You go home and get some sleep. Is there a doctor I should ask for by name?"

She gives him a name and her business card so he can flash it if he needs to, and he guides her behind the wheel. She says Tom or Sarah will be at the front of the dorm.

"Sleep in tomorrow," he tells her.

"Can't. Those women are going to be freaked out of their skulls. And one of them's in here because her husband likes to burn her with a fucking iron. If I find who did this..."

Not if I find him first, Hendrix promises himself.

He watches her taillights turn down East Street. Then he gets into his own car and points his headlights toward the hospital.

By the time he gets home, it's almost two-thirty. He has no idea why anyone would set fire to a women's shelter, but it feels like part of the job to find out.

Chapter Twelve

Hendrix checks out the Charity Jam poster in the display case for the fifth time, then walks across the parking lot to the traffic light by Corbin Avenue, where he can look up the hill at the houses lining both sides of the street. A dozen obese evergreen shrubs separate the parking lot from the sidewalk, and he wonders who takes care of them. A few cars enter and leave the lot near the Laundromat fifty yards beyond the rink, and the pizza joint has three cars parked against the building. It's cool enough so Hendrix's shoes no longer stick in the soft blacktop. Eight-thirty. The sun is beginning to sink behind those houses on the hilltop; in a few minutes, the streetlights will go on.

When Tori McDonald arrived earlier, she gave him her address and directions. Sure enough, she's in a condo less than half a mile from Cavos, where they ate lunch on Saturday, a fifteen minute drive from his own house.

He finds himself thinking about the arson at the women's shelter. The accelerant was nothing more exotic than gasoline, so it's useless as a lead. The displaced women are still at CCSU until the Fire Marshal says the building is habitable, but Hendrix doesn't see that happening. He doesn't see any connection between the fire and the roller girls or Danny Keogh, either. Kevin Draper doesn't even know the place exists, much less where it is, so he's not a suspect. But that means one of the women now hiding on a college campus has a very significant other, one who likes to play with matches.

Hendrix hates fires. It stems from his grandfather's experience at the Hartford Circus fire over 60 years before, not to mention his uncle's death when he himself was a kid. He remembers the funeral, firemen from all over Connecticut arriving in uniforms, his father and mother and himself sitting in the same church pew with his aunt and two cousins. Their eyes looked dull as cotton.

He weaves between the parked cars again. The black Mercedes on his left belongs to Roxy Heartless—she calls it the "Bitchmobile"—and the Hyundai two rows down is Annabelle Lector's. Tori McDonald's Civic is near the door. He thinks the green Chevy belongs to Grace Anatomy. Novocain Dancer drives the beat-up Nissan and the BMW belongs to Denver Mint Julep, Danny Keogh's girlfriend. He's not sure who drives the other cars, but he knows the names of most of the women now, even if he can't pick them out of a line-up.

Tori has said she's leaning toward lasagna for tomorrow night and she's told him to bring vegetables for a salad. Including zucchini. He wonders what she has planned for dessert.

He hates first dates and the guessing games while two people learn to understand what the other one is really saying. If they figure out each other enough to sleep together, he'll have to learn how Tori wants to be touched. She'll feel different, taste different, and smell different. Her skin will have different textures. How does she kiss, or like to be kissed? Jenny Della Vecchia liked to talk dirty in bed, but maybe social workers get more clinical.

It's only dinner, he tells himself. Yeah, right. At her place. And she told him to bring his zucchini.

He strolls to the back corner of the building to look through the chain link fence. He shines his Maglite into the gathering darkness, but sees only trees. Through those trees, he can see the lights of the houses down below. He stands motionless, listening for any sound, but all he can hear is an occasional car going by up on Farmington Avenue a hundred yards behind him.

Jimmy Byrne left a message on his voicemail. He's checked Kevin Draper out and found that the guy has never even had a parking ticket. He studied for two years at Tunxis Community College, but his classes looked more like a smorgasbord of fleeting interests than a planned major: a couple of computer courses, history, geology, golf, freshman English, and a refresher algebra class. The classes are so varied that Byrne can't even tell what the guy cares about.

He quit school just after turning twenty and took a job with the Bristol Department of Sanitation. He's been riding shotgun for curbside pick-up for five years now.

The only interesting item that Byrne turned up concerns Kevin Draper's parents, who are divorced. His father has two arrests for assault on his wife—now his ex-wife—and another for a fight in a bar when he and the other guy were both drunk. Kevin's attitude about women comes naturally.

Hendrix leans against the stone façade of the building; the crushed stones on the pillar scrape his back and he stands up again. At least the lower humidity has decreased the mosquito count. Weeding his garden the week before, he felt like he was being strafed by sparrows.

A large mass slows down at the light and starts to turn into the parking lot. It looks like it might be Kevin Draper's Hummer and Hendrix steps forward. The driver comes down into the parking lot just far enough to circle and turn back the way he came. Looking into the last rays of the setting sun, Hendrix can't be sure if the car was a Hummer or just some other big dark SUV. It turns left toward downtown New Britain anyway, and Bristol lies in the opposite direction.

Hendrix glides down the line of shrubs until he can smell the assorted aromas from the pizza shack. He wonders if they have one of the posters about the match taped on their front window. Tori says the girls go over there some nights after practice, but they're moving toward Vito's, which bought a full-page program ad in the program for the upcoming bout. He wonders what that program looks like.

Just after nine. In a few minutes, the women will emerge and he will have only two more sessions, Thursday night and the Saturday bout, before he needs to look for work again. He needs the money, but, more than that, he needs something to keep his brain occupied before it turns soft as the tomatoes in his back yard. He's certain that Shields has buried his grievance on his desk, so it may not see action for weeks.

He watches a woman trundle three large bags of laundry into the back of her car. She wears a baggy purple shirt and white spandex pants, and her cigarette glows faintly before she closes the door and waddles around to the driver's side. A minute later, he hears voices and realizes that practice is over.

Grace Anatomy, Novocain Dancer, and Tiny Malice appear in the lights and wave at him, then step toward their respective cars. Sure enough, Grace opens the door of the Chevy.

Roxy Heartless and Annabelle Lector appear, their bags over their shoulders. Hendrix watches Annabelle scan the lot before she steps out of the shelter of the doorway.

"It's OK," he says. "I've checked in back, too."

She hesitates for a second. Her face looks drawn and he wonders if she's sleeping worth a damn. The women support and protect each other here, but Kevin Draper violates everything these women believe in.

Tori emerges from the door, talking with Goldee Spawn. Molly Ringworm appears behind them.

Hendrix steps forward. To his left, a laboring engine revs up and headlights splash across the front wall of the building. When he turns, all he can see are two glaring white circles moving closer. His Maglite shows two shapes in the front seat, but he can't make out any details. Howling like a runaway train, the car turns parallel with the front of the building and the passenger leans out the window. Hendrix's flashlight beam reflects off metal.

"Get down," he shouts.

He throws himself at the women and hears a giant ratcheting as though someone is running a huge stick down a picket fence. His shoulder connects with someone and he, Tori, and Goldee tumble to the ground. He tries to stay on top of them.

The ratcheting continues and he hears the shots slam into the wall above them. He feels like he's back in that Albany Avenue stairwell; for the first time, it dawns on him that he's not armed. The shooting seems to go on forever. Someone is stitching the whole front of the building with an automatic weapon.

The car's engine cranks to an even higher pitch and Hendrix rolls over in time to get a glimpse of a boxlike sedan with dark patches on a rear fender. Dark blue? He can't be sure. It bores into the adjacent lot, swerves left, disappears beyond the pizza place, and swings right on Farmington Avenue. Slater Road, another main drag, is only a half mile away, and I-84 lies a half mile beyond that. The car will be miles away in five minutes.

Hendrix rolls to his feet and sweeps his eyes around the lot. The women look around fearfully before helping each other stand up.

"Everyone OK?" He realizes he's using his cop voice, louder and harsher, the one that demands instant obedience. "Did anyone get a look at the license number?"

Tori McDonald is looking off to her right and Hendrix follows her gaze. Molly Ringworm stands in the doorway, spider web cracks in the glass behind her. Her bag lies on the ground next to her, and she sags to her knees.

"Oh," she sighs. "I'm..."

She falls forward.

Hendrix dashes over. Doctor Goldee Spawn is a step ahead of him and Lugg Nutz appears in the doorway, his eyes wide. Hendrix shines his light on Molly while Goldee probes under the woman's torso. Her hand comes away red.

"Shit," she says. "Help me turn her over."

Hendrix puts the light in his mouth to free his hands. Molly's eyes are open and she blinks slowly as though gravity pulls her lids down before she remembers to resist. A red stain, already the size of Hendrix's fist, spreads on her white tee shirt, halfway between her breast and her belt.

"Call 911," He snaps. He tears off his own tee to stuff into the wound.

"Molly," Goldee says. "Can you hear me? We're going to take care of this. Just hang on, we've got help coming."

"Uh?" Molly's eyes roll toward Goldee Spawn, but Hendrix isn't sure she can see anything. He thinks the slug may have caught her liver. There's no exit wound.

"We're here, Molly. You're going to be OK." Goldee's eyes meet Hendrix's and he knows she doesn't believe it. The coach drops to the ground next to them, his phone in his hand.

"Tell them a police officer needs assistance," Hendrix tells him. "Say shots have been fired and we have a badly wounded woman. And tell them to move their ass."

Nutz speaks into his phone.

"It hurts." Molly's voice floats out in slow motion.

"Yeah," Goldee tells her. "We're gonna take care of it, Molly. Help's on the way."

"I'm so cold."

Her eyes roll back and she begins to convulse.

"Shit," Goldee says again. "Help me hold her down."

Hendrix straddles the woman's hips and feels her thrashing against him. He presses his tee shirt against the wound, but knows the woman is hemorrhaging internally. Lugg Nutz cushions her head so she doesn't slam it against the pavement.

"Does anyone have any towels or a blanket in your car?" Goldee says. "We need to stop the bleeding here."

Someone–it might be Denver Mint Julep–hurries over with two towels.

"Thanks," Hendrix says. "Now, everyone get back into the building. Come around to the right here, just in case there are slugs or shell casings the cops can use for evidence."

"Molly." Tori's voice shakes. "Who would...Why?"

"Tori, get the hell inside."

"He's trying to kill me." Annabelle Lector's voice is a wail. "He was trying to shoot me and he got her instead. It's my fault."

"Annie, get your ass in here." Roxy Heartless grabs her arm and steers her toward the shattered doorway.

"He'll get me next time." Annabelle's voice climbs another octave. "Molly...Oh, my God."

The others half drag, half carry her back inside as Hendrix, Lugg Nutz, and Goldee Spawn bend over the woman.

"Where the fuck is that ambulance?" Goldee demands.

They hear a siren seconds later, then another, and headlights wash over them. Two vehicles approach and Hendrix turns to see two squad cars escorting an ambulance. He stands and points to the left, hoping he can keep them away from the path of the shooter's car. With his other hand, he finds his wallet and his Hartford ID.

The first squad car jerks to a halt and Hendrix trots over with his badge held high.

"Can you leave your lights on? We need them here."

"What do you have?"

"A drive-by. The car was an old blue sedan, I think American, at least fifteen years old. Two people in it, the driver and the shooter, maybe someone in back, too. They had something automatic, fired a full magazine. They hit a woman over here, she's in bad shape."

"Was she the target?" The cop with the clipboard has two inches on Hendrix and probably forty pounds.

"I don't think so."

The EMTs kneel beside Molly and Hendrix sees them searching her chest with a stethoscope. He saw the same pose a month ago over Corazon Losada, and he has the awful feeling they're looking for a heartbeat they won't find. Goldee Spawn and Lugg Nutz step back and watch, their faces blank. Even in the sparse beams of the headlights, Hendrix can see that their clothes are soaked with Molly's blood. So are his own.

Less than three minutes later, the ambulance screams out of the lot and down Farmington Avenue with Dr. Goldee Spawn—whatever the hell her real name is—in back helping the EMT.

Hendrix tells his story three times and watches the cops from the other car meander along the front of the building and sweep their lights across the blacktop. Occasionally, one stops and puts down a white card. Hendrix finds another shirt in his car and rejoins the women inside, who huddle on the aluminum bleachers and hug each other. Some hold cell phones, probably calling home to say they'll be very late. Their eyes look glassy and several are crying.

Hendrix's adrenaline surge fades and he sinks next to Tori. His left hand and arm have a livid scrape from his dive on pavement and he feels it burning for the first time. When he closes his eyes, he sees the muzzle flash again, lighting up the whole wall. Then he remembers a month earlier when he lit up that kid like a flare. He orders himself not to puke in front of the women.

"Molly." Tori huddles into him and he feels her shaking. "Oh, God, why Molly? She's going to die, isn't she?"

"No," Hendrix tells her. "They're going to fix her up. She's going to be fine."

"Bullshit."

The cops gradually let people go home. Nobody got a good look at the car or its occupants, and nobody knows why anyone would want to shoot Molly Ringworm, whose real name turns out to be Kathy Sonstrom. After the cops finally write down Hendrix's badge number, they agree to check on Kevin Draper's whereabouts at nine-thirty that evening.

At midnight, Hendrix regains the parking lot. Three squad cars still command the area and officers and technicians crawl across the black top with flashlights and tape. They've taken enough pictures to fill a scrapbook.

"We've found a few shell casings," one of the techs tells Hendrix. "Nine millimeter. A lot of flattened slugs, too. They're for shit, but the casings might help."

Hendrix nods. Tori takes his uninjured hand.

"I need to go to the hospital. I've got to find out about..."

"They won't tell you anything if you're not family," he says.

Even in the dark, he feels her eyes. "If I have to, I'll say I'm her mother, Goddamit."

Before he can reply, her cell chirps in her purse. It's Goldee Spawn, who has sat in the waiting room covered in blood for the last three hours. She's finally managed to get a status report from the doctors who tried to resuscitate Molly Ringworm. She's found Molly's cell in her purse and called her brother and parents, too.

Molly was pronounced dead twenty-two minutes after being admitted.

#

"Shit, holy shit."

Emilio Losada drops the MAC 9 and the hot barrel hisses against the sole of his sneaker. The whole car smells acrid and a few casings rattle on the back seat. Tito's standing on the accelerator and fighting the steering wheel. The pizza place looms big as a fucking mountain before they hurtle by it and onto the street, Tito spinning the wheel the other way so the car rocks like a roller coaster.

"You get him? The cop motherfucker?" Tito asks. They're probably doing fifty on a city street, and still accelerating. Emilio doesn't know which will happen first, either they'll go airborne or the fucking engine will blow up and leave their raggedy ass stranded in New Britain with a smoking machine gun between his legs.

"I think," he says. "I don't know."

"You got someone." Manny brushes the hot casings off the back seat onto the floor. A few landed in his lap, but he's so stoked he doesn't even notice.

"Too bad we didn't find the place earlier," Emilio says. "I could've seen better in daylight."

"Bitch, bitch, bitch," Tito says. "You had the fuckin' map."

"I can't help it, they got some of the street names wrong." The only reason they even knew about the place was that reporter mentioned in her column this morning that Tracy Hendrix, suspended for shooting a teen-aged girl, is now moonlighting as security for the team. Bitches on wheels. Crazy fucking world. But they found the address on line, and here they are.

"He dove," Manny says. "He saw us coming, he tried to get those broads out of the way."

"Fucking waste," Tito says. "All those women, gotta be dykes. You shoulda took out every one of them."

"I wish I knew if I got that cop," Emilio says again. "He flashed that light in my eyes, I couldn't see nothing for a second. I just opened up."

He can't say to the others that he's never fired a gun before and the sound and the recoil almost made him shit himself. He still feels the gun trying to jump out of his hands, pulling his arms up toward the roof of the car. Lucky the others told him to aim low or he wouldn't have hit shit.

Tito swerves onto I-84.

"Emilio," Manny calls from the back. "Gimme the piece. Lemme wrap it again. Get it out of sight."

Emilio passes the gun over the seat, still hot. He can smell the smoke and oil, feel the heat coming off the barrel. If he closes his eyes, he sees the whole wall light up again, and those women scattering like wood chips and that shape in the white rectangle before they blew by the building like the angel of fucking death.

Something thrashes inside him. He puts his head out the window and pukes down the side of the car.

"Shit," Tito yells. "Fuck you doin'?"

"Shut up, Tito." Manny leans forward and slaps Emilio on the back. "You done good, bro. The first one is hard. But it's like your first pussy, you do better next time."

Emilio doesn't want there to be a next time.

They highball past WestFarms Mall. They're already miles away from the scene and the cops probably haven't even shown up yet.

Emilio wonders how many shots hit that cop. What does he look like now? The motherfucker shot his sister once with a shotgun. They wouldn't let him see her until she was in the casket and she just looked like a candle, so pale, so shiny. They wouldn't let him see the wound. Now he's shot at that cop like forty times. The bastard must look like a dog in the street, run over by a truck so its guts are splashed all over the fucking pavement, red and shit everywhere.

No, he doesn't want there to be a next time. Fuck you, Manny. Fuck you, Tito.

Then he realizes he may not have any choice. Now he's one of them. How the fuck did he get to this place?

He leans out the window and pukes again.

Chapter Thirteen

Hendrix cruises into the Hartford squad room the next morning riding on three hours of sleep and six cups of coffee. Savickas looks up from his desk and his white hair is the only familiar sight in the place.

"Trash, what the hell you doing here?"

"Investigating." He fills Vic in on the previous night. "The Bristol cops found Kevin Draper at home drinking with two buddies, and they all said they'd been there since about seven-thirty. Which means he's not the shooter. Not that I thought he was anyway."

"But who else would want the girl dead?"

"I don't think they were after the girl."

Hendrix and Tori picked up Goldee Spawn at the hospital, where she'd already notified Kathy Sonstrom's family about the shooting. They live in Florida, and she roused them from bed them with the most horrible news in their lives.

Hendrix drove them back to the rink, and they watched Goldee's tail lights disappear toward the highway. It's one-fifteen and the techs are packing up to go home, but their lights show the line of bullet pocks in the wall, moving up and to the left. Hendrix realizes the recoil of the automatic weapon may be all that saved several other women from being shot, too.

Tori unlocks her door. Then she turns around and buries her face in Hendrix's chest.

"Oh, God." He holds her until her sobbing runs down to hiccups and twitches. "I'm not going to be able to sleep tonight. I'm going to see Molly's face wherever I look. Even with my eyes closed."

"I know," he says. "But you need to rest anyway. Try to."

The warmth of her body against him makes him dizzy. He leans down and smells her hair, full of blood, sweat, and fear. But underneath it all, he smells her, too. He closes his eyes and lets her fingers clutch his arms for as long as she wants.

"Why?" she asks. When she looks at him, her eyes are terrified and shocked, but there's anger in there, too.

"I don't know," he tells her. "Not yet."

She finally climbs into her car and gives him a long look before she turns left out of the lot and heads for her condo...alone.

Back at his own house, he stands under scalding hot water for twenty minutes, trying to get the blood out of his hair and cuticles, but he can still smell it, along with the gunshot residue. Molly's frightened eyes float in front of him, too, just as he knows they will for Tori and a dozen other women.

After lying in bed for three hours, he makes coffee and looks at the Hartford Courant. The shooting merits four brief paragraphs in the CT NOW section, a transcription of the New Britain Police report. The paper would have been going to press before they could find any other information. He's faintly surprised that they know Molly is dead.

He brushes his teeth and sees a light in Paola Roccapini's kitchen. He knows that she sleeps only about four hours a night and has usually done two loads of laundry and most of her ironing before the sun peeps over the trees across the street, so he steps across the driveway to knock on her back door.

"Whoa, Spencer Tracy, you early this morning."

Her kitchen is spotless, but he can already smell bread baking.

"Ms. Roccapini, do you remember those young men you told me about the other day?"

"The Spanish ones. Sure, what, you think I'm getting old, I don't remember?" Her eyes are full of fun, but then she notices the lines in his face.

"You said there were three of them and that one of them had a bandaged hand. Do you remember anything about the bandage?"

"Uh, not really a bandage. More like a...it was a towel, I think. A big towel. "

"Was it big enough that he could have been holding something in his hand? Something he didn't want anyone to see?"

She narrows her eyes and looks out toward the driveway. He watches her talking to the boys again. Her eyes widen again and she nods.

"Yes. A big towel, could have been something in his hand."

"You said their car looked old, too. But do you remember any more about that?"

"Blue. Rust spots. Big old car. I don't know cars. My Dominick, he knew cars, but I don't know from a bicycle."

"Three boys, though," Hendrix asks again. "And Hispanic."

"Thassa right."

In the squad room now, Savickas chews on an antacid mint.

"You think these assholes last night were those kids? And they were after you?"

"I don't know for sure." Hendrix looks at Vic's PC and wishes he could get into one himself. "But the car might have been the same one, an old blue junker with rust spots."

He watches Vic process it. "Those kids knew where I lived Saturday. They asked my neighbor about me by name. But I never told her I was nurse-maiding the roller derby team.

That showed up in Carmen Ortega's column in the Courant yesterday morning."

Vic's mouth turns down. "Shit, that's right. I forgot about that. She's got a real bug up her ass for you. She mentioned you were a security guard now that Shields has decided that you're not fit to be a cop."

"Are they really an item?"

Vic rolls his eyes. "His divorce was final about the same time you shot that kid." He taps his fingers on his desk and looks back at Hendrix. "You thinking she's setting the Ricans on you?"

"Not sure." Hendrix digs in the drawer before he remembers that his gumdrops are long gone. "But I'm wondering if the shooter could be connected to Corazon Losada, or maybe one of the other assholes we took down in that raid. Can you check on that for me? See if they have any friends?"

"Sure. And why don't you talk to the steward again while you're here? I'm pretty sure Shields is stonewalling on your paperwork. Every time I bring it up, he just looks the other way. And we could sure as hell use you back here, Trash."

Hendrix tells him about the fire at the shelter, too, and they lob bad ideas about that around for another half hour. None of the suggestions is even worth pursuing.

On his way out, Hendrix turns the corner at the landing and almost plows into Carmen Ortega. She wears a translucent tee shirt and a turquoise jacket above outrageously tight jeans, and she's so close he can smell her breath mint.

"What are you doing here?" she demands.

"I'm investigating a murder," he tells her. "The murder you caused with your half-assed excuse for a column yesterday."

"What are you talking about?" Her eyes flicker and she tries to step around him, but he steps in front of her again.

"You told everyone that I'm guarding a roller derby team in New Britain."

She doesn't quite laugh in his face. "I'm glad to see all the money the city paid to train you is paying off."

"People need protection. That's what I do."

"Oh, yeah, I'm sure. Those women can take care of themselves, can't they?"

"It's not like it used to be."

And suddenly he hears himself parroting the Web site and Tori McDonald and all the other people he's talked to. Women supporting and encouraging each other, fun, health, and excitement. He sounds like an infomercial and forces himself to stop.

"Actually, Ms. Ortega, that might be a worthwhile story for your column. The women. They're doctors and lawyers and all kinds of white collar jobs now. They're smart and funny, too. And very articulate. You might get some great interviews, say something positive for a change."

"I say things that have to be said. You're a menace and you should never be allowed to carry a weapon, not even a nail file, for the rest of your life. And you should be spending it in jail for killing a girl."

The worst part of arguing with an idiot is that some people may not be able to tell which is which. "You're out to get me, aren't you?"

"That's the most ridiculous—"

"No." He steps in front of her again and forces her backwards. Her eyes widen when her foot reaches the edge of the landing and he crowds her until she has to search for the next step. He puts his face only inches from hers and keeps his voice low.

“You told everyone in the world where to find me, and someone tried to shoot me last night. But they missed me and killed a woman. A nice young woman, probably about your age, Ms. Ortega. Her name was Kathy Sonstrom and she skated with a lot of other nice women who like and support each other. She had no quarrel with anyone, not with me, and certainly not with you. But she’s dead now, just as if you pulled the trigger yourself.”

“You—”

Hendrix takes another step and the woman reaches for his arm. He slaps it away and she almost tumbles down the stairs. At the last second, he grabs her sleeve and jerks her back.

“A nice woman with parents and a brother and a sister. A nice young girl with dreams and hopes and friends. And you sent some asshole with a gun off to kill her. I hope you can sleep well tonight, Ms. Ortega.”

He roars onto the highway before he hears his own words echoing in his head.

A young girl with dreams and hopes and friends.

Just like Corazon Losada.

#

Tori McDonald’s condo nestles in a complex facing woods less than two hundred yards above the Berlin Turnpike. The tall trees absorb the traffic noise from the road, and the landscaping reminds Hendrix of the older areas of New Britain where industrial money built beautiful houses a century before. He hefts the grocery bag of vegetables while a slight breeze rustles the leaves; it’s so pastoral that he can feel the anguish of the last two days fading.

Tori answers his knock dressed in a candy-striped blouse and jeans, but she’s wearing a little more eye-liner and highlighter than she does at the shelter. The smell of serious meat sauce follows her from the kitchen.

"Hi." He hands her the bag. "Pepper, tomatoes, a summer squash, and a zucchini. The lettuce is still pretty anemic."

"Outstanding," she says. "I've got lettuce anyway. Come on in."

He holds up the other bag. "Wine. Red. I hope we're still doing lasagna."

"We are."

Tori's living room has a soft green carpet that reflects on softer gray walls, the same serenity as the woods outside. He suspects it helps her wind down after days of talking with battered women—or nights like the last two.

Tori holds up the bottle. "Should I open this now?"

"Sure."

"You want to help with the salad?"

She lets him retrieve a large bowl from a shelf that he suspects she can't reach without the step stool next to the refrigerator.

"Oh," she coos. "My hero."

"It's just part of the premium package we offer," he says. "You could see the whole list on our Web site, but it's still under construction."

She shows him the cutting board and a knife, then tears up half a head of lettuce and puts it into the bowl. "I've got six kinds of salad dressing. Just like a real restaurant."

"Whoa, decisions."

She uncorks the wine with an expertise that suggests she worked her way through school waiting tables, puts a glass where he can reach it, and leans back against the counter with another one. He slices the tomato, disturbingly red on the cutting board.

"How are you doing, Tori? Really."

"I've had better days." She takes a long swallow of wine. "My divorce hearing comes to mind."

She sips again. "Cooking is how I unwind. I just turn off my brain and watch my hands do stuff, or I'd go crazy. The fire, Molly—Kathy—it could have been me, if you hadn't tackled me and Goldee."

She watches him slice the pepper, too.

"So much for a restraining order. I hope they lock the guy in a dungeon with a bunch of scorpions and let him go slowly rabid."

"Kevin wasn't the shooter." Hendrix wipes the knife on a paper towel and slices the summer squash into poker chips. "The problem with being an asshole is that people start blaming you for everything that goes wrong."

Tori leans against the refrigerator. There's a little gold chain peeking through her open blouse.

"But the Bristol cops found him in his apartment, drinking with two other guys who claimed they'd been with him at the time the shots were fired. I'm willing to take their word for it. For now anyway, mostly because of the car."

"I didn't even see the car."

"It wasn't Kevin's Hummer. It was a blue rust bucket, a good fifteen years old."

He slides the tomato, pepper, squash, and zucchini into the bowl and looks around.

"Right there," she says. "To your right."

He wipes the knife blade on a sponge before he slides it into the slot in the block with five others while she brings out bottles of salad dressing and lines them up on the counter. She bends to check the lasagna, but straightens up so quickly she catches him checking out her ass. He flicks his eyes back to her face, but she cocks an eyebrow. He clears his throat and continues.

"Last Saturday, my next door neighbor told me that three Spanish teenagers came by my house in the afternoon. They knew me by name, but wouldn't say what they wanted. She says they were driving an old blue car with rust spots on the back fenders. And one of them had a big towel wrapped around his hand like he was hiding something. Maybe a gun."

"Who...?"

"I don't know their names, but I think it was the same car, so it's probably the same kids. Last week, a crime reporter for the Courant said some unkind things about me in her column, and she mentioned where I live."

Tori frowns and he remembers that she works with confidentiality issues every day.

"She's Hispanic and she tried to stir up flames about the shooting last month. Her column Tuesday morning mentioned that I was doing security for you, so someone could have found where I was last night."

"So you think you were the target? Someone trying to get revenge for your shooting that girl last month. And the bastard killed Molly instead?"

He can feel her rage fill the kitchen, even hotter than the oven.

"It's a possibility."

"So what are you doing about it?"

"I told my Lieutenant in Major Crimes. He's got someone checking out the people in that bust to see if anyone has a friend. He'll get back to me if he finds anything."

They stick the salad in her refrigerator and adjourn to the living room, which includes a gray leather couch and recliner. The coffee table is a glass square with a lower shelf hiding under dozens of magazines. It's more of the soft pastel look that feels soothing as the seashore.

“Have you found another place for the women,” Hendrix asks. “Or are they going to be at Central for awhile?”

“Probably Central. But Danny Keogh called me this morning. He’s already started working around the clock shifts to get the new shelter ready sooner. He figures they’ll be able to pour the concrete for the basement early next week. And he says everything will go fast after that.”

“He sounds like he’s really in your corner.”

“Yeah, I think so.”

A timer pings in the kitchen and Tori stands. “Lasagna’s ready.”

She bustles into the kitchen and he hears the oven door open and close again. He follows to dress the salads and help her refill the wine glasses.

The cooking dish atop the stove bubbles red and cheesy. Tori turns to him with a spatula in one hand and a knife in the other. She looks domestic as hell and twice as beautiful.

“Pick your victim.”

They move to the dining room carrying pieces of lasagna large enough to apply for statehood. Her table is set with blue and white cloth napkins rolled into wooden napkin rings, and what he suspects is her wedding silver.

“Whoa,” he says. “Do you always go out for dinner like this?”

“Only when the guest of honor brings his own zucchini.”

He takes his first bite. Ricotta cheese, meat, and Tori’s sauce with secret spices, some of which he can identify from experience, almost melt on his tongue. He resists the urge to close his eyes and moan.

“I forgot,” he says after savoring the aftertaste as long as etiquette permits. “You said you grew up a good Italian girl.”

“It’s OK?” she says. “Don’t say so if you don’t like it.”

“It’s terrific.”

He means it. The sauce is a lot like Ms. Roccapini's, too. Well, how many things can you put into a meat sauce? Tori wipes the corner of her mouth and looks at him.

"Annie called me this morning. She's a mess after last night. I told her about ten times that it wasn't Kevin—I figured I had to say it even if I didn't believe it—and that Molly's getting shot wasn't her fault."

She scoops the last bit of ricotta cheese onto her fork. "I don't think she believes me, though."

"Even if the guy stays away, she's got a long road back, doesn't she?" Hendrix remembers Annie's terrified eyes. He still thinks Kevin Draper is making her life hell.

"Yeah." Tori glances at his plate.

"More?"

"Sure. It's great."

"My mother and grandmother always told me the way to a man's heart is through his stomach."

"That's a cliché." He watches her hips disappear into the kitchen. "I expected better from you."

"I didn't say I believe it." She returns with their plates. "Actually, experience has led me to find a different route. It starts a few inches lower."

"Does it involve a zucchini?"

Her eyes look different now, and he doesn't think it's just the wine. "Sort of."

They put the dishes in her dishwasher and step onto her balcony. The sun is low enough to turn the trees into a rich emerald tapestry with a golden halo. Hendrix waits for someone to cue the violins, but apparently the guy is asleep at the switch. They both lean over the railing and watch the sun sink lower.

"What happened with your girlfriend?"

"Excuse me?" Hendrix almost drops his glass down two stories. Tori watches the trees.

"You're smart, you cook, you're good-looking, and you're definitely straight. You even know how to dress. You should have been snapped up long ago. And you're not divorced or you would have mentioned it Saturday when I said that I was."

Even though she's still looking at the trees, her wine sloshes in her goblet.

"You're really sharp," he says. "I'll bet that's why you're a social worker, isn't it?"

"No, I'm a social worker because I have this insatiable need to fix things. But I'm also incredibly nosy. You can tell me it's none of my business."

""We were about to get engaged," he says. "Then..."

"The shooting."

"Yeah."

She sits in a white plastic chair and motions to the one next to it.

"What was she like?"

He shrugs and sits. "Tall. Blonde. Green eyes. She was—is, actually—an artist."

"My evil twin, huh?" Tori sips carefully and still doesn't look at him. "When you say 'artist,' you mean a painter?"

"Yeah. She does kind of...abstract portraits. I don't know what the term is. More interpretations than realistic. They're very emotional."

"Uh-huh."

Hendrix sees Jenny Della Vecchia's face the night after the shooting. The night she stopped by to tell him she couldn't love a man who could take a life and to give back his key. He reminded her that he was a cop, and the dialogue rapidly disintegrated from there.

"She's very good," Hendrix says. "She's got a show coming up in a couple of months."

"Oh," Tori says. "Are you planning to go to it?"

"No."

"Good." She puts down her glass and still looks out at the trees, but now she sounds pissed. "Now tell me you're not trying to get her back, either."

"It's over." Hearing himself say the words comes as a shock even though he's known it's true for weeks.

"She didn't help you much, did she? You have a difficult, dangerous job, and she's second-guessing what I presume was a split-second decision."

"It was."

"You've got challenges all the time. We all do. You more than most people."

"Sure." Nothing like you, he thinks. Not one single thing she and Jenny have in common.

"No." Tori shakes her head. "I'm serious. Look at your name. Tracy Hendrix. You're named after a movie star and a rock star. So much pressure to excel from the very beginning, to be a star yourself."

"That's probably why I don't play guitar," he says.

"Or act?"

"Uh-huh."

"I suppose it could be worse," she says. "Imagine being named Casanova or Don Juan."

He lets that one go by. They sip their wine again.

"How come you're not seeing anyone?" he asks.

"I'm divorced."

"You told me that was years ago. Hasn't there been anyone since then?"

"You want more wine?"

"Maybe later."

She folds her hands in her lap.

"I was dating a guy, but we weren't really going anywhere. We said 'see ya' last winter. I guess getting the team and the space and everything together..."

"Sure."

"It's hard for people like me to find dates," she says.

"I can imagine. You're smart, you're funny, you're beautiful, you cook..."

"You left out straight."

"Right. That one. I knew there was something else."

She picks up her wine glass and sees that it's empty.

"I hate first dates," she says. "Checking each other out, trying to figure what's the right answer, trying so damn hard to be perfect."

"I know."

"I always catch myself wondering 'does he really mean that, or does he think that's what I want to hear so I'll sleep with him?'"

"There's such a thing as being too smart," Hendrix says.

She puts down her glass. "Sometimes you just need to sit back and enjoy the ride, but we read so much into everything now. Like every little thing means something."

"Yeah," he says. "Like inviting a man over to your place for dinner."

"Yeah," she says. "Just like that."

"And reminding him to bring his zucchini."

Her face turns red and he sees a tear trickle down her cheek.

"Yes," she whispers.

"I hate first dates, too." He takes her hand. "It's even harder for the guy, especially if he's been..."

Her fingers tighten on his.

"The rules change so damn fast." If he looks at her, he's afraid he'll start to cry.

"They do, don't they?" She takes a deep breath. "That's why I wanted you here. Home field advantage."

"There's a home field advantage?"

"I just decided."

He pulls her against his chest and realizes that she's not wearing anything under her blouse.

"We've done an awful lot of analyzing for one night, haven't we?" She slides her arms around his waist and he smells her hair. She tilts her head back and he kisses her, tasting a little lasagna, a little more wine, and a lot of Tori McDonald.

"Now why don't I take you into my bedroom so you can fuck my brains out?"

He tilts her face back and kisses her again.

"We could be looking at an awfully long night."

"Oh." She burrows into his chest and he pulls her even closer. "A girl can only hope."

Chapter Fourteen

Jimmy Byrne looks lonely, but the present surroundings have the potential to solve that problem. Hendrix slides onto the stool next to him as Tina Boxx bends over to show Jimmy her talents. She undulates subtly and Hendrix wonders why anyone would want to be either a proctologist or a gynecologist.

This morning, he woke up on the wrong side of a strange bed and put everything together when Tori McDonald lifted her head from his chest.

"You OK?" he asked.

She snuggles against him. "I feel a little dumber than last night."

"Must have been that home field advantage."

"I guess." Her voice sounds soft and slow, like a sleepy kitten. "That does mean they finish first, right?"

"Close enough."

He closes his eyes and feels her warm breath against his chest. Her plans don't seem to involve moving off him any time soon.

"Don't you have to go to work?"

"The place burned down, remember? We're all taking turns at the dorm."

Her hands slide across his stomach and he feels himself respond.

"I went crazy shopping yesterday," she says. "I bought a spare toothbrush. Why don't we take turns in the bathroom, then you can come back to bed and do me again."

An hour later, they look at each other over coffee. She's offered to scramble eggs or make something more intricate, but he's content to sit and look at her in a tee shirt and cut-offs.

He's not going to tell her he'll call. Hell, he'll see her at practice in less than twelve hours.

She puts down her cup and looks at him for a long time.

"You're right," she says. "Sometimes I think too much."

"It's the price you pay for being smart," he tells her. "That's what I've heard, anyway. I don't have that problem, myself."

"I love a man who can use his mouth for more than talking about himself."

They'll definitely do this again. His turn to cook.

Byrne slides a five between Tina's plastic heels. "You're looking good."

"You too, Jimmy. A life in the gutter brings out the gleam in your eyes."

"Doesn't it, though? Sometimes I think about asking for a transfer to vice and narcotics, but why mix business and pleasure?"

"Mess up the cosmic order," Hendrix says.

Tina turns around and Hendrix wonders how many credit cards her chest maxed out. Her smile looks so mechanical that he waits for a click, but the song ends and she scoops up the bills from patrons of the arts and disappears before he hears it.

"You said you had something for me." Hendrix needs to get Byrne on task before the next girl gets in range; he should be in the Advocate's annual poll as Chick Magnet of the Year.

"Maybe." Byrne orders another ginger ale. If they were on the other side of the building, they could drink beer, but then the girls wouldn't be naked, so what's the point?

"I checked out all the assholes on that raid," he says. "Most of them have already been busted before, but the girl was different."

"Well, yeah." Don Henley's "How Bad Do You Want It?" blasts through the house speakers and a girl with red eyeliner and leather biker shorts above knee-high boots struts onto the platform. "She was only fourteen."

"Yeah, and she's been around the block. She'd been picked up as a runaway a couple of times, and a shoplifting thing about a year ago. Her mother's a real piece of work, too. Vice has her on their speed dial as both a hooker and a crackhead. Probably some crystal, too, which might explain how the girl got involved."

"Does this story have a point, Jimmy?" The fetish monster grinds toward them and Hendrix sees Tori McDonald in her jeans and candy-striped blouse from last night, ten times as sexy, even before they took turns undressing each other.

Byrne watches the woman thrust her hips a few times before he faces Hendrix again.

"Corazon Losada has a seventeen-year-old brother. He's squeaky-clean and he lives with his father. It looks like Dad has busted his ass to keep the kid in school, and he's been showing up, getting decent grades. But some of the gang-bangers keep coming around, trying to recruit him, especially the last month or so."

The girl takes off her leather sports bra. Ten-penny nails pierce both her nipples.

"What does the kid look like?" Hendrix watches Jimmy look at the woman, Frieda, across his ginger ale.

"He's about five-ten, thin, and doesn't wear Gangsta-gear. Prep is more his style, like khakis and a polo shirt. Everyone says he's very polite and respectful around old people. Like us."

It's not enough to talk to Ms. Roccapini again. "Does he drive an old beater? Rusted out dark blue?"

"He doesn't have a car. His father does, but it's a red Nissan, eight years old."

"You find any other possibilities?"

Byrne watches Frieda unzip her biker shorts, all the way down her left hip. "I'm still looking."

"OK. Thanks."

Byrne forces his eyes off the stripper. "Vic is pushing the union to light a fire under Shields. He wants you back yesterday, Trash. We all do. Really hot summer, people get mad, they treat each other mean."

"That's what's happening with the roller derby, too."

Byrne hasn't heard about the fire. When Hendrix tells him, his face turns serious.

"How much longer you working with these women?"

"Tonight." Hendrix finds a five and holds it up for the woman, who pushes her breasts together to grasp it. "And their bout is Saturday. If nothing happens by then, I'm probably going to bail. Besides, if this shooter is really after me instead of them, they're better off without me around."

Byrne drops a bill on the platform and lets his eyes roll over Hendrix again.

"You're not carrying. You should."

"I will tonight."

"You need back-up, call me."

"The New Britain cops know where the place is." Hendrix takes the first sip of his Coke, room temperature by now. "They've been over there the last three of the last four practices. They know half the girls by name."

"So weird," Byrne says. "I talked to you two weeks ago, I thought roller derby was a dinosaur joke."

“You and me both,” Hendrix says. “Who knew?”

On the way home, he grabs a burger from Wendy’s and eats it in the kitchen. He wonders if Tori McDonald is eating any of her leftover lasagna and how it tastes the second day. He brushes his teeth and goes to his bedroom closet, where he opens a small safe and withdraws his Sig Sauer semiautomatic. He checks the clip, then tucks it into a holster on his left hip and drapes a blue shirt over his tee. His other gun is his Smith & Wesson .45 from when he wore a uniform. It’s too big to wear concealed, but he wraps it in a towel and transfers it to his glove compartment.

The towel reminds him of those boys the other day and he’s tempted to call Byrne for back-up tonight after all. Then he decides he’s jumping at shadows.

He pulls out of the driveway, turns left onto Shuttle Meadow Avenue, and follows Corbin all the way across New Britain and down the hill to the light at Farmington Avenue. Across the street, he sees the ugly gray box that has become the home of the New Britain Whammer Jammers. A car pulls in while he’s waiting at the light, and he recognizes Lugg Nutz behind the wheel.

Under his shirt, his gun feels big as a fire hydrant.

#

Annie Rogers cruises through the light at the intersection and lets her eyes sweep the parking lot. That security guard, Hendrix, weaves through the cars and she K-turns so she’s facing out toward the street again. She’d like to be closer to the door, but if he’s here she feels a little safer.

“Good evening, Ms. Rogers. Or is it Annie?”

He wears a blue oxford-cloth shirt hanging open over a white tee and she can see that he’s got nice pecs. Something in the way he moves makes her realize that now he's wearing a gun under his shirt.

"Annabelle Lector, darn it."

Whoa, good job, Annie. Scare the kittens.

She hurries inside, where the fans are already on.

"Annie, Annie, Annie." In her skates, Tina G. Wasteland has six inches on her and they clutch each other like the ship is sinking beneath them. Molly Ringworm is dead. The only reason Annie forced herself to come tonight is because she knows everyone else hurts too, and maybe they can help each other get through it.

She leans back and stares up at Tina, who looks old enough to be her mother now, lines around her mouth, more lines around her eyes. Annie knows "sleepless" when she sees it.

She's spent the last two nights wrestling with nightmares that alternate between Kevin Draper fucking her up the ass and a cannon exploding every time she comes through a doorway. Her hands are so sweaty she can hardly grip her purse strap.

She dumps her stuff on the bleachers and digs for her helmet and pads. Her hands don't work right and she has trouble getting the knee pads over her feet, which seem to have grown overnight. She bites her lip and tells herself that's impossible. Kevin is miles away and the guard outside has a gun.

More girls come in and hug each other. They all look like they've been crying. Goldee Spawn looks like she's running on fumes and Tina spends extra time with her.

DMJ's boyfriend strides through the door with her and joins Lugg Nutz, who still has a bandage on his chin from when Kevin hit him last week. The announcer, Lee Da Vocal, appears, too. Maybe the other men have come to help the security guard. Annie feels secure enough to tie her laces. She digs into her bag and finds her mouthpiece and water, too. No water yet. She'll have to pee, and it's a royal pain getting the tights down in this frigging humidity.

"Annabelle, are you OK?" Roxy Heartless cruises over. She has her helmet in her hand and her blond hair tucked into a scrunchie. Her eyes gleam. Tonight, they'll all be ready to kick ass, anything to exorcise the pain and fear.

"I guess so. But what if—?"

"No. You're fine, you're good." Roxy takes her hand. "Well, that's bullshit, isn't it? We're all really fucked about Molly. But your dickwad ex-boyfriend wasn't the shooter. I just talked to the guard. He's a Hartford cop, and he says they're looking at someone."

Roxy's voice is like that trumpet for the grown-ups in the Peanuts TV specials. Wah-wah, wah-wah. Annie nods even though she can't process a single word.

"OK, everyone's here." Lugg Nutz raps his clipboard against the bleachers for attention. "Listen, I know we're all upset about Molly. This is going to be a short session, and Tina has a few things to say before we start."

Annie forces herself to listen to Tina G. Wasteland, who rolls slowly back and forth while the others sprawl on the bleachers, their skates clinking against the aluminum.

"I...God, this is hard. I feel like I watched my sister die the other night and everything is shit. But I've talked to Kathy's family and told them how bad we feel about...Well, anyway."

Annie remembers that in her real life, Tina G. Wasteland is a social worker. She's used to putting people's lives back together, but that's on the clock. This is her own life now, and it's the same shit. How bad does that suck?

"The funeral is going to be in Wethersfield tomorrow morning at ten. If you can get there, I'd really appreciate it. Kathy was our sister and she worked hard for this team. We owe her a decent farewell."

Annie reminds herself to get her black slacks out of the closet when she gets home. See if they need ironing.

"I've ordered flowers from the team. And I've got everyone's home address here. Some of us live close together, so maybe while we're here tonight we can figure out how to carpool."

Annie looks at the announcer and DMJ's boyfriend. Their faces are grim, but she suspects they'll both come to the funeral, too. She wonders if Danny Keogh could be a skater, too, like Lugg in the men's league. Annie bets he's ten times nicer than Kevin Draper ever was. Well, DMJ looks together enough so she wouldn't put up with a loser.

Not like me, she catches herself thinking. She forces herself to listen when Danny joins Tina.

"I just want to add to what Tina's said. We're all deeply sorry about this, but we're pretty sure the shooting wasn't related to the roller derby or the problems you've been having. Jerry and I will set up the speakers for Saturday night, then we're going outside to help watch the parking lot."

Annie feels a wave of relief surge over her. Danny Keogh glances toward DMJ before he continues.

"Um, we're making another contribution to roller derby in Molly's name, too."

Murmurs fill the bleachers. Then someone raises her hand.

"Mr. Keogh? DMJ says that you're working double shifts at the new shelter. Do the police know anything about that fire the other night?"

Tina sags for a second before she answers.

"I don't know what's going on with that." Her voice feels heavier. "The police think that was someone whose significant other was taking refuge from him, but they haven't told me whether they have a suspect."

"But I read in the paper that your building was badly damaged. Is that true?"

Danny Keogh steps in. "The building inspector feels the place is not fit for occupancy now. I've put people on twenty-four hour shifts to get the new site ready as fast as we can. And—I know this sounds sick, but it's the truth—we hope that publicity will bring out more people for the bout Saturday. Raise more money."

"What about the women who were staying there?" someone asks. "What about them?"

Annie tunes out the babble and plays with her mouthpiece. She watches Danny Keogh and Lee Da Vocal check cables and adjust speakers. Lee taps on a microphone and the thump echoes around the room. They give each other a thumbs up and disappear through the front door.

Annie looks toward her purse, sitting on the bench next to her gym bag. She doesn't want that purse out of her sight.

Practice is a disaster. Lugg's whistle shrills and he tries to work everyone into different combinations. They have to replace Molly Ringworm, who was one of their best blockers.

They're trying to work Tiny Malice in as a third jammer, too, but nobody's on the same page. They might not even be in the same library. Usually, Annie gets into the feel of her wheels on the floor, the whole room filling with an intoxicating mix of adrenaline and estrogen. Tonight, she feels like she's lost in quicksand and dragging herself around big aimless circles.

The other girls seem to feel the same way, a bunch of women in gym clothes and bulky padding. In their helmets and mouth guards, they look like Star Wars rejects. They skate like robots, too, and nobody seems to understand English.

At eight-fifteen, Lugg blows his whistle one last time and waves everyone to the bleachers again.

"That's enough," he says. "You've had a tough week."

He holds up Tina's clipboard. "Some of you have already paired up for rides tomorrow. Why don't the rest of you look this over before you leave. I can drive if someone in Wallingford or Meriden wants to come with me. Or Berlin."

Meriden. Annie sees Grace Anatomy nodding, too. They can go as a threesome. She and Grace talk to Lugg and figure out when he'll swing by for each of them. She packs her gear, hugs Tina and Roxy one more time, then walks toward the exit, the lowering sun lighting up pink streaks in the new glass.

New glass. She remembers that awful racket from two nights ago. Her fingers grip the handle in her purse and she forces herself to push through the double doors to the parking lot.

It's sticky outside again, but she steps onto the blacktop and forces her eyes to focus on her white Hyundai. When she reaches it, she'll lock her doors and start the engine. She'll drive back to Meriden and circle her own block three times in each direction. If she sees a black Hummer, she'll drive straight to the police station. If there's no black Hummer, she'll run to the door and up the stairs—fuck the elevator, he might be waiting there—to her apartment, lock the dead bolt, slide the love seat in front of the door, and try to sleep with the covers over her head.

A black Hummer appears near the Laundromat and cold terror uncoils in her stomach. The security guard trots over to head the car off and she sees something in his hand. She's not sure if it's a gun or a flashlight, but the Hummer stops a good fifty yards away and Hendrix steps up to the driver's window. Lee and Danny are coming from other corners of the lot to join him. She forces herself to start walking again.

From the corner of her eye, she sees movement off to her left. Kevin Draper charges at her, his shaved head big as a full moon. She tells herself to run to her car, but her feet feel stuck in tar like a bad dream. She drops her gym bag and sound slows down. Her car is right there, but Kevin is big as a tank, his mouth open as he says something that sounds like "Biiitttcchhhh," and he's reaching out for her with those huge hands and she feels her back bump against her car as she drops her purse and brings up her right hand. He sees what she's holding, but it's too late for him to stop.

The carving knife slides into his chest so easily she can hardly believe it. His eyes widen like he can't believe it either, but he drives her back against her car door and knocks the wind out of her before she can scream. She forces herself to push him back and hold onto the handle of the knife with all her strength. His hands clamp around her neck and she tries to suck more air into her lungs, but he's crushing her throat. Then he lets go and reaches for the knife. His hands cover hers and he tries to pull them off, pull the knife out, but it's stuck. He tries again, but she locks both hands on the handle, slippery with blood. Her teeth dig into her lip with the effort and she tastes her own blood, too. She brings her knee up to brace against him so she can pull the knife out and stab him again because he's so big and she's so scared and nobody's coming to help her.

"Annie, you bi..."

The rest dissolves in a frothy spew that coats her face and chest. The knife moves a fraction of an inch and she wrenches it free, another red geyser erupting all over her before Kevin's head sags down between her breasts. He slides down her torso and his hands clutch at her hips like he's trying to pull her shorts off. She pushes him and he collapses on the pavement, his hands trying to hold back the blood pumping out between his fingers.

His mouth moves again, but his words gurgle under the blood. His eyes look wide and furious, then the rage turns to something else and she recognizes it because she's seen it every time she looks in her mirror.

It's fear. And she knows that she's killed him, even before his hands flop away from his chest and that fear in his eyes turns to nothing at all.

The world around her becomes a montage of women screaming and men shouting. Someone tries to touch her and she whirls, the knife still in her hand.

"No, Annabelle, no. Put it down. Just drop it. Let it go."

Goldee Spawn and Lugg Nutz kneel over Kevin Draper and other footsteps pound toward them. Kevin's blood on her clothes makes Annie shiver and her vision funnels down to a fine point.

"Everyone get back." She thinks that's Hendrix. "Give them room to work." Danny and Lee come into her line of vision and Denver Mint Julep and Roxy Heartless grab her.

"Annabelle, it's us." Roxy puts her face in front of Annie's. "We're your friends. Just drop the knife."

"I've killed him," she screams. "He was going to kill me but I killed him first."

"Annabelle, shut the fuck up. Don't say another word." Roxy's hands clamp on her arms and shake her like a toy. DMJ looks tall as a steeple.

"It's all right, sugar. We're with you. We saw it." Her voice wraps around her and Annie feels herself slowing down. She feels the knife fall from her fingers.

"You crazy bitch. You killed him."

Through her tears, Annie sees a black beard above a red tee shirt. Who the hell is this?

"You crazy fucking cunt."

Lee Da Vocal grabs the guy by the throat and lifts him clear off the ground.

"You say another word, I'll tear your fucking head off and stuff it up your ass."

Annie sags into DMJ's arms and sobs her guts out.

By the time the ambulance shows up, Annie is on her hands and knees, vomiting against the front of the building. Hendrix has herded most of the others back inside except for Lugg and Goldee, who are still doing CPR on Kevin, and Danny and Lee, who are restraining the asshole who was screaming at her. Roxy Heartless hovers over Annie, and every time she opens her mouth to do something besides throw up, Roxy tells her to shut up again.

One of the cops approaches Hendrix, pausing to watch the ambulance beside Kevin Draper's body.

"Jesus, you guys getting a bulk rate or what?"

#

Hendrix has enough juice left to drive around his block twice and approach his house from the opposite end of the street before he pulls into his garage and drags himself to his back door. The gun he never drew while Annie Rogers stabbed her ex-boyfriend to death feels heavy as a cinder block.

Kevin Draper was DOA, Annie Rogers is being held for manslaughter, and Lynn the lawyer has called one of her colleagues to represent her. Danny Keogh, one of the seventeen witnesses, has already promised to pay the guy's fee.

Mitch Donahue, who drove Kevin's Hummer to distract everyone, has an attitude that makes his dead friend seem like Dr. Phil. Of course he'd help his bud. Kevin's a great guy and he still wants the stupid bitch back, damned if he knows why. When the officer questioning him points out that Kevin has a restraining order against him, the asshole rolls his eyes like some drama queen.

The cops release him with a clear warning to stay away from everything and everyone connected to the roller derby. The officer in charge gives him a fifteen-minute head start before letting Danny Keogh, Jerry Machowski, Denver Mint Julep, Goldee Spawn, and Lugg Nutz leave. Hendrix decides that means he's on their side.

Tori McDonald melts into one of the benches across the far wall and Hendrix wonders if he has the strength to carry her home when a man with a three piece suit and hair the color of a shiny new penny comes through the door brandishing a briefcase. Roxy Heartless greets him and they look at each other with the affection of two sharks divvying up a wounded dolphin. He looks at her gym shorts and bloody tee, and his face doesn't change at all.

She points toward Annie, rocking and chewing her knuckles in an interrogation room, and he nods. She vanishes through the door and Hendrix shakes Tori's shoulder.

"We can leave now." He's too young to feel this old.

She stirs and looks at the clock. After midnight again. "Are they holding Annie?"

"Her lawyer's here, a snake in a Brooks Brothers suit. But he won't be able to arrange bail until tomorrow morning."

"Christ." Tori sways on her feet. "Put her on a suicide watch. I'm afraid what will happen if they leave her alone."

He's thinking the same thing. He waves the lawyer over and repeats their concern.

Twenty minutes later, the cops drive them back to the rink and he holds Tori's door for her.

"Can I pick you up tomorrow, give you a ride to the funeral?"

Her eyes look like she can barely focus. "Thank you."

Her taillights disappear down Farmington Avenue. He wonders how many of the women will descend on a bar together after the funeral and tie on one colossal drunk. Maybe he'll join them.

He stumbles upstairs to take a shower, then collapses into bed. For the rest of the night, he feels himself trying to run across the endless parking lot before Annie Rogers can jam an eight-inch carving knife into her boyfriend's chest. He never makes it.

Chapter Fifteen

Georgia Leigh Pitcher feels Danny's hand squeezing her own while they walk from the parking lot of the First Congregational Church toward the wide stone steps. It's callused and rough, but she likes having a boyfriend who can screw more than a light bulb. Danny can plane her doors, cut her log, roll her dough, and ring her chimes. He cleans up real nice, but he looks more himself in a tee shirt and jeans. She looks better in black, though, and, right now, they're in mourning.

Several other women who also wear black mill on the sidewalk and Georgia tries to recognize people she's never seen in make-up before. She has a flawless memory for names—a job requirement—but she didn't know Molly Ringworm's real name was Kathy Sonstrom until Tina G. Wasteland told them at practice last night.

Tina is really Tori McDonald, in a black pants suit with a delicate gold chain winking at her open collar. She looks like she's keeping herself together with sheer grit and crossed fingers. Hendrix, the security guard, stands next to her and seems to be trying to recognize people, too. Georgia eases up to hug Tina and feels the smaller woman's fingers dig into her back.

"God." Tina's voice throbs and Georgia squeezes her tighter to pack the pieces back together. "It's too nice a day for something like this."

The shiny black hearse parked at the curb says otherwise. Danny shakes hands with the guard but neither of them says a single word. Georgia can work crowds the way other people stir their coffee but she feels like she's on the outside of a vault, looking in through an invisible grate.

Then Tina and Hendrix make eye contact and Georgia can feel the sparks. She knows that vibe from 'way back. Well, shoot, it's about time Tina found herself a good man, and Georgia's not willing to share hers.

A blonde woman a few inches shorter than Georgia drags over a tall man: Goldee Spawn, whose husband is also a doctor. His suit looks custom-tailored and even more expensive than Danny's. When he shakes hands, he forces his hand up into the webbing between her thumb and index finger so she can't squeeze.

"Are you a surgeon, Doctor?" She lets her drawl leak out, just a lil' bit.

Grace Anatomy looks completely different with her jet black hair in a French twist that she must have started assembling at dawn. A blonde woman wearing pin-stripes and barracuda eyes strides over and Georgia exchanges a hug with Lynn Kulak, AKA Roxy Heartless, the only other woman she can give a real name. Lynn the Lawyer looks like she wants to punch someone.

"Is Annabelle...?" Georgia asks delicately.

"Court convenes at ten. My partner is trying to arrange bail."

"So she won't be here?"

"She's a mess." Lynn bites the words off like she's snapping a bread stick. "Tina and I had them put a suicide watch on her last night. Restraining order, my ass."

"But she'll get bail."

"Oh, yeah. But they'll probably jack it up higher than the AIG bail-out." Lynn's eyes turn even colder. "Before my colleague got there last night, Annie told me that Kevin Draper forced his way into her apartment last week after Hendrix sent him away. He raped her."

Georgia forces down the hot ball of rage that boils up in her chest.

"Has she told them that?" Danny is talking with Lee Da Vocal, who cleans up well, too. "I'm not an attorney, but it sounds to me like that would suggest self-defense."

"Matthew is keeping it up his sleeve for now," Lynn says. "If it comes out, I want that asshole who drove the Hummer last night to go on trial as an accessory. If he hadn't distracted the men, Kevin Draper would still be alive and Annie wouldn't be in jail for a crime the system forced her to commit."

Two more women hug Tori McDonald. She seems to gather strength from their touch and Georgia knows that's what she loves most about roller derby. It's not the hitting or the speed. It's knowing that everyone has your back. She tells herself they'd come to her funeral, too, and the thought catches her off-balance. She still has too much to live for. Well, so did Kathy Sonstrom.

"Poor little girl," Lynn says, almost to herself. "She never asked to be a dick magnet."

"She's a sweetie," Georgia agrees. But they couldn't help her in time, and now she's in trouble she doesn't deserve. Life does not play fair. Not ever.

"Sweet doesn't begin to cover it." Lynn waves to two other women in black. "Jizz wouldn't melt in her mouth."

"I do declare, Lynn. Where did you learn to talk like that?"

"Hartford Superior Fucking Court."

Tiny Malice and Novocain Dancer work their way through the growing crowd at the foot of the stairs. Nobody wants to be the first one into the church to see the shattered family sitting in the front pew.

"I've talked to Sugar Plum." Georgia feels herself blush. "Danny. I've persuaded him to pay your colleague's fee."

"Not going to ask how you did that." Lynn's eyes warm up a few degrees. "I wish she'd cut the guy about two feet lower. Let him bleed out on the pavement with his dick in his hand, then give it to his asshole friend to hang on his rear-view mirror as a warning."

The Wharton School taught Georgia the way of the world, but Lynn's passion still makes her take a step back. Near the steps, Hendrix talks with one of the other girls, who shakes her head. Then he talks with Lee the announcer, who shrugs. They both look at the sky and check their watches like the guest of honor is late. Which, unfortunately, is not the case.

Inside the church, the grief and shock overpower the flowers and perfume. The minister recycles Platitudes for Dummies and Georgia is sure he never met Kathy Sonstrom in his entire life.

When he turns to her family and friends to speak, their memories are real and painfully uncensored. When Tori McDonald peers over the podium and tells how Kathy morphed into Molly Ringworm and supported everyone else and laughed with them and took out an opponent with a hip, Georgia feels the small woman's voice shaking in her own chest and feels Danny's arm squeezing her tightly against him.

What if it were me in that coffin? It shocks her, even though he's been trying to buy her a diamond for the last month. My Lord, she thinks, he really does love me. The tears she's held back all morning slowly rise to the surface and she fumbles in her purse.

Two men who resemble Kathy join four other pallbearers, and everyone rises as they wheel the casket down the aisle. Two hundred tissues rustle and people reach out to each other. The roller girls move to the front of the church and follow the casket, an honor guard in black, and Georgia Leigh Pitcher realizes that all the love in the world can't fix diddley.

The cars follow the hearse to the cemetery, where Georgia's heels sink into the soft turf around the grave. The women hold hands and Danny still holds her close, but she's never felt more alone. She joins everyone else tossing a handful of dirt onto the brass and mahogany casket. It feels like a pitiful way to say good-bye.

On the way back to their cars, Lee Da Vocal draws abreast of them. He's still several inches taller than Georgia when he leans close to his boss.

"They called me bright and early, and they tell me we're going to make it."

"Excellent," Danny tells him. "I'll be by later."

Georgia watches Tori McDonald burrowing into that blond guard's side and his lips brush her hair. She thinks they only met two weeks ago, then remembers that she went home with Danny the night she met him. Such things do happen. Sometimes, they even last.

Danny kisses her good-bye in the church parking lot and she aims her hood ornament at the Continental Bank. When she slides into the parking lot half an hour later, she sees men working on the site of the new shelter and hears the trucks going in and out and the compressor and the jackhammer roaring.

She has lots of work to finish before closing today.

Tonight, she'll go to dinner with Danny Keogh, and then they'll go back to his house. After what this horrible morning has taught her, she knows that she will hold him even more tightly than her deep dark secrets. She doesn't like to think of herself as a bad person, but in a few more days, she's going to break Danny Keogh's heart.

#

Hendrix expects Tori to fall asleep again on the short drive back to her place, but her eyes are wide with caffeine and her hands keep wrestling with each other.

"Who would do this?" she asks over and over. She alternates it with variations on "Poor Annie. I hope she makes bail."

Hendrix doesn't have answers to either comment yet, but he's got the afternoon and tomorrow morning to find out. He doesn't want any surprises at the bout, not with a possible six hundred people around who could get hurt instead of him. He's not that eager to get hurt himself, either.

He walks her to her condo and watches her fit the key into the lock on her first try.

"Promise me you're going to rest, OK? You can't do anybody any good by driving yourself nuts. Not Kathy, not Annie, and certainly not the rest of the team. They need you ready to rock and roll tomorrow night."

"I know. Thank you." She hugs him and he doesn't want to let go. That seems to be her strategy, too, and she follows it up with a kiss that she definitely didn't learn in high school. Must be that graduate social work. He spends the walk back to his car wondering if she'll stay at his place after the bout. It's closer.

Half an hour later, he walks into the squad room in his black suit. A few people look up and ignore him, as though the suit makes him invisible. Then Savickas recognizes him and comes over.

"What the hell are you dressed up for?"

"The woman who took that shot instead of me was buried this morning." Hendrix looks at the computer on what used to be his desk.

Vic straddles a chair. “You have a look on your face that says you need my password.”

“You’re really brilliant for your age, Vic, did anyone ever tell you that?”

“Only my ex-wives. I was smart enough to marry them both, then smart enough to divorce them both.”

“Can’t keep a good man down, can you?”

Vic looks at him closely. ”You look like you bought the winning Powerball, then left it in your pants when they went through the washer.”

He tells about Annie Rogers, too. Vic digs in his desk and finds a roll of mints.

“They’re paying you how much for this gig?”

Hendrix looks up Mitchell Donahue first. The guy has no record. Unfortunately, being an asshole isn’t a felony yet; maybe the legislature will get around to that before the session ends. The New Britain police are checking everyone connected with the women in the shelter for possible arsonists, so Hendrix pulls the list of real names Tori McDonald has given him for the Whammer Jammers and goes through them one at a time.

Three of the women besides Tori are divorced—including Lynn Kulak, AKA Roxy Heartless, but one of the ex-husbands has remarried and another now lives in Atlanta. Five of the other women are married, and Tori has mentioned that two of the husbands are referees. Her ex-husband lives in Rochester, New York.

Hendrix leans back and sees pixels dot the ceiling when he looks up at it. He blinks, then gets a cup of coffee and drops a dollar in the collection. He’s not a real cop right now, even though he’s doing real police work.

The thought is still rattling around in his head when Harmon Shields strolls through the arch and stops directly in front of him.

"What the fuck are you doing here?"

"Police work. You want to watch me, Harmon? Maybe learn something?"

"You are suspended, Hendrix. You have no business in this building."

"I've grieved the suspension, Harmon. You should have the paper work on your desk. Maybe your girlfriend can read it for you."

Shields opens his mouth, but Hendrix keeps going. "You're the one who gave her my address, aren't you? That's against department regulations, but how else would she find where I live? I use my cell phone on my business cards. My Internet, cell, and cable are on the same carrier so I don't even have a land line. But Carmen Ortega knew where I live. She knew about my security gig in New Britain, too. And the night after she published that information, someone tried to shoot me. They killed a young woman."

"What are you saying, Hendrix?" Shields tries to look threatening, but his pallor and squeaky voice undermine the effort.

"I'm saying that you're responsible for the death of a woman who had no quarrel with you. Or anyone else as far as I can tell. She just had the incredible bad luck to walk through a door behind me as someone opened fire with an automatic weapon."

"Trash..." Vic touches his shoulder and Hendrix realizes that everyone else in the room is listening. He hopes nobody has a camera phone. On the other hand, it might be cool if this showed up on YouTube. He's often pondered the wonders of going viral. He's told himself he'll get a new cell phone one of these days, just so he can take movies and send them out.

"I'm cool, Vic. And I'm almost done."

"That's the first intelligent thing you've said, Hendrix."

"Chief, can I say something here?" Vic stands with his hands at his sides. Shields talks over him.

"You have thirty seconds to get out of here, or I'll fill out the forms to have you permanently terminated from this department."

"Paper," Hendrix says. "You want to look at paper? Go re-read the IA report on Corazon Losada. I fired in self-defense. The IA officers declared it a clean shoot within 72 hours. You were wrong to suspend me then, and if my grievance goes through, you're going to be pounding a beat again, Harmon. It might be good for you, learn how to be a real cop."

"Trash..."

Hendrix slows down and Shields looks around the room. Nobody seems to be on his side.

"Deputy Chief," Vic says. "Why don't you let me handle this? I promise Detective Hendrix will be off the premises as soon as he finishes the special assignment I gave him."

Shields gapes. "You did what?"

"Yes, sir. Major Crimes is swamped, and I called Detective Hendrix while he was in the middle of conducting personal business—you can see that he's dressed in a suit—and he agreed to come in and help."

Vic takes a deep breath. "I know that's against your orders, but we felt that the case warranted special measures."

Shields is waffling, but has no way out. Hendrix looks between the two men.

"Why don't I wait in the hall while you discuss this? Vic, I figure another half-hour on line is all that's worth looking at. Someone else may be able to work free in the next few days."

He takes three steps toward the door and his footsteps are the only sound in the room.

“Why don’t we discuss this in my office, Lieutenant.” Savickas follows Shields, stopping just long enough to point at Hendrix, then the PC.

Hendrix mouths “I owe you.” Savickas mouths back “no shit.”

Hendrix waits until both men are out of sight before he resumes his seat.

“Shit,” one of the other cops says. “Hendrix, you must be sucking Vic’s dick.”

“Not for weeks,” Hendrix tells him.

He checks Lugg Nutz, AKA Roger Colosimo. Nothing. Who the hell else is there to be involved? He brings up Emilio Losada, and finds no record whatsoever, not even juvenile. Hendrix checks the DMV records to confirm what Byrne told him. Sure enough, the kid’s father’s only car is nothing like what the shooter escaped in.

He’s running out of names. For the hell of it, he checks Danny Keogh and finds dozens of hits on-line for charity and construction. He checks financials and finds the guy is worth an easy eight figures, even in the recession. His construction company currently has eleven different projects going on, and about a hundred workers. That’s just construction. He also owns a moving and storage company, a plumbing supply company, and three apartment complexes. In 2004, he got a parking ticket in downtown New Britain.

Hendrix wonders if someone else bid on the property where the new shelter is going up. He checks the New Britain records and navigates through the realty jargon. There was another bid for the space, but it was nearly ten percent lower. Hendrix wonders if the guy has an ad in the Whammer Jammers program.

Roller derby. Jerry Machowski, the foreman at the construction site, is the announcer. Hendrix checks him, too.

Jerod Artur Machowski won a Bronze Star in Desert Storm when he was only nineteen. He came back and attended classes at the University of Hartford, but never graduated, going back to construction full-time instead. He's worked with Keogh for nine years.

Hendrix is getting desperate, and Vic will probably return with Shields any second. Machowski is his last guess. He goes into the guy's financials. His credit cards—all five—are at or near their maximum. Hendrix looks at the amount.

In a typical work week with no overtime, Jerry Machowski is making over sixteen hundred dollars. That's nearly sixty grand if he only works seasonally. But his credit card balances total a hundred thousand dollars. How does a guy run up that kind of debt?

Hendrix sips his coffee. It's room temperature.

#

By the time Hendrix finds his car again, slides behind the wheel, and checks his cell, the last three days are catching up with him. The battery is dead, which is pretty much the way he feels, too.

Back in New Britain, he drives around his neighborhood looking for old blue sedans before he pulls into his garage. He wonders how long he'll have to keep doing that and hopes that Vic or Byrne can come up with something before the Whammer Jammers' bout, now only some thirty hours ahead. Across the hedge, Ms. Roccapini's tomatoes look even more obscenely red and luscious than his own. He doesn't have cukes, but hers look big enough to put on wheels.

He plugs in his phone and changes into jeans and a tee, then cracks a beer and sits at his kitchen table to mull over what he knows. Someone has damaged the women's shelter badly enough so it can't be used, but the women are still together, so whoever did it probably wasn't trying to isolate one woman as a target. No matter how he turns that piece of the puzzle, he can't make it fit with the problems that have beset the roller derby. Kevin Draper certainly didn't set the fire, and he's dead now, so maybe the skaters' problems are over. Except that they've lost two skaters in the last four days. And Kevin Draper didn't shoot Kathy Sonstrom, either.

From what Tori says, Danny Keogh's offer to match the gate the following night could potentially cost him thirty thousand dollars, maybe even more than that. Sure, it's only a grain of sand on his massive beach, but it's a tidy sum. Is someone after Danny? No enemies showed up in Hendrix's search, and it seems so far-fetched he didn't even look very hard. Danny's working class ethic still shows up on him like a three-day beard. He seems to admire the roller girls, and not just because he's sleeping with one of them.

Hendrix remembers the tall brunette hugging Tori and watching the funeral proceedings. Denver Mint Julep. She's a banker. Did she help Danny get a loan for the construction of the new site? No, that's stupid. The shelter has a grant to defray the cost, and Keogh Construction is picking up a lot of the slack, a leading contributor. Besides, the shelter was already on the architect's drawing board before Danny even got involved in roller derby. But he got involved through Jerry Machowski.

Hendrix gets another beer. Jerry's in hock up to his eyebrows, but how did he get there? What does that have to do with anything else, especially the roller derby?

Kevin Draper was a jerk, but his grudge appears to have been specifically against Annie Rogers, and not against the whole team. Hendrix wonders if the judge has granted Annie bail and what her emotional state is right now. He suspects that both Lynn Kulak and Tori McDonald are already checking on her.

Hendrix closes his eyes and visualizes the angles again. Molly—Kathy—came out the door behind him, and when he dove to shield the other women, she was directly in line with the car. She took a shot meant for him, but he has only a wild-ass guess to say that the shooter is trying to get even with him for Corazon Losada. Maybe he owes Carmen Ortega, the Courant writer, an apology. No, that would mean apologizing to Harmon Shields, too, and he'd rather drink battery acid.

He rinses his second beer bottle in the sink and puts it in the drainer.

Maybe Tori McDonald has slept through the afternoon and is up to a sandwich somewhere.

No, he tells himself. *You don't want to take her to dinner, you want to take her to bed again.* He remembers Wednesday night, the smell of her skin and the smoothness of her breasts, the taste of her mouth on his, and that little shuddering sigh when she came. Then the way she curled into him and locked her fingers into his until they both slept like bears in winter.

Yes, he wants to sleep with her again. Now he knows better how to make her happy, and he wants to make her very happy. That will make him happy, too.

Not to mention that she's smart and funny. And cute as hell. Unlike Jenny Della Vecchia, she doesn't even expect him to be perfect.

The sun is no longer beating on his garden, so he steps outside. The weeds already have his peppers under siege again and he spends the next half hour counter-attacking. How do weeds grow so quickly? He makes a small pile of dirt digging down to the impossibly resilient roots. When his hands hurt, he looks back down the row and can't even tell where he's been working. He drags his hose over and positions the end on that pile of dirt, then turns the water on at the slowest possible trickle and goes back into the house to shower.

He watches the brown line of dirt wash off him and form concentric circles as it spins down the drain. It sticks in his mind, but he's not sure why.

He towels off, puts on a fresh tee and jeans, and checks his phone. It's fully charged now and he checks his email. Nothing from Vic or Byrne. Nothing from anyone else, either.

The image of dirt spiraling down the drain still hovers before his eyes. He looks out at his garden, and decides all he wants for dinner is a large salad. The funeral is still too fresh in his mind. People crying and walking together in black and throwing dirt on the casket.

There it is, again. Dirt.

He wonders if Tori is still resting. She's a psych major; does she know anything about dream interpretation? But this isn't even a dream. He's wide awake, and he can't get dirt out of his mind. Gardens, graves, gossip? What else is dirt? Money is dirty. Playing dirty at sports. Penalties. The roller girls.

Tomorrow night will be his last night watching them unless something else happens. With Kevin Draper dead, he doesn't think it will. If someone is really after him, they won't try to ambush him in front of hundreds of witnesses. Even if they're that stupid, they'd never get their car through the traffic.

The car? No, that's rust, not dirt.

Tomorrow after the match, he'll ask Tori to come back here and spend the night with him. He'll make dinner for her Sunday, too. If the relationship isn't going to go anywhere, he wants to find out quickly. He thinks she feels the same way.

Dirt. Are there poems or songs about dirt? All he can think of is "Dirty Deeds Done Dirt Cheap." Book titles. The movie The Dirty Dozen, but that's forty years old. He saw it on DVD once.

Is it a song? A dream? He's not a big reader and he doesn't think it's a quote he should know. He goes to his backyard and moves the hose a few feet so the water drifts down into the second row.

Piles of dirt.

He gets his mail from the box and sorts it out. A sale at Macy's. A copy of the notice from the union that his grievance has been filed. A credit card bill, which reminds him of Jerry Machowski again. Hendrix sees the two sides of the guy, one as Lee Da Vocal, the announcer for the Whammer Jammers, the former singer with the microphones he tested the night before. The other is the construction foreman with rock-hard biceps and tanned face under a hard hat, directing traffic at the construction site, compressors running for the nail guns and the jackhammer, men checking blueprints and measuring two-by-sixes for framing, trucks of dirt rumbling down the street...

Truckloads of dirt.

Why are they still digging? Danny said they're ready to pour the foundation and they're erecting the building's frame. They should have finished the digging long ago. OK, there's the water pipes they had to move from the bank side of the foundation to get a clearer line, but...

The bank. Digging. Triple shifts. They've got guys working night and day since that fire.

Hendrix goes into his bedroom and sets his alarm for ten o'clock, then strips and gets into bed. He forces himself to close his eyes, but now the possibilities play out like a video on his eyelids.

Maybe he's finally found the right questions.

And maybe he can answer them tonight.

Chapter Sixteen

Danny's wearing a blue blazer over a white tee, jeans and sneakers. He still feels like he's been dropped down a garbage disposal and reassembled with a few pieces in the wrong places, and Georgia doesn't look like she feels any better. They're sitting under the blue and white tent at Max Fish in Glastonbury, trying to save what's left of the day that started off with a funeral, and their attempts at conversation fare slightly worse than playing Frisbee with manhole covers.

He talks for a few minutes, she nods like she's almost heard him, then she talks and he does the same.

She went straight to the bank from the funeral and everyone called her "Morticia" until they found out why she was wearing black. She checked the financials on-line six times during the day. She signed off on a mortgage.

"I looked out the window, sometime in the afternoon, Sugar Plum. I saw you and Lee the announcer over by the work site with your lil' heads bent over something, I guess it was a blueprint."

She went home from the bank and changed into her "Summer Tourist disguise," white linen blouse, khaki cargo shorts, and sandals.

He watches her foot bobbing up and down.

“When did you paint your toenails pink?”

“Oh.” She looks at her feet. “After I got home this afternoon. I needed to change something, and the couch is too heavy to move by myself. Or the hutch.”

“You could have called me.”

“I figured you’d be over later anyway. And by the time I’d decided on the color, I thought I was hungry.”

They both thought food would help, but they’ve played with their salads for so long that the server finally comes over and asks if she should bring out their entrée. Danny looks at his glass, the bourbon the color of sand now that the ice cubes have melted. Even the cherry looks pale. Georgia’s wine glass looks full, too; only the hint of lipstick on the rim tells him she’s even touched it.

They’ve sold almost three hundred tickets for the bout tomorrow night, twice as many as they usually sell in advance, and the ad was in yesterday’s Courant. After the last few nights, it’s really hard to give a shit.

“We even had a picture,” he says.

“Uh-huh.” She picks up her wine glass and puts it down. “Annabelle passing someone at the bout last month. I think that was my caboose in the background, too. Looked big enough.”

“Your caboose is just fine,” he tells her.

“Thank you.” She squeezes his hand and tries to smile. He can see her effort.

“Tina’s a right good jammer,” she says. “But she can’t do it all by herself. Tiny Malice is going have to carry lots of weight tomorrow night.”

Danny remembers that Annabelle Lector was supposed to have her bail hearing this morning while they were at Molly’s funeral. He meant to call and find out how that went. Georgia seems to read his mind.

"Roxy called Tina and she called me this afternoon," she says. "Annabelle's out, but both of them are worried about her. They're afraid she'll try to hurt herself, so I believe that Roxy's staying with her tonight."

"Christ." Danny's glad the girls are taking care of her. He wonders if Annabelle's going to skate tomorrow night. They need her, but she's probably going to be a basket case.

"Uh-huh." Georgia picks up her wine glass and puts it down for the third time.

All around them people are eating and drinking and planning the rest of a beautiful Friday evening, a dramatic break in the record heat wave, and all Danny can do is keep imagining Georgia Pitcher on the ground with a bullet in her, instead of Kathy whatever, and the thought turns his stomach to ice.

"Lugg thinks we're gonna get whupped real bad," Georgia says. He can tell she's upset because the drawl, which she usually takes care to stifle, keeps oozing out, and she's only had about one mouthful of wine.

"None of this is your fault," he says. "If you can pull together, you'll give them a good game. And the crowd loves you."

He looks at his drink again. "It has to be the worst luck I've ever seen in my life."

"Real ugly karma," she says. She watches the server arrive with her tilapia and his swordfish, lay them down with a flourish, and step back proudly.

"I imagine Lugg's right."

Danny tells himself this isn't what was supposed to happen, and he tries even harder to believe it. Jerry Machowski talked him into going to roller derby. He went to the after party and Denver Mint Julep followed him home. Now he can't get her out of his mind.

He didn't plan the girl dying Tuesday night. He didn't plan that asshole attacking Annabelle Lector last night, either, and he still sees the guy lying on the blacktop, blood flowing out of his chest, the girl screaming over him with that carving knife in her hands.

And God help him if Georgia finds out what he has planned. She'll pluck his eyes out on toothpicks and drop them into her salad. If she'd died the other night, he can see himself throwing himself into the grave on top of the casket and singing some frigging aria. He can't even sing in the shower.

For the first time, he understands just how deeply he has allowed himself to screw up. Jerry's in even deeper. After all, he set the fire. They were so stupid they didn't even understand how much they could lose. Or maybe they didn't have anything that mattered then. He didn't expect to fall in love.

He's lost before, but now for the first time, it terrifies him.

"We're really working at this tonight, aren't we, Sugar Plum." Georgia's voice flutters in the slight breeze.

"We are, aren't we?"

"We've never had to work at it before, now I feel like I'm doing a real bad play in front of a real tough crowd."

She runs her fingers down the stem of her glass. "I keep hearing Tina this morning, talking about how much we all loved Molly..."

Danny realizes that neither of them has even picked up a fork yet.

"Her family. Her parents aren't even old yet. Her brothers and sister, I don't think they're my age. And they're burying their baby." It comes out "bay-uh-beh."

He reaches across the table and finds her hand. "Let's get out of here."

When the server comes, alarm in her face, they assure her that everything is fine, but he declines a doggy bag before leaving a generous tip and escorting Georgia through the walkway in the perfectly manicured hedge and out into the parking lot.

They window shop around the circle: Talbot's, Pendleton, Ann Taylor—Georgia has an Ann Taylor Visa—Chico's—ditto—Smith and Hawken, a funky gardening store in the center of the shops, architecture like the Alamo with glass doors, rakes so expensive even the Pentagon can't afford them—which may be why it's closed now, and neither Danny nor Georgia can keep dandelions alive anyway—but don't step inside even one of them. Georgia wraps her fingers around his tighter than she ever has before, and she leans her head on his shoulder.

Over the trees to the west, the sun turns the puffy clouds an obscene pink. The night hasn't even started in Glastonbury, east of the river and south of Hartford. In Hartford, the dance clubs and bars haven't even shifted out of first gear yet.

They walk back to his car and Georgia buckles her seat belt. "I'm not much fun tonight, am I, Sugar Plum? I'm sorry."

"I'm not holding up my end, either," he says. She's the most wonderful woman he's ever known and he's this far from losing her. And he can't stop.

"What would you like to do now?" His voice feels less exciting than mud. He reaches for her and she takes his hand in both of his.

"I want to go back to your house," she says. "I want to go to bed with you. And I want you to promise you won't let go of me all night long."

When he realizes that she's trying not to cry, he knows that he's even closer to losing it than she is.

#

Hendrix wakes up thirty seconds before his alarm is set to go off and realizes that he's sleeping on the other side of the bed and he's been dreaming about Tori McDonald. He lies on his back and enjoys the last vestiges of her fading into the darkness and realizes that after spending one night with her, he has to struggle to call up Jenny Della Vecchia's face. He tells himself that if he were a better person, he'd feel guilty about that. But he's not a better person, and there's work to do.

He rolls to his feet and pulls on a long-sleeved black tee shirt and black jeans. He takes black socks and his black sneakers from the closet. His Sig Sauer with the thirteen round magazine sits on the nightstand and he clips the holster onto his belt above his left hip. He thinks about taking a back-up gun, too, but decides against it. A charming smile and people skills have their limits, but if he gets into a shoot-out, everything is fucked anyway.

In the kitchen, he finds a roll of gaffer's tape and covers his belt buckle and the reflective patches on his sneakers. He puts his shoes on and finds a navy watch cap in his closet. It'll be hot, but any stray light will find his blond hair. He tucks his mini Maglite into his pocket, turns off the kitchen light, and goes out the back door.

As usual, Paola Roccapini's back porch light is on. He's never sure whether she's discouraging prowlers or summoning gentlemen callers. A light in an upstairs window casts a faint orange glow and he wonders if she's reading. He's figured out that the woman needs even less sleep than he does. Well, after all, she's only eighteen and a half.

He cruises down the driveway with his lights off. He should have checked the street first, but if someone is waiting out there, they won't park the car in front of the house where he can see it anyway. He turns right and turns on his lights when he reaches the stop sign at the end of the block.

He takes the first left, then the next, and coasts down Kimball and onto Arch. The street is alive with people shopping, sitting outside drinking, calling out to friends and strangers alike in Spanish. This section of New Britain is mostly Puerto Rican. A mile down, where Main Street runs into Broad, the language turns Polish, but Hendrix won't get that far. He turns left on Hart and follows it uphill, then turns right near the hospital and cruises into Walnut Hill Park.

The Museum of American Art is downhill to his right, and he plans to park under the old trees near it. The museum is closed and the old houses around it are mostly business offices so nobody will notice a strange car in the area. He hopes.

Five minutes later, he kills the engine, makes sure his phone is set to silent, and takes the change out of his pockets. No rattles. Then he closes the door quietly and tucks his hair under the watch cap. West Main is two hundred yards to his right, Continental Bank a block down and to his left, and the site of the new Patience Randall Shelter directly behind that.

West Main crawls with traffic all night, every night, so he stays away to avoid being caught in someone's headlights. He only walks halfway down the block before he cuts into a back yard, keeping his fingers crossed that nobody has a dog that will wake up the whole neighborhood.

His luck holds. Ten minutes later, he emerges between two houses and sees the Tudor-style apartment building across the street. He zigzags from shrub to shrub and sees the bank's well-lit parking lot and ATM drive-through. He forgot all about those damned lights.

He moves closer and hears voices. Two men in jeans and hard hats sit on a pile of dirt next to a wheelbarrow. He can't get by them without being seen, but he sees the gleam of cigarettes and hopes they're just taking a break. There's no moon, but that damn' parking lot makes up for it.

Minutes later, the smokers grind the butts under their heels and move away, pushing the wheelbarrow into the back left corner of the frame for the new building. Hendrix follows as closely as he dares. They go around a wall of sheetrock and vanish.

He moves behind the same wall, putting his feet down carefully and with his eyes wide, straining to pick up every stray beam of light from the parking lot, passing headlights, and anything else that might be around. He'd love to turn on his Maglite, but he doesn't dare until he knows where he's going.

There's no one here. He listens to traffic sounds and an occasional owl flapping overhead. He waits for two minutes, then risks shining his mini Mag on the ground in slow sweeping movements. He takes a cautious step and does it again. He realizes that he's already sweating and his heart is hammering. The dark pushes down on him until every breath is an effort.

There, in the corner. A black tarp hangs over two beams. He moves it aside and sees a hole, about five feet across. Faint voices float from the distance, along with a muffled percussive sound he can't quite identify. He risks aiming his light down the hole and sees sheets of plywood covering most of a gradual grade, footprints on each side of it. Sure, they can't move a heavy wheelbarrow up soft dirt, so the plywood gives them a solid surface with more purchase.

The hole points toward the bank, no more than forty yards away.

Now he knows why a truck of dirt went by while he talked to Jerry Machowski. The digging should have been completed weeks ago if the team is putting up the frame and preparing to pour the cement for the basement, but Danny Keogh said he had men working around the clock to get the shelter built faster now that there was a pressing need for it. That's why someone set the fire: to give him an excuse to dig at night.

And now they're running out of time. They have to finish before that basement covers their tunnel.

Hendrix hears voices again, along with a rumble that he recognizes as a full wheelbarrow. He retreats and watches the men dump the dirt onto the pile, then return to the hole.

He follows them, staying close enough behind to let their noise cover his own. The tunnel is about five feet tall, and they've stuck planks in the roof to support it. It's narrow, almost as narrow as the stairwell he encountered on that drug raid weeks ago. But that one had light, and this one is dark as a coffin. He doesn't want to die here, not like Corazon Losada.

Thirty yards in, he touches another tarp. Beyond it, he sees work lights and realizes that he can't follow any farther without being seen. Or can he? It takes them a few minutes to load the wheelbarrow.

He pulls the corner of the tarp aside. If he stays low, he can get closer. The pounding is clearer now, and he recognizes the sound of pickaxes in the dirt. He wonders if they've done any blasting. During the day, they probably use a jackhammer to break up as much hard soil as they can, but that's risky at night. Besides, the men he saw didn't wear ear protection and the pneumatic racket would be deafening.

He hears the rustle of paper.

"We're there," a voice says. "A hundred-fifty-one feet is right here. Now we go straight up four feet. We'll do that and stop for the night."

"How much time will we have tomorrow?"

"They close at one. We can drill if we have to and set the charges then. The match starts at seven and the fun will start at seven-fifty. We can blow then and start unloading."

The scuffling sounds stop again. "OK, take it out."

Hendrix realizes they're bringing out another wheelbarrow and crawls back through the tarp. He reaches out a hand to find his way back and walks straight into a wall. He can't even see his hand. He gropes for his mini Mag, but it slips through his fingers. He drops to his knees, but the ground is rutted from the wheelbarrow and it must have fallen into one of the tracks. He can't find it.

He searches frantically. There's no way he can get out of the tunnel in the dark without being seen, and that's not a great choice. If these guys are carrying, he's got nowhere to go. If they aren't, he'll blow everything once they know he's found the tunnel. The ruts feel deep as graves and he gropes blindly, the tunnel closing in around him. His armpits feel sodden and his hands feel stiff and awkward. He can't hear the wheelbarrow yet, but the tarp deadens sound. They're probably only about fifty feet away. He envisions one of them with a gun and a bullet whistling by his ear. Or between them. He doesn't have a shotgun now.

He reaches back and lifts the lowest corner of the cloth, praying that in their lit portion of the tunnel, they won't be able to see.

There. Four feet ahead, his little gold Mag catches a stray beam and he fixes his eyes on the spot as he releases the fabric again and thrusts his hand forward. It finds a cylinder and he clutches it tight, turning the top until a spear of light shoots out. He follows it down the dark tube like he's being born again, reaching the plywood just as the wheelbarrow pushes the tarp aside. He dashes up the right side of the grade and feels cool air on his face.

He bursts into the world again and scrambles to his right, around the sheet rock, and toward the shrubbery. He lowers his head and dives into the shrubs, trying to control his breathing so they won't hear him panting clear back in Hartford.

The men empty their load and return to their tunnel. Hendrix waits until his heart and breathing are almost normal, then he stands up and trots down the street toward his car. He smells of earth and sweat and his clothes stick to him like clammy hands.

When he reaches his car, he opens the windows and drops his gun on the seat beside him. Nobody is in sight. He starts up and turns left to go around the park. Fifteen minutes later, he's back in his own neighborhood and he does his usual turn around the streets for strange cars before he glides down his driveway. He peers through the windows of his garage before he emerges into his back yard. His garden smells fresh and moist, not dank and rotten like that tunnel. He's tempted to put the hose on again overnight, but he'd forget about it in the morning, especially since now he knows he'll have other things on his mind.

Paola Roccapini's back porch light is still on, but her bedroom light is off. Hendrix goes in his back door, locks it behind him, and finds his way through the darkened house to the stairs. He takes another shower then returns to his bedroom and looks at the clock.

It's almost one-thirty, too late to call Tori McDonald. But not too late to call Jimmy Byrne.

Chapter Seventeen

Hendrix is sitting in the IHOP working on three slices of bacon and a stack of blueberry pancakes when Byrne strolls in. He seems disoriented because the servers are fully clothed instead of doing table dances, and his chin looks rough enough to file nails.

"Long night?" The IHOP is only a little over a mile from Tori's condo—she's on the way, too—and a strip joint lies a mile in the other direction, one where Byrne has at least two girlfriends. If he can drive all over the state to get laid, Hendrix doesn't worry about asking him to drive this far for breakfast.

"Yes, bless her heart." Byrne smiles at the server, then registers her age and orders Belgian waffles and black coffee. The girl probably only got her driver's license that month, but he automatically watches her walk away. Routine has its place. "She was very...appreciative. Grateful, even."

"Grateful?" Hendrix spreads marmalade on his toast. "I always figured that women who dance naked for a living get all the action they can handle. So to speak."

"Not even." Byrne looks around the place again as though he's never seen sunlight. The paleness of his skin makes Hendrix realize that it's a remote possibility and tries to remember if he's ever seen his partner's reflection. "Lots of guys wouldn't dream of asking a stripper out. They think a woman like that is...unapproachable, like the Homecoming Queen."

"The Homecoming Queen is supposed to symbolize a virgin." Hendrix watches the server plunk a steaming mug of coffee in front of Byrne.

"Yeah, I know, and she keeps her clothes on, too. But lots of strippers, they're thrilled if a guy like me asks them out. Especially if you don't mention money. I just suggest a drink or a salad somewhere and let her drive."

Hendrix ponders the ambiguity of letting the woman drive while Byrne adds cream and sips again. "I think a stripper is the Homecoming Queen's anima, like in Jung, you know. Sort of the evil twin."

"Since when do you know Jung?" Hendrix never ceases to be amazed by Jimmy Byrne, who looks like he outgrew his belief in Santa Claus only last Christmas but seems to live in strip joints. He's not sure Byrne really has an address, only a cell phone number.

"I was a psych major. But clinical stuff bored the shit out of me. Field studies are more my speed."

Tori McDonald appears in the doorway in a crisp white shirt and jeans, her purse nestling against her side. Annie Rogers carried a carving knife in her purse, but Tori's eyes light up with no hint of malice when she sees Hendrix. He reflects for the first time that introducing her to Byrne might be a bad move. Too late now, though. Every step she takes makes her look more beautiful in that Girl Next Door way that he's never appreciated before.

Byrne manages to convey the impression that he's had all his shots, and Tori sits next to Hendrix. She orders coffee and one scrambled egg with a glass of grapefruit juice.

"That's all?" he asks.

“I was very bad last night,” she says. Byrne’s ears seem to rotate toward her. “I had about half of that lasagna from the other night. I even micro-waved it. My mother would write me out of her will.”

“Some things you don’t tell your mother. Besides, don’t marathon runners eat pasta the night before a race?” Hendrix sees Byrne processing the information that he’s had dinner at her place. “You’re just getting ready for tonight.”

Byrne sips his coffee, but is clearly reading ‘way too much into the conversation.

“Tori’s the Captain of the roller derby team I’m watching,” Hendrix tells him.

The server appears with Byrne’s breakfast before he can say anything, and Hendrix feels grateful.

“Tori, I’ve thought of a few more things that might be important. Whose idea was the charity bout tonight?”

Tori studies the napkin dispenser while Byrne pours syrup over his waffles. “I was batting ideas around because I knew the shelter needed major renovations and we didn’t have the money.” Sitting next to him, she smells fresh as strawberry shortcake. “Then when DMJ hooked up with Danny, he got on board pretty quickly. She worked her feminine wiles on him.”

“As long as she’s using her powers for good...” Byrne doesn’t know any of the people involved, but he follows the boy-girl stuff perfectly.

“When did you get together on the idea, do you remember?”

“A couple of months ago. We already had a bout coming up in July, and by then Danny was really smitten with the team. And DMJ, of course.”

“’DMJ?’” Byrne asks.

“Denver Mint Julep,” Hendrix explains. “It’s her rink name because she works at a bank.”

"Of course." Byrne reaches for his coffee and Hendrix turns back to Tori. If she were any smaller, he'd warn her to hold her juice glass with both hands.

"So did he offer to match the gate right up front?"

"No... that sort of evolved. We talked about raising money for the shelter, but we're a non-profit, so we couldn't afford to share with anyone else. Danny suggested that if we made more money, we could split. Then he came up with the matching thing a week or two later."

The server appears with Tori's scrambled egg.

"He's been trying to get publicity, but most of the media think we're still dykes from the fifties like the WWF. We pay for an ad, but trying to get an actual story isn't working yet. None of the papers called me or Lugg."

Byrne mouths "Lugg?" Hendrix nods but doesn't want to interrupt the flow.

"But it's on your Web site, right?"

"Oh, yeah. And the price and stuff about the new shelter." She puts down her fork. "We're going to dedicate the match to Molly, too. For what that's worth."

Her eyes replay the shooting. He remembers that he thinks he's the target and realizes that the assholes may show up again at the bout tonight.

"That's a great gesture. Listen, you said people have already paid in advance, more tickets than you usually sell. How do you handle ticket sales at the door?"

"What do you mean?"

"How complicated is it? Do you just have a few people at tables selling tickets and handing out programs, or what?"

"Yeah, pretty much. A few of the girls have family who help out, husbands, boyfriends, someone like that. And we have two cash boxes with change."

"You mean this is all cash?" Byrne makes his first contribution to the discussion.

Tori shrugs. "We only have six or eight home bouts a year. It's not enough business to pay the fees for Visa or MasterCard."

Hendrix and Byrne look at each other. "So tonight, at twenty-five bucks a pop, you hope to have six or seven hundred people?"

Byrne reaches in his pocket for his cell phone and uses the calculator.

"You're talking over seventeen thousand dollars. I hope you have police there."

"We do. We're a public gathering for entertainment. And the New Britain police like to come. We sell dynamite goodies at the concession stand."

Hendrix gives Byrne a warning look before he can say anything.

"How early do you open?"

"The girls get there at five to warm up. We open the doors at six and a lot of the crowd is family and friends, so we mingle and chat with them before the bout. That starts at seven."

Byrne shakes his head. "I'm still working on that seven hundred people part. Do you really get that many?"

Tori flicks her napkin across the corner of her mouth. "We've worked up to about five hundred regulars. New Haven does seven hundred. Sometimes, even more"

"There's roller derby in New Haven, too?" Byrne looks astonished.

"Uh-huh. We just formed up here last winter because it was a long drive a few of us. One of our skaters is in Ellington and another is in Old Saybrook."

"So Danny Keogh just got involved a few months ago," Hendrix repeats. "And I think it was because of Lee Da Vocal, right?"

"Right." Tori's fingers tap on her glass. "Maybe February?"

More and more bad ideas occur to Hendrix about what could be on tap for the night.

"I've got a favor to ask you," he says. "I think there may be some trouble tonight."

She turns to him and the social worker eyes come into play. "What kind of trouble?"

"That's just it. I don't know. But there's stuff that seems to revolve around the bout. The fire at the shelter, the guys that shot Molly, some other stuff I've just found out..."

She opens her mouth, but he raises his hand.

"I don't have any details, just a bad feeling. Do you and Lugg usually get there early to unlock the doors?"

"Yes."

"OK." Hendrix looks at Byrne. "I'd like you to give me your key so we can go in there early and check things out. The lights, the AC, stuff like that."

He wants to tell her the rest of it, but it's better if she doesn't know.

"I'll give you the key back when you come in."

When she hesitates, he touches her cheek. It's soft and warm. "I'll explain whatever still needs explaining tomorrow. Right now, there's still too much I don't quite understand myself."

She still hesitates.

"We can talk about it over dinner. My turn?"

He feels Byrne watching. Tori's foot brushes his under the table.

"OK. You want me to bring wine this time?"

"Sure."

"What time?"

"Why don't you come at five, we'll eat at six."

"OK." She digs in her purse and peels a key off her ring. "It sticks a little, but if you jiggle it a couple of times, it works fine. Do you know where the lights are?"

"I've watched you open up for the last few practices."

She stands. "I just remembered something else. We were going to have the bout two weeks ago, but Danny asked if we could push it back so he'd have more time to get the word out. Fortunately, Raleigh had the week free. I don't know if that means anything or not, but I haven't seen stories in any of the papers."

Sure, Hendrix thinks. He needed more time to dig the tunnel.

Tori extends her hand to Jimmy Byrne. "Detective."

Byrne watches her leave before he turns to Hendrix.

"Something you forgot to tell me?"

"Now that she's gone, there's lots more."

He tells Byrne about the tunnel and the "distraction." Byrne clicks his tongue.

"Bet there are guys digging now," he says when Hendrix finishes. "Too bad we can't swing by and arrest them."

"Make life easier tonight," Hendrix says. "But if we take them now, we can only charge them with trespassing. Until they actually go into the vault and come out with something, we're screwed. And they didn't use any names last night. It's hard to believe Machowski and Keogh aren't involved, but I can't prove it. If they are, I want to make it stick."

"What do you need from me?" Byrne lets the server take their plates and refill their coffee.

"Come with me to the New Britain PD. I want them to put some guys on the bank and grab people when they come out tonight. I could do it myself, but you're not suspended so you might have more cred."

"OK." Byrne shrugs. "But they sure as shit know you after the last few nights."

He drains half his cup in one long swallow.

"Do you think the asshole who shot at you the other night will show up and try again?"

Hendrix reaches for the check. "I didn't mention in front of Tori, but yeah. It's possible."

"Well, someone trying to shoot a Hartford cop sure as hell comes under our jurisdiction, doesn't it? If I come to the match, I'm investigating, aren't I?"

Byrne digs into his own pocket for the tip.

Chapter Eighteen

Looking around the arena, Hendrix realizes that Danny Keogh wasn't kidding. The atmosphere feels like a cross between a high school basketball game and the Guilford Craft Show. Over four hundred fans have already come in, most of them bringing their own folding chairs and setting up just outside the lines defining the track's tight turns. Hendrix and Byrne both wear baggie white shirts with vertical red stripes so they can pick each other out in the mob, but everyone else is dressed in jeans or shorts, too, topped by a tee or a polo shirt, so they've just become two more eggs in the carton.

Byrne checks out the table full of tee shirts, some of which have alarmingly explicit designs of well-endowed demons or clever double entendre with graphics in case you don't get the joke. Women and a few men with multiple piercings hawk homemade jewelry, art work, ice cream, and beer. Hendrix is surprised they sell beer until he reflects that the ambiance here resembles NASCAR, too. The whole room thrums with camaraderie.

Lee Da Vocal tests his speakers at the far end of the space. In dark slacks and a gray sport coat with a red shirt and black tie, he could be the lead singer for a lounge act. The baked goods include some of the biggest muffins Hendrix has ever seen, even factoring in Byrne's girlfriends. His glucose level spikes just walking by the table, but Byrne picks up a cupcake that belongs on a bowling alley and hands a bill to the girl with the pink pageboy cut and a nose ring.

The scorers have set up the scoreboard, a laptop with what looks like it might be PowerPoint, and a folding screen in the corner, angled so everyone can see it. The spectators greet each other like old friends—maybe they are—and Hendrix sees women and a few men with tee shirts that advertise CT Roller Girls. Apparently the Yankee Brutals and the Stepford Sabotage from New Haven have come up to support their sisters. Three weeks ago, Hendrix didn't know that this world existed, and now he's ready to apply for citizenship.

Music comes up on the speakers and Hendrix sees a pudgy DJ in a red shirt open over a white tee with the Whammer Jammers logo: Block "W" followed by a hammer. The first song is Pat Benatar's "Hit Me With Your Best Shot," and a mix of heavy metal and classic rockabilly follows. A few of the crowd dance along the edge of the rink and hold hands like back in high school.

Danny Keogh watches the women from both teams skating laps and talks with Lee Da Vocal. Then he walks over to the bench on the far side and talks with the tall brunette that Hendrix knows now is Denver Mint Julep. On skates, she's at least six-three.

Hendrix and Byrne let themselves into the space with Tori's key and spent nearly an hour checking everything out. The back doors are locked from the inside, and they found nothing that looked like an extra wire, a smoke bomb, a flare, or any kind of electronic gimmick in Machowski's speakers—their first guess—under a table, or connected to the metal bleachers.

The vending machines in the lobby seem fine, too, and nobody was in any of the bathrooms. He and Byrne have stashed their

Smith & Wesson forty-fives above the dropped acoustical tiles in the men's room. The guns are too big to conceal under their shirts, but great to have if things get ugly.

They looked at the fire alarms and extinguishers and the panic bars on the two glass doors on the front of the building, too. The door on the left is closer to the entrance to the rink, and two tables sit ready, four folding chairs behind them.

Hendrix is no electrician, but the circuit breakers and lights seem fine. He and Byrne turned the AC on low and let it run while they inspected the place, and no fumes gave them headaches, sinus problems, watery eyes, or dizzy spells.

He replays last night's conversation, but all he knows is that something will happen at seven-fifty, which should be during half-time. Maybe a herd of dinosaurs will race through the building, but where would you hide them? And who's doing it? He still assumes that Machowski and Keogh have set this up.

"Tina! Gold-eee! Kick ass!"

Hendrix sees four guys who seem to have escaped from March Madness. They wear maroon and gold rugby shirts—the New Britain Whammer Jammers took the same colors as the local high school—and bright red wigs that remind him of Ronald McDonald. They've painted their faces ochre and would be perfectly at home at a UConn basketball game if they changed the colors to blue and white.

The crowd gets bigger and louder, the anticipation like Springsteen at the XL Center. Hendrix feels himself start to sweat. It's becoming more difficult to weave through the chairs and people juggling food and beer. Dozens of people—probably those who know how uncomfortable the bleachers are—have set up their own folding chairs along the edge of the rink. Lee keeps reminding them that children under eighteen aren't allowed to sit on the edge of the rink for safety reasons.

A trio of teen-aged girls examines the tee shirts, paying special attention to a wolf bending over to display a human tush that Hendrix thinks he's seen at The Cavalier Lounge.

"Freakin' cool." The girl with the cobalt blue ear piercings seems to be their leader. "But my mom would kill me."

"You could wear it under something," one of her friends says. They're still discussing it when Hendrix moves on. A woman with her hair in green pigtails shows purses to a man and woman who look old enough to have grandchildren. The stones set in the leather remind Hendrix of costumes for the Grand Ol' Opry.

The first wave of cupcakes and muffins has vanished and even more impressive ones have taken their place. One of the plastic barrels near the beer counter is already filling up; people have read the sign that says "Please recycle. We need the money for our road trips."

Two girls approach him with bright eyes and hopeful smiles. "Would you like to enter the wheel roll?" When he admits that he doesn't know what that means, they release an explanation that sounds like a tape loop on fast-forward.

"See, we put a target on the center of the rink at half-time, and everyone rolls their wheel"—they hold up a roller skate wheel, about the size of a normal donut—"from the edge of the track. The one who comes closest wins a prize."

"What's the prize?" Hendrix looks around and realizes that dozens of kids have the wheels. For the first time, he realizes how many children are here; it's like a day at the circus, too. Every family event he can think of rolled into one.

"Um, we have two tonight." The blond girl looks like a cheerleader during the school year and her sentences all end with that upward lilt that sounds like a question. "One is a fifty-dollar gift certificate to Vito's over on Main Street."

She glances at her partner, who explains that the other one is a free massage at a local chiropractor. Hendrix wonders if physical therapist Grace Anatomy arranged that one.

"Only five dollars?"

He digs in his wallet and hands her a bill. She writes his name on a clipboard next to the number that's painted on the wheel. Hendrix tucks the wheel into his shirt pocket and feels like one of the family.

Byrne finds him. "Have you seen those Hispanic guys?"

"No. Where?"

"I don't know where they are now, I lost them in the crush. But they came in together a few minutes ago. Two of them looked like Gangsta cartoons, do-rag, home-boy shorts. The third one was wearing a white shirt and khakis."

Hendrix feels a burst of adrenaline. "Not that we're racial profiling, of course."

"Shit, no." Byrne watches a woman in black with white tights bend over to adjust her knee pad. The name on her jersey is Donna Naytrix. "But they're the only Latinos I've seen."

Hendrix walks by the tables where women are selling tickets and handing out programs and pushes his way outside. The parking lot overflows into the Laundromat next door and he walks up and down the aisles looking for an old blue sedan with rust spots. No luck.

He returns to the building and recognizes Goldee Spawn talking with a mother and daughter. She waves at him, but her face is tense. The Whammer Jammers can't avoid thinking about Molly Ringworm.

Hendrix finds the New Britain cop talking with the EMTs, who are also required at every bout. "My partner spotted three Latinos here a few minutes ago. I can't find a car that looks familiar outside, but they may mean trouble."

The guy looks young and sharp. All the stuff on his belt makes him look chubby, but his face is thin. "I've worked three of these bouts before, I don't think I've ever seen a Hispanic here."

"You do all the matches, then?"

"Not all, but whatever I can. When we heard that they sold beer, we figured some assholes would get drunk, but I haven't had a single problem yet. These girls are fuckin' great."

Hendrix watches people reading the programs and decides they must be the newcomers like him. The regulars seem to know the girls and the rules and gladly explain them to everyone in earshot.

"This other team looks good," a fat man in a Mets jersey tells his bearded companion. "You see them warming up? Our girls, they skate laps and wave their arms and bend their knees a little. This other team, did you see? They were weaving in and out in formation. And they'd jump up and land together. They're a lot more specific, like they already know what they want to do."

"They look big, too." His partner watches the women in black and white sail by.

"Yeah," says Mets. "And faster than goosed greyhounds."

Iron Maiden fades from the speakers and Lee Da Vocal greets the crowd, his voice a cross between Frankie Valli and Michael Buffer. He reminds everyone they have five minutes left to buy a wheel for the wheel roll and please use the recycling bins for their empty bottles and cans.

He thanks all the patrons who have contributed to the program, forty-eight pages long, forty of them ads for restaurants, realtors, boutiques, you name it. Hendrix's high school yearbook didn't have as many ads, and they sure as hell couldn't have sold the hot pants with the logo "Roller Derby saved my soul." The ad calls them the official booty shorts of the Connecticut Roller Girls.

Hendrix wonders whose ass is filling out the picture. If it's the same model from the tee shirt, Byrne might know her.

"Ladies and gems, let me please remind you that this bout is to support the new Patience Randall Women's Shelter, so every dollar you spend on a wheel roll or at our refreshment or gift stands will help finance this building for women in the Greater Hartford area. And don't forget to get in the drawing for this beautiful guitar, too."

One of the girls holds up a red acoustic guitar, and Hendrix sees a banner displaying the logo of a local music store on the wall behind the DJ.

A waxy face catches Hendrix's eye and he turns in time to recognize Harmon Shields in a navy polo and jeans. He's escorting Carmen Ortega, who wears a red tee shirt and cut-offs that show miles of spectacularly tanned legs. They don't see him, but he wonders if Carmen is here to check out the derby after their little dialogue the day before.

The crowd is ready to rumble. Hendrix still hasn't seen the Hispanic boys. The jewelry table is behind him and Lee Da Vocal at about three o'clock, which puts the two exits at ten and one. An outside exit is directly beyond the door on his right, but the one on his left takes another left beyond the vending machines and down a short hall to the ticket tables. Bathrooms are between the vending machines and the ticket sellers.

Danny Keogh was right. There must be eight hundred people in here; Hendrix can't even raise both arms without bumping someone.

Lee Da Vocal introduces the seven referees, who have names as outrageous as the skaters. After they get their share of good-natured booing, Lee introduces the Raleigh Riot, who skate laps around the track, raising a fist as he calls each woman's name. The crowd applauds politely. Lee waits for the visitors to coast to their bench near the score screen and nods at the DJ, who cranks up the sound until the speakers squeal like a dentist's drill.

"Whammer Jammer, lemme hear you, Dickie!"

It's the old J. Geils song, and the locals take the rink in a roar that makes Hendrix think Lady Gaga and Kobe Bryant must have entered the building. The women circle the rink like their guests, but when Lee calls each one's name, cheering fills the space for an entire lap. These fanatics do indeed love their roller girls. Hendrix is surprised to hear Annabelle Lector's name, but sure enough, the tiny brunette in the red fishnets raises a fist. The Raleigh Riot skaters stand by the corner of the rink and the teams slap five as the Whammer Jammers roll back to their bench.

Lee lets the women come to a complete stop before he steps in with the timing of a singer used to gauging audiences.

"Ladies and gentlemen, before we start, we need you to listen for just a minute. Tuesday night, we lost one of our skaters in a tragic incident, and we need you to help us pay our respects. The Whammer Jammers are dedicating this match to their blocker and fallen sister. Would you please give us a moment of silence for Molly Ringworm."

The crowd goes silent as if someone has flicked a switch. The New Britain team stands by their bench holding hands, and it's so quiet Hendrix can hear someone sniffling. He remembers Annie Rogers screaming that she was the target, but he knows she's wrong. He looks for the Latino trio again. He wants to see them before they see him, and prays to God they won't pull guns in this crowd.

"Thank you, friends."

The starting five for both teams roll onto the rink and take their positions.

"How many of you have never been to a roller derby bout before?" Lee asks. "Let me see your hands. Come on, no reason to be ashamed. We all have our first time."

Hundreds of hands wave. Lee tells the virgins—that's what he calls them—to check their programs for the basic rules, and the two teams skate around the track in a slow motion demonstration.

"A jam can last up to two minutes." The crowd absorbs lots of the echo and Hendrix keeps scanning the faces. "The pivots—in the striped helmets—set the pace, and the jammers—wearing the stars—have to pass everyone else and take the lead. That's how they score points."

Tina G. Wasteland moves ahead and the crowd cheers. She waves and a referee raises a fist and points at her with his other hand.

"The referee has just told the scorers that we have a lead jammer," Lee explains. "Now, for every opponent that Tina can pass again, her team will get one point. In case you can't figure it out, the other team doesn't want her to do that, so they'll try to stop her."

The teams mime hip and shoulder blocks and Tina eases through the pack, the referee signaling each point.

"OK," Lee says a minute later. "There's more, but you'll catch on. Oh, in case I didn't mention it before, roller derby is a full-contact sport."

The screen flashes the time, 30:00, and the skaters retake their positions, a pivot from each team, then three blockers behind them, and the jammers—Tina for New Britain—several strides behind them. The referee blows his whistle, and the pivots and blockers begin to move. Three seconds later, another whistle sounds and the jammers accelerate to catch up.

Hendrix knows he should be watching the crowd, but he has to see if Tina can actually get by all those women who look big enough to put her in a shopping bag.

#

Georgia—Denver Mint Julep—knows Sugar Plum is standing about half-way between the score screen and Lee Da Vocal, but she can't look for him now and doesn't want to see him anyway. She needed three matches to break him of hanging out near the Whammer Jammer's bench where she saw him the second she came gliding off the track. She needs to stay focused on what Lugg is telling her and how to get past that girl with a butt even bigger than her own and an elbow that she must sharpen last thing before she comes out of the locker room.

Lugg said they might get whupped tonight, and the first few minutes suggest that it could happen. Lee Da Vocal's voice bounces around the room like a Superball in heat and the crowd cheers, all of it blending with the metallic roar of the skates. The ladies trade pleasantries with each other, too, but nobody has aimed the "C" word at DMJ. Yet.

Tiny Malice comes on and Tina gets a break. She's probably already got bruises all over her teeny little body. Annabelle's there, but DMJ's worried about her. She looks like she hasn't slept in three days and if her pupils were any bigger, she could use them for dinner plates.

"Annie," Goldee says. "That was two weeks' worth of Valium. How many did you take?"

She doesn't hear Annie's answer. Tina flops next to her on the bench and Lugg tells Novocain to speed up next time if Raleigh's jammer breaks on top. Tina's having an awful time keeping on her skates, never mind taking the lead. The Raleigh blockers are going after her as soon as the ref whistles. DMJ and Grace are getting pulled out of position to protect her, and then they get whomped when the Riot blockers clear the way. DMJ hasn't seen so many fast women in one place since she graduated and moved out of the sorority house.

"Molly," Lugg shouts. "We owe this one to Molly."

Molly was their best blocker, and DMJ sees Annabelle bite her lip. Her hands keep clenching and unclenching.

"You got to put Annabelle in for a few minutes, Lugg." Tina sucks down water and wipes her forehead. "We need a breather."

"I'm trying to let her get it together, first." DMJ knows Annie's here because sitting home would make her even crazier. Tina and Goldee offered to join her last night so she wouldn't be alone after spending the night in jail. The poor little girl's probably half out of her mind.

Lugg watches the next jam, the Raleigh team like Jersey barriers on wheels. They seem to be everywhere, but now Tiny Malice breaks out and Grace Anatomy clears a path for her. The crowd noise gets even louder and DMJ hears herself screaming, too.

Sugar Plum is out there somewhere, and she knows he's got to be happy tonight. She'll make him even happier later.

"First squad," Lugg shouts. "Get out there."

Grace, Goldee, DMJ, Novocain, and Tina surge back onto the track. DMJ smells hairspray wafting off her opponent. Any thicker, she'd be a fire hazard.

The whistle shrills. DMJ lowers her hips and tries to push back against Barbie Troll, but the woman has better position on the inside. She feels the tension in her thighs and tries to push off, seeing a black shape no bigger than a wasp whisk by before she can do anything about it.

"Shit," she says to herself. She feels an elbow digging into her ribs and pushes back.

Whistle. Referee pointing at her. Damnation. She slides to the outside and follows the pack around to the penalty box. Got to be more discreet about hitting back.

She coasts outside the lines for most of a lap. If you go to the penalty box, always skate in the same direction around the track so you don't cause a collision. By the far turn, she passes a stack of PBR cans that the fans are erecting. A beer can pyramid. They call them beeramids, and this one is already nearly waist high. They first heard the term in Montreal last spring. The track is a little wider by the turn, but if you get crowded, there's nowhere to go but through the cans. The racket goes on forever.

On the Whammer Jammer bench, she sees Annabelle watching the action, but her head bobs like one of those dogs in the back of a car with a spring in its neck. She looks seriously stoned, and DMJ remembers Goldee's screaming about the Valium.

Shoot, if they'd killed Danny, she'd load up on pills, too. But who'd hold her and care for her then?

"Annabelle?" Lugg sticks his face almost in Annie's. "You with us?"

"Oh, yeah." Annie nods and her head keeps moving.

DMJ looks at the scoreboard and is amazed that they're only behind 15 to 9. And that only eight minutes has gone by. It already feels like halftime.

The Raleigh jammer puts her hands on her hips to call off the jam. She's just scored four more points. The next squad goes in and DMJ feels useless, her butt on the hard metal penalty bench.

Lugg Nutz is saying something about if Tina breaks on top, slow down so she can lap easier. He tells the blockers to move their guy to the outside, use the centrifugal force of the track to help them so Tina can slide up the inside. It sounds dirty and DMJ remembers Danny Keogh holding her tight last night. She thinks she called his name while the waves of pleasure washed over her.

She finds her water bottle and watches the clock run down on her penalty. She's good to go, gonna kick some Raleigh ass, you bet.

She's never seen so many people at a match and wonders how many will come to the after party. Danny's already said they'll go to Vito's and he'll buy the first round. She'll want a beer and a couple of slices when this is over; she always burns off enough calories so she could afford one of those humongous cupcakes. If she could lift it.

Lugg Nutz waves Annabelle Lector onto the track and she finds the line next to the jammer from Raleigh, Bertha Denation, who looks twice her size.

Goldee Spawn soars by with the striped cap in place, moving a little more slowly, and DMJ realizes that means Annie must have the lead. Better living through modern chemistry. Sure enough, she comes around the turn three lengths in front of Bertha and her huge brown eyes seem to be looking for the orange line that marks the edge of the track. Another black-suited skater drops back, but Annie cuts inside and the ref raises a finger.

"Yes, yes, yes!" The girls on the bench are up on their skates and Annie swoops around the bend. They all watch as Roxy Heartless and Goldee Spawn lean against Raleigh skaters, forearms moving just a little, pushing toward the outside. Goldee seems to be getting position and DMJ wonders if those high-priced bearings make a difference. Or maybe it's Goldee's clit ring, you never know. Wheels roll like thunder, the crowd noise cascading over them. Lee's voice is lost in the mix.

One of the skaters goes down, rolling into a ball, her arms and legs scrunched up tight so nobody runs over them. They practice falling small every night. Tuck and hide. The only serious injury DMJ remembers is a year ago when someone couldn't tuck in time and another skater ran over her hand and broke her fingers.

That's why we've got the EMTs here, Sugar.

Annabelle comes around the far turn with an even bigger lead and the referee waves a whole hand. Five more points. She puts her hands on her hips to shut down the jam and DMJ looks at the screen. They're only down 27 to 24 now.

"Good for you, girl."

She gives the little girl a pat on the backside, then she's back on the track.

She puts a hip into her opponent. The woman's arms windmill and one foot comes up and she almost falls. She's 'way off the track, though. Now if Tina can just get around...

But Novocain Dancer is trying to speed up the pack and DMJ realizes that means the Raleigh jammer has broken on top. Grace drops back and DMJ sees her tracking the bitch when she comes into the straight-away. She jitterbugs past the Raleigh blocker and drops back a step.

It looks like slow motion. The jammer moves into the straight-away and Grace is right there, her black braid like a flag as she slides to the inside and forces the jammer toward the line. Farther, farther, and here comes the corner, and there's nothing left but that big pile of cans like an iceberg. DMJ and the others whip into the turn, but the cans clatter for hours, even drowning out Judas Priest blasting through the speakers.

Lugg waves them to the bench and they grab their water bottles.

Ten minutes left and they're only down by twelve.

#

Emilio can't find that cop, but he's sure he's here somewhere. There are so many fucking people, and they're all screaming like maniacs about the chicks on the skates, seriously getting into it. He feels the excitement, but he's got too much on his mind. Tito and Manny are around somewhere, but they've told him he's going to take the cop out himself. He thought that happened the other night, then he saw the paper the next day and knew he killed that girl. Shit.

Corazon. He didn't care for her much and only saw her like once a month anyway because Papi decided his ex-wife was a loser and Corazon wanted to stay there. You sleep with the dogs, Papi says, and you wake up scratching. So his stupid little sister gets killed trying to waste a cop. She's doing drugs, selling, probably selling herself, too. She's his sister, but she's a skank.

And then Tito and Manny say if he's gonna be a man he's got to flame the cop that killed her. He's trying to get through school, get out of that whole plan, but they're gonna make his life one big toilet if he doesn't throw down with them. They're assholes, but they're gang assholes, lots of guys stroll with them, so what choice does he have? Corazon, dead and buried a month, is probably laughing her ass off at him from the grave.

It should have been over Tuesday. They promised him if he took out the cop, that's it, he's a man, nobody gets in his face. He tried. He thought he did it. Then they see on the Web that he missed and killed that girl. The good part is nobody saw Tito's wheels, the paper doesn't say anything about a car, so they're still good. But Tito and Manny say they got to try again, and it's no good at his house because now that old lady got a good look at him and they don't want her telling the cops what they look like. Shit, she saw the car, too.

And now he's here with a nine weighing down his pants, the barrel rubbing his bone every time he takes a step, walking through these screaming people watching some chicks skate around a fucking circle and how's he ever going to find the cop now? He's probably not even dressed the same and the picture in the *Courant* is for shit, little tiny thumbnail of the guy in his cop hat. Like he's wearing a fucking uniform tonight. If he's even here.

Of course he's here. He's the fucking security guard, isn't he? And there's a New Britain cop out there, too, Tito didn't think about that, did he? No. Like Emilio should be surprised.

They had a moment of silence, Molly something. The guy calls it a tragic incident. Emilio almost shit his pants. He didn't even know her and he killed her. For the first time, he wonders how Hendrix the cop feels. He didn't know Corazon, but he killed her, too.

Emilio wonders if he can find Hendrix, get him off in a corner, just ask him, "Did you mean to kill my sister?" What would the guy say? Would it be the truth? Would Emilio even be able to tell? Maybe only if the guy says yeah, he meant to light Corazon up like a torch.

Corazon. Stupid bitch. Probably sucked off every guy in the neighborhood. Fourteen-year-old whore. Fourteen-year-old druggie. Fourteen-year-old dead. And he's supposed to kill someone else to make it even?

How does he get into this shit?

A pretty girl brushes by in cutoffs almost up to her ass. Hot, very hot. She's the only other Puerto Rican Emilio's seen here. She looks around like it's her first time at the circus and he knows how she feels.

The New Britain team is behind 44 to 35, but they're catching up. He looks at that big brunette girl, almost Corazon's size, maybe. It's hard to tell, on skates they all look like giants.

Emilio moves through the crowd again. It's only a few minutes left in the half. Maybe Hendrix will get a snack, a beer or one of those muffins. Maybe he should hang near the food.

A girl his own age moves by, holding hands with a little girl no more than seven or eight. The little one has a tee shirt, Red with yellow sleeves, draped over her shoulder. Her sister bought her one of the roller derby tee shirts. What's it like to have a sister you want to give presents? Emilio never wanted to give Corazon anything but distance.

Two guys go by, screaming for the Whammer Jammers. They wear clown wigs, big bright red, and they got their faces painted yellow. Fucking weird. The whole room is so loud Emilio can't even think. Music, that fucking announcer, the whistles, the skates, everybody cheering like New Year's Eve. He just wants to get into Tito's junk car and haul ass back to Hartford. But Tito has the key, not him.

Emilio looks around for Tito and Manny. Where the fuck are they?

And where the fuck is Hendrix?

#

Hendrix feels like he's watching a huge family wedding, all the uncles and cousins and siblings who haven't seen each other since the last time one of the clan was getting hitched and all the kids are a little taller now but everyone knows and loves everyone else, including the Raleigh Riot, and the crowd roars at every elbow and hip check. Skaters swoop by and referees whistle, women fall to the floor and bounce up again with fire in their eyes. Hendrix keeps moving and watching the crowd, but it's the most fun he's had with his clothes on in longer than he can remember.

"Aww riiight, Grace!" The guy must weight four hundred pounds, wearing a Yankees' cap and a tee shirt big enough to project the PowerPoint scoreboard on his back. Hendrix smells his sweat when he slides by him. Where the hell is Byrne?

He's figured out that the action never stops. If someone calls off a jam or the two minutes expire on one side of the rink, the next squad is already lining up in front of the benches and they start as soon as the previous players roll off the track. The program says a lap is about 130 feet, which means these skaters cover a quarter of a mile during a two minute jam. Maybe more. On skates, the bigger women like Novocain Dancer and DMJ both tower over Hendrix, but with six inches of wheel added, even Tori and Annabelle look big. He catches himself watching Tori's ass when she rounds the turn near the pile of beer cans.

Raleigh leads, 46 to 34.

Hendrix forces his way to the edge of the track with the hardcore fans. A skinny man in jeans and a safari shirt has a press pass dangling around his neck and tries to focus a camera as the women power toward him. They're gone and he looks at the back of the camera to check his shot. Hendrix guesses it's either terrific or a blur.

He sees Annabelle Lector sitting on the bench, her fists clenching and releasing as she watches her teammates. He realizes again that the system has failed her. She probably should have been in Tori's shelter. No, that means she might have burned the other night.

Hendrix looks at Lee Da Vocal, who controls the crowd as carefully as a NASCAR driver drives on a wet track.

He can't find those Puerto Rican kids. He didn't see their car out in the lot, so maybe they aren't here after all. And maybe they aren't the ones who shot at him—if it was really Latinos who have a MAC 9. If someone opens fire in this crowd, no telling how many people will be hurt. He knows how easy it is to conceal a weapon: he and Byrne are walking proof.

The muffins and cupcakes on the tables smell more seductive than Tori McDonald's hair, and people jam up in front of them even during the bout. Hendrix is finally getting used to the terminology of calling the games bouts instead of matches. It conveys more aggression, but it's a misnomer. There's plenty of action, but none of the WWF sideshow he saw on TV.

He moves beyond the recycling barrels and into the lobby, where two of the red and yellow clowns feed coins into vending machines. The ticket sellers sit at the tables counting the cash, but nobody gives them a second look. Everyone is watching the action inside.

Byrne materializes by the jewelry table again.

"I saw one of those PRs a while ago." He has to put his lips against Hendrix's ear to be audible. "The straight arrow. I don't know where the homeboys went."

"He was alone though?"

"This last time, yeah." Byrne wets his lips. "He's dressed invisible. You won't even notice him until you trip over him."

Three minutes left in the half, Raleigh leading 54 to 46. The crowd is going crazy.

"Have you seen the cop?" Hendrix thought he'd be in the lobby or near one of the doors.

"Not for a while." Byrne watches one of the guys in red wig and yellow face cheer when DMJ sends a Raleigh player out of bounds. The ref whistles at her and she rolls her eyes before cruising around toward the penalty box.

"I gotta tell you, Trash. You told me about this, I thought you were bullshitting me."

Ted Nugent's "Free For All" explodes through the speakers. "I was over on the other side awhile ago, near the bench. These women can actually carry on a conversation."

A doctor, a lawyer...Hendrix wonders if the Whammer Jammers have a merchant and a chief. DMJ's a banker, does that count?

One minute left in the half, and he hears Lee Da Vocal reminding people that they'll have the wheel roll and the drawings at half-time.

Hendrix drifts out to the lobby again. Tomorrow, he and Tori McDonald will talk over veal picatta. And she'll spend the night at his place. He forces his mind back to the skating.

Where is that cop? Or those other Puerto Rican kids? The two red and yellow fans he saw at the vending machines emerge from the men's room and look toward him, then wander toward the entrance. Maybe they're going out for a cigarette. Dozens of people will probably join them in a few minutes. Hendrix remembers seeing barrels with sand in them by each entrance.

The cop isn't in the hall yet. Again. Still. Hendrix feels tension like when he rushed up that stairwell with Sturges and Byrne.

After the chaos back in the arena, the men's room is like a morgue. Feet show under the stall, the legs wearing blue trousers. OK, here's the cop, attending to a call of nature. Mystery solved.

Hendrix is two steps toward the door when it dawns on him that the cop's pants cover his legs. He's still wearing them.

He taps on the door. "Officer? Everything all right?"

No answer. He tries again, then does a pull-up to look over the stall door. It's a terrible breach of restroom etiquette, but his cop alarm is screaming louder than the crowd and how hard is an apology if he's wrong?

The cop is slumped on the toilet seat. His chin rests on his chest and his hands dangle between his thighs. His trousers are still belted around his waist.

Hendrix reaches up to dislodge the tile and pulls out his other gun, the forty-five. He speed dials Byrne.

"Jimmy, I just found the cop. He's unconscious in the men's room and I don't think he did it all by himself."

"Fucking swell." Cheers obscure Byrne's voice and Hendrix realizes that the half has ended. "How you want to handle it?"

"I'm going out the side door to check the parking lot. I'll come back in the main entrance and meet you by the vending machines. Keep your eyes open. If Machowski is running something, it may be now."

"Got it."

Hendrix slips out of the door and sees people walking toward him, many already pulling out cigarette packs. He's tempted to call the New Britain police again for back-up, but that might be premature. He tucks his gun under his shirt and pushes through the outer door.

The sun pours down the hill and directly into his eyes. Cars jam the lot and traffic hisses by on Farmington Avenue, but nobody's out here except the smokers. He sees a few cars up by the Pizza place, but none of them looks like his junker.

His watch says seven-fifty, and he remembers the conversation he heard in the tunnel.

It's show time.

#

Danny feels even more overdressed than usual, everyone around him ready for a backyard barbecue or painting the garage—his preferred mode—and him in a navy blazer and white shirt over charcoal slacks and a tie with black and blue art deco prisms on it. Georgia told him it will look funky and professional but not phony like one of those scary types campaigning on TV now. Danny's roots are still working class; if he sees a guy with white hair in a three-piece suit, he wants to go after the bastard with a claw hammer.

The crowd is humongous and happy and wired like eight-year-olds on Kool-Aid and chocolate, and the Whammer Jammers are busting their ass. He's amazed they're only down nine at the half, especially without Molly Ringworm, one of their best blockers, and Annabelle Lector, who looks like she's tranked into another galaxy. Danny was amazed she came tonight until he watched Georgia and the other girls envelope her in a group hug that's probably the only good thing that's happened to her in the last week.

That's why New Britain needs a newer, bigger, better shelter for women. Danny's no saint, but guys like those motherfuckers the other night make his teeth grind.

Jerry introduced him to the crowd and they got some good pictures that may or may not show up in the newspapers tomorrow. If nothing else, they'll stick them on the Web site and try to get more donations. Danny said a few words, Georgia suggesting that a couple of sentences would be better than some canned speech, especially since she knows he's a social animal, but only in small groups. Jerry's the voice of the Whammer Jammers, so let him carry the weight. As usual, she's right. Jerry's working the crowd like a stripper on her last song of the night.

He's juggling something else along with the crowd, too, and Danny can tell he's watching the clock. Something's coming up, but he doesn't want to know the details.

The women disappear into the dressing room and the game clock switches to 20:00, the half-time break. Danny wonders what kind of strategy Lugg can pull out of his ass in twenty minutes. The Raleigh team is faster than the Whammers, and has lots more experience. Tiny Malice has talent as a jammer, but not enough seasoning, and the blockers don't know her timing yet. Georgia—DMJ—has opened a path for her three times, but she's been too early twice and got sent to the penalty box for holding.

Jerry calls for the wheel roll. Over a hundred people, most of them kids, kneel along the orange line at the outer edge of the track and two of the referees lay the five-foot plastic square with a bulls-eye at the center. Two of the girls who were selling the raffle tickets for the guitar join Jerry and one of the women who handed out the programs draws a number. She announces it, but Danny can't translate through the echo.

Jerry explains the rules for the wheel roll and Danny heads for the beer table. In ten minutes, the girls will return and he needs to wet his mouth to cheer more. He doesn't care if people think he's crazy cheering for a bunch of chicks on wheels. He loves this, and the people around him clearly do too. He's guessing a good eight hundred people, which means he's writing a pretty hefty check. They'll have to get a picture of him handing that over to Tori McDonald when she's cleaned up, too. He'll wear the dark suit and Tori will do business casual. Maybe they can get Georgia in the picture, too, in hot business-babe chic.

The guy pops the cap on a PBR and Danny lets that first cold sip fill his mouth and trickle down his throat. Five minutes before they start again. Maybe he should hit the john while he's got the chance. Behind him, he hears Jerry count off for the wheel roll.

"One...two...three."

The rattle of the wooden wheels fills the air and Danny steps into the lobby. The men's room is down and to his left.

Ahead of him are the guys he's noticed before, three of them with red wigs and yellow faces, the real hardcore fans, jammed up by the vending machines and looking toward the exit to the parking lot. One of them is holding a white plastic trash bag and two of them have guns. One guy with a gun has a woman by the hair, terrified in a tight tee shirt and tighter cut-off jeans. He's telling someone to drop it or he'll kill the bitch.

Danny follows the guy's gaze to his left and sees Hendrix, the security guy. He's holding a gun, too.

The robber shoves his gun under the chin of the girl, who is sobbing in helpless terror. She looks like a Latina.

Danny feels someone come through the door behind him, stop, and then try to push him out of the way.

"Yo, motherfucker. Let her go."

#

Tito and Manny are around somewhere, but Emilio can't find them. You'd think Tito's do-rag would stick out in this Anglo crowd like a fucking lighthouse.

Emilio wonders if they've gone back to the car and left him here on his own. Then it occurs to him that if they did, they may already be back in Hartford and left him here with his dick in his hand. No, they wouldn't do that. They were Corazon's friends, they wouldn't do her like that.

That's when it flashes to him that they were doing her. And now they've got her brother out here with a gun he's never handled before and ready to kill some cop he might or might not recognize if the guy comes up and kisses him on the mouth. There are a lot of blond guys around. Emilio thinks they may be Polacks.

He wants to buy a Coke, but he's trying not to talk to anyone any more than he can help it. They're the only Hispanics here, so people might remember them. He wanted to get close to the track and watch the skaters because he thought Hendrix might do that, too, but then he saw the skinny asshole with a camera and all he needs is to have someone take his picture when he's here to kill a cop.

More fucking white boy music comes up on those speakers, loud enough to make his balls drop. "Come On Feel The Noyze." Some fag metal band.

Maybe Hendrix isn't even here. Maybe he's out in the parking lot.

The women sail around the turn and two of them drop to their knees and slide to the bench. Their faces are flushed and shiny with sweat. They look so full of life that even if they aren't beautiful—like you can tell with those fucking helmets and mouth guards like boxers—Emilio thinks they look hot. He's never been with a woman, but some of these skaters make him want to start.

Tito and Manny told him once he gets his bones, he'll get someone to bone, too, no problem. Women love a warrior. That's how Tito says it. Like he read it in some book. Like he can read. Emilio's not sure Tito can name the colors in the rainbow.

Two minutes left in the half. When it ends, Emilio thinks he'll check the parking lot. Maybe the guy's out there again, watching the cars instead of the game. That must suck, missing all this cool shit. Maybe the women buy him a beer after it's over. Maybe only if they win. Maybe Emilio should buy one to take out to him. But he doesn't look a day over seventeen and they'd remember him.

Where the fuck is everybody?

Emilio's gun feels heavy, weighing down his pants so he feels like they'd see the crack of his ass if his shirt didn't cover it. He wishes he could pull it out and get used to the feel of it, but he can't.

The half ends and the women skate out to wherever the locker rooms are. How long is the half time here? Do they have bands like football games? No, that guy with the microphone is telling everyone to get their wheels ready for the wheel roll, whatever that is. Dozens of little kids and their Papi or Mami come up to the orange lines and kneel like they're gonna pray.

The echoes bounce all over the room, it's crazy. And now some guy in a nice jacket thanks everyone for coming and donating to something, Emilio doesn't quite hear it. Now all of a sudden he's got to pee. He'll go to the men's room, then go outside.

Lots of other people are heading for the door, too, and some of them have cigarettes in their hands. Shit, if they're all out there smoking, they'll see him when he shoots the cop. Well, he'll just have to run like hell. Tito parked the car a block down the street so they wouldn't see it here, he can probably get there fast and they can pull out of the lot before anyone can catch him.

But what if Tito and Manny have split already? Then he's really fucked.

He's about to go back in when he remembers he's got to pee, his bladder like a fucking reservoir, like he's gonna burst.

The guy who thanked everybody for coming strolls into the lobby a few steps ahead of him. He's got a beer in his hand and stops to take a sip. Emilio hears the announcer behind him, counting to three like it's really hard to do, like you should admire him. Maybe he can give Tito lessons.

Emilio sees those Halloween assholes in the lobby, the ones in the Ronald McDonald shit. Three of them, he thinks there were four, but now he only sees three. And they're holding a girl. She's even hotter than the babes on skates. One of the assholes has a gun stuck under her chin and he can see in her eyes that she's scared he's going to kill her. Emilio realizes that the girl is that Latina he saw earlier, the only other Puerto Rican he's seen here.

And when he sees this girl, all young and pretty and scared, it's like her face is even younger, like she's in her teens again. Like she's his sister.

"Yo, motherfucker," he shouts. "Let her go."

He pushes past the guy with the beer and pulls the gun out of his pants.

"Drop that fucking gun."

He figures he can scare this asshole, make him let the girl go. Maybe she'll want to thank him, but he can't stop for that, she might remember his face and he's still got to find Hendrix.

"Yo," he says again. "I said drop it." Like in some movie.

Ronald McDonald moves the gun from under the girl's chin so fast Emilio can't even get his own gun up to fire. He sees the flash, then the pain in his chest is like a fucking house has sucker-punched him. He tries to bring his gun up to shoot back, but his hands don't move and now all he sees are the lights in the ceiling. He hears another shot, and now he can't even see the lights, just this really bright beam, like he's looking down a tunnel.

At the other end of the tunnel, he sees someone.

It's his sister, Corazon.

She's laughing her ass off.

#

There's nobody in the parking lot yet. Hendrix swings through the first row of cars and approaches the main entrance again with his gun hand under his shirt so he doesn't freak anyone out. Before he steps through the glass, he sees those guys in the wigs and painted faces coming toward him and one of them has a big white trash bag. When they see him, they stop dead.

Oh, shit. He sees metal in someone's hand and whips out his own gun. The clown posse retreats and he speed dials 911 before he opens the door.

"What is the nature of your emergency?"

"We've got an armed robbery in progress at 700 Farmington Avenue, and an officer is down. Another officer needs assistance as fast as you can get troops here."

He passes the ticket sellers, who still huddle under the table. He speed dials Byrne, praying that the guys haven't gone back into the arena where they've got eight hundred potential hostages.

No, they're ahead by the vending machines, Byrne at the far side with his gun up, too. Hendrix sees Danny Keogh frozen three steps inside the door to the arena and hears Lee Da Vocal over the speakers. The wheel roll has started and everyone's attention is on that. He's sorry he's missing it, but right now he's where he was a month ago, at the point of a gun. Being familiar with it doesn't make him like it any better. And the guy in front has a woman in a red tee plastered against him, his gun forcing her chin toward the ceiling.

"Drop it or the bitch is dead."

Danny Keogh takes a step, then stops when the other guy levels a gun at his chest. Hendrix tries to be the voice of reason, but feels like he's asking a volcano to play nice.

"Let her go, guy. You're not making things better for anyone."

"Put down your gun and let us walk out of here or I'll kill the girl on the spot. You guys are cops, you don't want a hostage to die. Bad public relations, you know?"

Byrne is trying to move where he has a clear shot at the guy holding her, but the other guy raises his gun.

"Stay put, Jack."

The first guy turns toward Hendrix and moves the girl in front of him. Hendrix recognizes Carmen Ortega, her eyes huge and terrified. She looks like she expects to die any second.

"Put down your gun," the guy holding her says.

"No." Hendrix wonders how long he can keep this up. As long as it's an intimate little gathering, maybe they can discuss this like adults, but if someone comes out of the arena, he's fucked big-time.

"Last warning, asshole." The guy pulls the reporter up by her hair and Hendrix hears her sobbing hopelessly. Out of the corner of his eye, he sees Keogh shift like he's thinking about throwing his beer bottle at the guy and prays he won't try it. If he does, someone's going to die for sure, certainly the girl, but probably at least one or two other people. His attention stays on the hand holding the gun under Carmen's chin. If it goes off, it will splash the top of her head and most of her brain all over the ceiling.

"Yo, motherfucker. Let her go."

A young voice. Hendrix sees a young Hispanic in a white shirt and khakis push past Danny Keogh. His left hand points at the girl and his right hand pulls a gun from his waistband.

"Drop that fucking gun." The kid tries to look bad. He just looks young, but Hendrix would admire his nerve if he had time to think about it.

"Yo, I said drop it."

Ronald McDonald Number One shoots the kid in the chest. As soon as his weapon no longer covers the girl, Hendrix brings up his forty-five. Before the kid hits the ground, he shoots Ronald through the ear and sees his head explode. The acrid smell fills the room and his ears ring. Byrne gets off a shot as the other two guys spin toward the far door and Hendrix thinks he wings the one with the bag, but then they're out in the parking lot.

Keogh looks at the kid with a red splotch the size of a golf ball on his chest. Hendrix can tell the kid's only chance is if his name is Lazarus, and who's going to put money on that? Keogh shoves the dead Ronald off Carmen Ortega, crumpled into a fetal crouch under him. Hendrix hears the first screams from the arena, but Byrne is already out the door and he needs to back up his partner. He remembers that there was a fourth clown.

He's driving the car. A blue SUV glides in front of the building with its doors open and the two guys push through the smokers and dive aboard. Byrne bursts through those smokers as the vehicle begins to accelerate again, Hendrix only steps behind him.

"Hey," someone says, but Hendrix shoves him off.

"Everybody on the ground," he shouts. "Now." He sees cigarettes fly as people drop to the pavement.

Byrne dashes to his left and Hendrix runs toward the line of cars on his right. Maybe they can bracket the guy and shoot out his tires. Where the hell are the New Britain cops?

A shot erupts from the back of the SUV and Hendrix hears it slap against the building behind Byrne. He fires a shot at the rear tire and sees a muzzle flash from the passenger door. When the slug whistles past his ear, he decides fuck the tire.

Byrne fires off his Glock's entire clip so fast it sounds like a continuous burst. The back window of the SUV dissolves and Hendrix squeezes off three shots at the passenger window, but the car is still accelerating up the driveway at an angle so he doesn't have a good shot. It veers to the right, toward the shrubs. Byrne must have hit the driver.

The car is doing about forty when it runs up the hill and goes over the embankment. The passenger wheels are at least a foot higher than the driver's side, and it reels into Farmington Avenue, straight across the intersection, rolling onto its left side and skidding into a telephone pole. The pole buckles and the traffic light, hanging on a cable from it, crashes to the pavement.

Hendrix is fifty yards away, but he sees the fireball and feels the heat when the gas tank erupts. He speed dials 911 again.

"Jesus Christ, you again?"

"Yeah," he says. "I thought you'd like an update. We need fire apparatus, too. And ambulances. And tell those cops to hurry, will you? We need someone to direct traffic at the corner of Farmington and Corbin. You've got a light out."

Byrne slaps another clip into his gun and dashes up the driveway. Hendrix takes his time. He's pretty sure no one in the SUV is going to be running anywhere.

Chapter Nineteen

At midnight, Tori McDonald walks into the New Britain police headquarters. She's wearing a black silk shirt and faded jeans, a necklace with stones that Hendrix thinks might be jade nestling in her open collar. She's also wearing two inch heels, but he still has to lean toward her so she can reach his lips. When her freshly-showered body leans close, he's aware of the blood, sweat, and gunshot residue coating him and his clothes.

"Are you all right?"

His ears have stopped ringing from the shots and he hears her perfectly. She's doing that social worker control thing like she did at the shelter fire, but he can see that she's ready to tuck her thumb in her mouth and pull the covers over her head. It's been a rough week. He's glad she wasn't in the lobby to see him shoot a man through the head. Carmen Ortega took it pretty well, considering that choice B involved the guy shooting her through her own head.

"I've been worse," he tells her. "Been better, too."

Carmen has interviewed him, Byrne, the EMTs who tried to keep the kid alive, and the first cops on the scene of the fire. She's also thrown up twice. Harmon Shields, his face waxy as ever, maintained a low profile after identifying himself as a cop, too, but told Hendrix that she talked him into going to the bout with her and they both loved the first half.

Videographers and anchor types swarmed down on the rink, too. It's not the kind of publicity the New Britain Whammer Jammers were looking for, but anybody who reads the Courant or has Internet access will know about them tomorrow morning. Hell, it's probably on-line right now.

Tori sinks to the chair next to him, a hard wooden affair that may date from the Spanish Inquisition. "That reporter gave me her card. She wants to set up interviews with Danny, me, and most of the other girls. I think she's really smitten with us."

She looks at him. "Or maybe she's just still in shock."

Hendrix gets them both more coffee. All around them, phones ring, people chatter, and computer monitors glow. Two rows over, Jimmy Byrne props his feet on a desk and chats with a cop with a red face.

"What happened inside?" Hendrix asks. "I got kind of tied up."

"Don't tease me, please." Tori's eyes look wistful. "It's only our second date."

"Third." He puts an arm around her and she leans against him.

"We played the second half," she says. "Nobody could leave, anyway, and we figured it was the best way to keep the crowd occupied. Lee talked them down and kept things sort of going, and Danny and the EMTs took care of the kid and the reporter."

Downstairs, the robbers who walked out of the bank tunnel and into the arms of New Britain's finest are still talking. They seemed even more stunned than Carmen Ortega. Officers are filling out warrant applications for both Daniel Keogh and Jerod Machowski.

Tori sips her coffee and makes a face. Hendrix should have warned her that cop coffee is akin to heavy duty motor oil.

"We lost, by the way. They knocked us ass over fishnets. Blew us out in the second half, won by about forty."

"That's too bad," he says. "But you were missing a lot of players. And your mind sure as hell wasn't on it. "

"DMJ was amazing. She went out there the second half like she had something to prove. You should have seen her. But they were just too good and too fast."

"This time," he tells her.

"Yeah." She adds a little cream and sugar to the mess in her cup and tries again.

"Who was that boy the robbers shot? Danny said he tried to save the reporter."

"Do they know his name?" he asks.

"His Hartford Public High School ID says Emilio De Soto, La Sota, something like that."

Hendrix feels the pieces fit. "His sister is the girl I shot in that drug bust last month. I think he missed me the other night and shot Molly instead."

"He's in the hospital, too."

Hendrix can't believe it. "He's still alive? He took one in the chest from about eight feet."

"From what the EMTs were saying, they don't expect him to make it."

Hendrix sits quietly and lets that sink in. Tori's hand creeps over and finds his.

"A bunch of us went to Vito's after the bout."

"I thought you'd go up for pizza, just across the lot."

"There were a lot of us. Most of the girls and Lugg and Jerry. Lots of family and lovers. Jerry and Grace Anatomy looked like they were hooking up. Some of us needed something a little harder than beer, too. Besides, Vito's has a full-page ad in our program. I sold it to them, of course."

"Of course."

She watches the activity swirling around the room and seems to remind herself that she doesn't have to make sense out of it.

"I was there, looking at all the couples and nearly-couples, and thermo-couples, and I remembered meeting you there a few weeks ago. It seems like years."

"Lots of things have happened since then."

"Tell me about it. I was sipping on a margarita, but it didn't taste right without you there. It was like that's our special place already, which I know is silly, but..."

She's blushing and he feels himself perk up a little.

"So, are we still on for tomorrow?"

"Oh, I don't know. What's for dinner again?"

"Veal picatta, pan-roasted potatoes, garden vegetables, my special secret dessert."

"What the hell," she says. "I've already bought the wine."

"Well, I guess that's it then, isn't it?" He watches the cop on the computer across from him turn away from the screen and rub his eyes. "And I bought another toothbrush."

"We can't let that go to waste, can we?"

Byrne talks into his cell phone and looks at the clock. It's after one, so maybe his date for the evening will be getting off soon. So to speak.

Hendrix remembers that all four of the red and yellow clown thieves are dead, the one he shot and the three in the SUV.

"What about the money from the bout?"

"It burned up in the car fire," she says.

"Hell." He leans back in the chair. "You busted your ass for that money. And you lost the bout. You ought to get something."

"We will. Before he and DMJ went home, Danny said he'll write us two checks. We had eight hundred and seventy-one people in there tonight, at twenty-five bucks a pop. And three times that for the shelter."

"They didn't go to Vito's with you?"

"They looked like they had some serious business to attend to."

Has Danny heard about the bank arrests and taken off? Does he have Denver as a hostage? Hendrix isn't up to another hostage crisis.

When will that damn warrant be ready?

Tori doesn't know about the bank robbery, and he doesn't want to mention it. To her, Danny Keogh is still the Patron Saint of the Whammer Jammers. Hendrix sees him checking out the boy, then Carmen Ortega. He gets the feeling DMJ is a fairly good judge of men and wonders if he's guessing wrong here. He never heard a name in the tunnel, and maybe the thieves are throwing out Danny's and Jerry's names to save themselves. No, that's even crazier than suspecting them in the first place.

Tori yawns and her whole body quivers with the effort. "Sorry. I'm kind of worn out."

"You should go home, get some rest. I'm probably going to be here for most of the night."

They've taken his gun and Byrne's. They did the same with the shotgun he fired last month in Hartford. They've said they'll take swabs and return them tonight, but that could mean another four or five hours.

Tori stands and he stands with her. His whole body feels heavy.

"If it's OK with you, could we make it earlier tomorrow? You come around four, we'll eat at five? I'm going to want to get to bed early tomorrow night."

She leans into his chest, the way she did three nights before. This time, she's wearing something under her shirt.

"That's pretty much what I had in mind, too."

Half an hour later, a cop with his tie loose and bags under his eyes escorts Byrne over to Hendrix and notices their matching shirts.

"You guys sing, too?"

"Not on duty." Hendrix says.

The cop smells of cigarette smoke. "We won't find a judge to sign anything until tomorrow morning, especially since one guy lives in Rocky Hill and the other one in West Hartford. You want us to call you?"

Hendrix nods. "I want to be in on the end of this."

Byrne agrees. "I'll take Machowski if you want the boss," he says.

"Deal."

It's two-forty. Hendrix wonders if Tori is asleep yet, but it's only ten minutes down Arch Street to his own place, and he's not sure he can hold out much longer than that.

Chapter Twenty

Danny's in the kitchen listening to the coffee maker burble and staring into the refrigerator at the apples, grapes, oranges, and blueberries in his crisper. Georgia is a fruit freak, preferably over yogurt, which he has in more flavors than he knew existed before he met her. He never touches the stuff himself; it looks like refrigerated snot.

When they got home last night, she didn't say a word, just took him by the hand and led him upstairs to his bedroom, where she slowly took off his clothes, then helped him take off hers. She guided him onto the bed and he doesn't remember the next few hours very clearly except that somewhere around three o'clock in the morning when he could scarcely remember his own name, much less speak it aloud, she whispered,

"Do you still want to marry me?"

"Yes," he managed to say.

"When I realized tonight how close I came to losing you..." She buries her face in his shoulder. "If those men had shot you..."

"They didn't," he whispers.

"I don't even remember the second half of the bout." She kisses him and he tastes their lovemaking on her mouth. When she curls up against him, he knows he's luckier than any man deserves to be.

"I love you, Sugar Plum."

He buried his face in her hair and fell asleep.

The doorbell rings and he walks from the kitchen, wondering who else is awake this early. Sunday morning, not even solicitors are up at nine. Besides, they use the phone or send spam.

Two uniformed police officers who look like they'd rather be at the dentist stand on his porch. Hendrix, the security guard, hovers behind them. His eyes look heavy enough to use for paperweights.

"Mr. Keogh," the taller uniforms says. "We hate to disturb you this early, sir."

"What's this about?" Danny feels bad news approaching at a gallop, but he doesn't see any paper in their hands.

"Well, sir, it's kind of complicated. May we come in?"

Hendrix is deferring to the locals, but he seems to be pulling the strings. Danny steps back and finds his cell phone in his jeans pocket. His lawyer is just a speed dial away.

The cops look around the living room. Danny can see that the natural beams in the ceiling impress the hell out of them, even Hendrix. Well, it's one of the perks of owning a construction company. You can get good materials and workers, make your own house into something out of a magazine, not that his neighbors on Boulevard in West Hartford are any different.

"Sir, you know detective Hendrix here, don't you? From the Hartford Major Crimes Division?"

"Major Crimes?" Danny forces his voice to sound sleepy. "You mean that robbery you stopped last night?"

No, sir, this is something else, but we think the two things are connected." Hendrix looks at the living room furniture, lots of wood and leather, and earth tones. Danny never thought about it until Georgia praised his taste. She might not even want to change it when she moves in.

The shower shuts off upstairs. Danny knows he needs to get rid of these guys before Georgia hears anything.

The cops stand next to the leather couch. None of them seems interested in sitting down and having coffee, and Danny's not in the mood to offer.

"Mr. Keogh, last night the New Britain Police arrested four men at the site of the new Patience Randall Women's Shelter."

"What were they doing over there? Stealing tools or equipment?" He reminds himself that this is news to him, he has no idea what they're talking about.

"No, sir, they dug a tunnel. It looks like they started where you had to put in the new pipes to bring the water system up to code, and went under the parking lot and into the vault of the Continental Bank. Detective Hendrix here found the tunnel the night before last and alerted the local authorities."

Keep breathing, Danny tells himself. Maintain eye contact, speak slowly. "So, what does this have to do with me?"

"Well, the men said something about a distraction at seven-fifty the following night, when they were going to blast through the floor of the vault. That's the same time the robbery took place at the roller derby match."

Georgia's footsteps pad down the hall. If she hears any of this, Danny knows he's so screwed.

"I was there, officer. The thieves took a woman hostage and shot a kid. Detective Hendrix here shot the guy, and he and his partner broke up the robbery." He looks at Hendrix. "Great job. I haven't looked at the paper this morning, but I'll bet you're on the front page."

Hendrix tips his head slightly, but the cop continues. "Yes, sir, and that's our point. The robbers claim that you and a Jerod

Machowski—your construction foreman?—planned the whole thing. They say it was your idea."

Danny feels his bowels loosening.

"That's crap. I don't know anything about this."

"Well, sir, that seems hard to believe. I mean, it is your construction project."

"I've got projects going on in six towns right now. I'm in charge, yeah, but I have foremen on each site. That's their job, to supervise. I can't believe Jerry would do something like this."

"Well, Detective Hendrix found that Mr. Machowski has over a hundred thousand dollars in credit card debt, and the men tell us he's a big gambler. On-line poker, stuff like that."

"I can't believe this." Danny realizes he's the only one sitting and stands again to regain more power. "These guys get grabbed, of course they're going to name Jerry and me. What would you expect?"

"Tori McDonald tells me that you moved the bout back two weeks." Hendrix speaks for the first time. "I think that was so you had more time to dig the tunnel, and then you could use the bout as a diversion. One of the thieves says Jerry set the fire at the shelter. That gave you an excuse to have men at the site at night, too, crews working around the clock so the new shelter would be done sooner. And finish the tunnel."

"I do not fucking believe this." Danny looks at the cops, who don't look back at him, and Hendrix, who does. "I hope you clowns have a warrant to come in here with this shit."

The cops shuffle around like toy soldiers. Denny understands that there is a God in heaven and vows that he'll go to church next Sunday. Then another idea flashes in his mind.

"Are you harassing Jerry Machowski with this bullshit, too?"

"Officers are visiting him in Rocky Hill," Hendrix says. "My partner is with them."

"But I'll bet you don't have a warrant for him, either, do you? Frigging assholes get caught, they say we're in charge. I'll bet a judge told you guys to go pound sand, didn't he? But you decided to play this horseshit game. What, you didn't make you quota on parking tickets this month?"

The West Hartford cops look at each other, then at Hendrix. Hendrix has something in his eyes, something mean, and Danny realizes again that the guy can probably take him. If he's as mad as he looks, he could probably even take Jerry, too.

"You got bounced from the Hartford PD, right? For shooting a girl? So now you're playing cops and robbers to get your badge back? Forget it, guy. You assholes have ten seconds to get out of here. And you will definitely be hearing from my attorney."

The cops move toward the door, but Hendrix doesn't move an inch. His eyes look like chips of ice.

"I'll be watching you from now on, Danny. For as long as it takes. And I'll be back."

Danny closes the door behind them and realizes that he's dripping with sweat. But they're gone. They couldn't get a warrant. Now, if Jerry can tough it out too, they're home free. But they don't have the money, either from the roller derby or the bank. Jerry needs his share to pay the gamblers. If he keeps his mouth shut, Danny knows he can help him out on that. Fair's fair.

Besides, he and Jerry didn't take part in the robbery. All they can charge them with is conspiracy. He's not sure what the max is for that, but it's probably less than for a robbery.

He's halfway across the living room when Georgia appears at the top of the stairs.

"Danny? Sugar Plum?"

She's wearing a black tee shirt that says "Show me the money" and faded jeans, and she has her overnight bag over her shoulder.

She comes down the stairs looking ten feet tall and the radiance around her almost makes him squint.

"Where are you going?" He forces his voice to stay casual. "I thought you'd want breakfast. I've got coffee on, and I've got all kinds of fruit."

"What those police were saying." It comes out "Po-leese." "About you robbing a bank."

"No, they had it wrong. Some guys tried a robbery, they got caught, they must have figured they'd get a break if they threw my name out there."

"Sugar Plum. Daniel." She's never called him "Daniel" since that first night together. She stands like a gunfighter, her eyes never leaving his, and they've never looked so cold before. "This is me. Please don't do this to me."

"Do what? I told you—" She walks toward him and stops just out of reach. In sandals, she can stare at him eye to eye.

"Oh, Sugar Plum." Her voice is still slow and low, but it's steady as a brick, no wobble at all. It's the most horrible sound he's ever heard. Something precious has gone away, right now, before his eyes.

"It's funny, isn't it?" She seems to be finding the words one by one. "If someone had come up to me yesterday and told me that my lover was a bank robber, I would have laughed in their face. I never would have dreamed it, not even in my worst nightmares. Not even once."

Maintain eye contact, he tells himself. If you can meet her eyes, she'll believe you.

"But now that I hear those policemen say it, I can feel it. It's true, isn't it?"

"No, Georgia. You have to believe me."

Something moves in her face. That wonderful face, the one he wants to wake up and look into every morning. Yes, her cheekbones are still a little soft, and her upper teeth are a little too big, but still...the warmth, the intelligence, the humor...

The distance.

"A bank, Danny. I work in a bank, remember? Robbing a bank is the most disrespectful thing you could possibly do to me. And it's even my bank."

Her voice feels like it's pounding him into the floor.

"God damn you."

"Georgia." He reaches out to her, but she steps back. "I love you. There must be something I can do to convince you. Some way I can help you believe me. Just name it."

"There's nothing." She looks around the room like she's never going to see it again. "It's like I just walked in and found you with another woman."

"Georgia..."

She faces him again.

"I'm coming back this afternoon to pick up my clothes. Please promise me you'll be out of the house from noon until...three? I'll leave your key here on the coffee table."

When she closes the door behind her, he's not sure his legs will carry him all the way over to the couch.

#

When he gets home, Hendrix steps into his garden and picks two blazing red tomatoes, only slightly brighter than his face still feels, a shiny green pepper, a summer squash that matches Goldee Spawn's hair, and a zucchini. The day is cloudy for a change, so he won't put the hose on tonight. He's probably going to have other things on his mind, anyway.

Paola Roccapini waves at him over the fence. She's seen the picture in this morning's Hartford Courant, and recognizes that nice polite boy who was looking for him last week. Emilio Losada died at two-fifty that morning, just about the time Hendrix pulled into his driveway. He manages to evade her other comments and is glad she didn't read the article that also mentioned he shot a man through the head. It would play hell with the dynamics of their flirting. If she sees Tori's car in the driveway later, that will probably have the same effect.

He dumps the vegetables on his cutting board and goes upstairs to take another shower and shave more carefully. Caffeine and frustration have kicked in and he's wide awake. He knows Keogh and Machowski planned the tunnel, and it makes sense that Jerry Machowski or one of his crew would set the fire too, but there's not a speck of physical evidence. If they've never tried anything like this before, they've got beginner's luck up the ass.

Byrne tells him that Jerry Machowski has even bigger balls than his boss, and he's still free, too. When he and two Rocky Hill cops knocked on the door, a woman he saw on skates last night opened the door wearing what looked like one of Jerry's shirts and a black braid that fell to her waist.

"Oh, something else," Byrne remembers. "Vic called me this morning. The chief saw the story in the paper and asked him what you were doing in New Britain. When he heard that Shields still had you suspended for that shooting, he went ballistic. You'll probably get a call tomorrow to come back in."

Hendrix can't help gloating. "Shields left me a voicemail this morning. He even sounded like he was trying to apologize. I'm guessing Carmen had something to do with it."

Carmen has called him, too.

"I need to thank you again." Her voice sounds more tentative than he's used to hearing. "I learned a lot last night. And I remember what you said about taking it personally when someone tries to shoot you."

"Uh-huh." He's watching the coffee drip into his carafe. On three hours sleep, it's a challenge.

"And then I remembered what you said about not having a lot of time to decide."

"It happens fast, doesn't it?"

"It does," she said. "I'm glad you chose the way you did."

"I'm glad that you're all right," he says.

"Well," she says. "Maybe that's a relative term." He can almost feel her blushing over the phone. "I talked with the captain of the team last night. Tina?"

"Right. She mentioned that. That you want to interview her and some of the others for a story. That's great, they can use the publicity."

"Yes. And I still have roller skates in my closet. I asked her how long she thought it would take to get back in shape."

"Really?" Hendrix wonders who's kidding whom.

"She told me it's like good sex. You never quite lose it."

She hangs up and Hendrix pours himself a cup of that coffee.

"So," Byrne says. "I guess we're going to have to dig clear to China to hang anything on the builder and his buddy. Maybe we can check their phones."

"Not without probable cause," Hendrix reminds him. "And I'm pretty sure how far we'll get with that."

"Shit," Byrne says.

"Yeah," Hendrix agrees. "Shit."

Byrne sighs. "Goddamn strip joints aren't even open on Sunday. I'm going to have to watch fucking baseball all day."

Tori's due in half an hour. Hendrix lays out the pans and cutting board and selects a knife to slice up the vegetables. It's smaller than the carving knife that Annie Rogers plunged into Kevin Draper's chest. He tells himself he should have been able to prevent that, but can't think of anything he could have done differently. Tori hired him to protect a bunch of skaters from getting their windshields smashed, and now Kevin Draper is dead. So is Molly Ringworm. And Emilio Losada. And four robbers.

In the worst of all possible worlds, Annie Rogers is looking at jail time. At best, maybe she's in for long-term therapy.

He shreds lettuce and distributes it into two bowls. As long as restraining orders have the weight of tissue paper, women will need a refuge like the one Tori's spearheading. Maybe she'll be able to help Annie.

And maybe Danny Keogh will bankroll most of it—until they can find the proof they need to put him away.

His phone vibrates in his pocket and he pulls it out and checks the number.

It's Jenny Della Vecchia.

"Handsome." Like they've never even been away. "Are you all right? I saw the *Courant* this morning. About another shooting..."

"I'm fine." He realizes that he can't think of anything else he needs to say. "Thanks."

"That's good. I know I...we...well, I didn't want you to be hurt. I never wanted..."

Is she crying?

"Jenny, are you OK?"

The pause is so long he looks to see if the call is breaking up.

"Trash, Trace, Tracy. I fucked up. I made an awful mistake. And I'm sorry. I'd like...I mean, I was wondering..."

"I don't think so, Jenny."

He hears her waiting on the other end and realizes she's bracing herself even harder than Danny Keogh did that morning.

"You're an artist," he says. "Your whole life is about things that are beautiful. My life is a cop. I wallow in things that are ugly. When we get together, we speak different languages."

"We're both intelligent people, handsome. We can change."

"Jenny, we look at the world from opposite sides. You can bring me beauty, and I appreciate that. But I can't give you back anything you can use or need. You need someone who can give you more good stuff."

She's not crying now. "You've changed."

"We both have. Or maybe I just see what we are now."

"No, a month ago, you couldn't see yourself so clearly. Who is she?"

"Excuse me?" He looks out the window, where the sunshine creeps around the corner of the roof and eases toward his garden.

"You've met someone else, haven't you? What's her name?"

Now's a good time to hang up, but he and Jenny had two years together and talked about having forever. He can't just hit "End" like she's a TV show he's tired of watching.

"Her name is Tina G. Wasteland," he says.

She thinks he's goofing on her, and her voice sounds hurt when she speaks again.

"I hope she turns out to be a bitch on wheels."

"Oh," he says. "You wouldn't believe."

Tori appears at his back door wearing eye-liner again, and lipstick. She carries an overnight bag along with a bottle of Chardonnay.

"I don't believe this." She puts the bottle on the counter next to the refrigerator "I should have realized it when you told me the address, but it didn't register. You live next to my grandmother."

The world jumps the tracks. "You're kidding."

"Uh-uh." She points to Paola Roccapini's house. "The one who taught me how to cook. Along with my mom."

He thinks of Paola Roccapini. "So that's why your lasagna was so good."

"Yeah, I use her recipe. For lots of things."

One or both of them is going to get an earful tomorrow. "She's very cool, bakes bread for me all the time."

Tori finds his corkscrew and opens the wine so it can breathe.

"What do you think she's going to say if she knows you spent the night with me?"

"She'll probably give me hell for trying to steal her boyfriend." She looks at her gym bag. "I'm going to do it, too."

"Cocky, aren't you? Think you're really up to it?"

Tori moves close to him again and puts her arms around his neck. "I think you like your girlfriends a little older than eighteen."

"There's that smart social worker thing again."

He pours two glasses of wine and ushers her into the living room, where they both sink to the couch.

"That reporter made you and your partner look like the greatest team since Butch and Sundance, didn't she?"

"Not the most objective reporting, given the circumstances."

"No." She sips her wine. "She wants to come out for the team, now, too."

"Yeah," he says. "She called me this morning and mentioned that."

"We need skaters now." Tori looks at her glass. "I'm glad you saved her, of course. But I'm even more glad I didn't see you shoot that man."

"You've seen too much of it in the last week," he tells her. "We both have."

"We're going to help each other put it behind us, aren't we?"

"We are."

She kisses him and leans back again. "It feels good not having to pretend, doesn't it? We already know lots of the bad stuff about each other."

"It does," he says. "We can take our time and enjoy the trip a little."

“It’s Sunday,” she says. “We don’t have to be anywhere else today, right?”

“Right.” He watches her eyes move slowly around the room. He’ll give her the tour later. “I think we’re where we need to be.”

They let the world slow down around them. Tori puts her feet on the coffee table.

“Did you see the paper this morning? About that robbery in New Britain?”

Fortunately, the paper went to press too early to have any mention of the thieves accusing Danny and Jerry of planning the whole thing. But Hendrix was amazed to find that they came out of the tunnel with less than fifty thousand dollars. He thought they’d have at least twenty times that much.

“New Britain’s a happening place,” he says.

Tori lets her foot brush against his and he reminds himself that the veal will burn if he gets sidetracked. Such a tragedy. Tori sits up again as another thought strikes her.

“Lynn—Roxy—called me this morning. The guy she called to defend Annie got a call from the cops, and he thinks he can get her off. Or at least, get her a good deal.”

“Really. That’s great.”

“Yeah. They found a message on Kevin’s phone. He’d deleted it, but they managed to dig it out. You remember he said someone told him that Annie and Lugg were getting together?”

Hendrix remembers. “She said it wasn’t true, though. And so did he.”

“Yeah. But they found it. They tracked the caller, too, and I don’t know what the hell to make of it.”

“Why?” Hendrix realizes she’s trying to assemble a puzzle that now has an extra piece. “Do you know who it was?”

Tori blinks as if she's looking into a blinding light. "It's Georgia Pitcher. She called him the day he showed up and punched Lugg."

"Georgia Pitcher..." He knows the name, one of the skaters.

She nods. "Denver Mint Julep. Danny Keogh's girlfriend."

"Holy shit."

He feels himself standing and realizes that they've read it all wrong. Danny Keogh's girlfriend is manager of the Continental Bank.

And she set Danny up.

Chapter Twenty-one

By noon Monday, Geneva time, Georgia Leigh Pitcher has deposited two-point-three million dollars in her Swiss account. The suitcases with the GLP monogram stay with the Swiss Bank, and she's already back at the airport and awaiting her one-forty flight to Paris.

She left Bradley International Airport in Hartford and passed through Geneva customs as Elizabeth Brennan—the name on the passport she's used the last two times she's visited Europe on bank business—and will depart as Melissa Davenport, the name on her traveler's checks. Her new luggage bears the initials MLD.

She listens to the multi-lingual announcements in the terminal and proves to herself that her French is still up to speed. Maman would be so proud.

Poor Danny is too nice a man for a life of crime, so she's done him a huge favor. When she walked out of the bank Saturday afternoon and dropped two garbage bags into her car, she left most of the safe deposit boxes in the vault open. Those poor men in the tunnel, working so hard and so long, and finding so little. The police will almost certainly figure out where the money went—especially if that Hendrix man is with them, he's just much too smart—but they can't do anything about it now.

But how in the world did the police ever find out about that tunnel? That's the question that kept her awake on her trans-Atlantic flight. If they'd been in and out according to plan, nobody would have been the wiser until this morning. Lucky for her she was flying out Sunday afternoon anyway. By the time Danny came back to discover her clothes were still hanging in his closet, she was an hour out of Bradley.

Note to self. Don't let your lover check your phone messages while you're in the shower. It was early June when Jerry M reported that the new water pipes would put them fifty-three feet closer to the vault, and apparently they just couldn't resist temptation. Well, she figured that out about Danny the first night she followed him home.

He's really a nice man, and he really does care about the roller girls. If he doesn't go to jail, maybe he'll still sponsor them. She hopes so.

She wonders if he's left any voicemail messages. Her cell is still back on her coffee table in Farmington. If he or the police have been there yet, maybe someone has watered her plants. Fortunately, she never got the cat she'd like to have. Someone would have to feed the poor dear, and she couldn't afford to tell anybody that she was going away.

A tall man in an impeccable charcoal suit bows and smiles. Probably mid-thirties, with eyes like broken glass and almost certainly pictures of the wife and kiddies in his wallet.

"*Bitte*?" she says. He straightens up.

"Sorry. Excuse me. I just..." He moves farther down the bench and speaks to a blonde woman in jeans and with green toenails. She apparently does speak English. Georgia realizes that the German felt foreign in her mouth. *Papa würde sich furchtbar schämen.*

Papa would be dreadfully ashamed.

A young couple with a baby comes in speaking French, and she watches the little girl, curly blonde hair and lovely blue eyes, too small to be walking yet. Marie, and her mother is Lisette. Sweetums seems to have a few more words than she has teeth, but she can't be even a year. She wears an adorable blue and white checked dress and she's still in diapers. Cute as a bug. Georgia wants a child some day. Maybe even children.

The speaker announces her flight and she picks up her purse. She hopes Annie Rogers will be all right, too. She had one wing low Saturday, but the girls take care of each other. She didn't expect that man to come after her, and certainly didn't think Annie'd have the spunk to carry a knife, but she had to give that detective something to watch, especially after he talked to her and she realized how smart he was.

She settles into her window seat and greets the older couple next to her, going to visit their son and daughter-in-law. The man pulls out pictures of their three grandchildren. Can you imagine, someone still has an old-fashioned camera that uses film. They settle down to regale her with stories of these wonderful children and she hangs on every word. Such nice people.

The plane lifts off as gently as blowing fuzz off a dandelion.

Melissa Davenport orders a glass of wine and settles back to look out the window.

Tomorrow, she will have her long brown hair cut to the nape of her neck and dyed a strawberry blonde.

She wonders if they have roller derby in Paris.

If they do, she's already got her name picked out.

Rive Gaucho.

Left Bank.

The End

Acknowledgements

My daughter and Webmistress Hazel Smut Crunch, formerly of the Queen City Cherry Bombs, inspired this book. She also let me use her name as an introduction to the local skaters and tweaked the questionnaire that eventually went all over New England.

The Yankee Brutals and the Stepford Sabotage, the Connecticut teams skating out of New Haven, generously invited me to a practice session where I interviewed coaches, trainers, and skaters without the heat of a bout swirling around us. Other skaters from teams throughout New England answered my questions at length online, too.

So, thanks to:

Girl Fawkes (who also posed for the cover), Dee Nasty, Dirty Kat Box, Irate Pirate, Lady Braga, Milla Low Life, Parker Poison, Pearl Jammer, Pixie Bruiser, and Rinko Starr.

Chopsaw, who oversees the officiating for the CT Roller Girls, and Patricide, a referee, explained the rules for me, and Coach Rat Furee Crotchless discussed strategy and conditioning.

Dee Stortion, who owns the Bruiser Boutique in Nashua, NH, discussed the equipment and explained about the different grades of bearings in the skates.

Hitman Hank, announcer of the CT bouts, gave me a fan's take on the sport, as did several husbands and other spectators. Mr. Mutation, the CT Roller Girls DJ and husband of Gene Mutation, elaborated on the same theme.

Nancy Shelton, manager of Roller Magic in Waterbury, CT, gave me more insight into the sport's history and appeal.

Jennifer Waltner and Georgia Wilson read various drafts of the book in progress and offered helpful and encouraging feedback.

Sgt. Christine Mertes, Information Officer of the Hartford (CT) Police Department, answered my questions about procedure.

Myron Gubitz translated the German.

Any errors that still exist are my failure and not theirs.

About The Author

Steve Liskow is a member of both Mystery Writers of America and Sisters in Crime, and serves on panels for both groups. His stories have appeared in *Alfred Hitchcock Mystery Magazine* and several anthologies, and *The Whammer Jammers* is his second novel. A former English teacher, he often conducts writing workshops throughout central Connecticut, where he lives with his wife Barbara and two rescued cats.

Visit his Web site at http://www.steveliskow.com

Coming Soon

Cherry Bomb

Hartford PI Zach Barnes searches for the missing daughter of a wealthy CEO and uncovers a thriving trade in teen sex-trafficking, blackmail, and murder.

CPSIA information can be obtained at www.ICGtesting.com
Printed in the USA
LVOW04s1307061014

407438LV00002B/182/P